"With luscious settings and compelling characters, this stellar follow-up to *Bad Medicine* takes us back to the 1970s—its music and its mores—and immerses us in Jimmy Marino's life as he embarks on 'adulting' with his sweetheart, Sarah. Remnants of his previous life resurface (literally and figuratively), and he discovers the truth of Faulkner's saying, 'The past is never dead. It's not even the past.' A terrific read!"

-Kim Suhr, author of the *Nothing to Lose*

"After a precious artifact is deliberately set free, its legacy still haunts desperate treasure seekers. Fans of *Bad Medicine* will relish Sheild's return to the prairies of the 1970s to take up the tale of a lost generation searching for true worth. Another page-turning thrill ride."

-Lisa Lickel, author of the *Buried Treasure* cozy mystery series

"Pete Sheild has done it again . . . adventure, betrayal, and love all wrapped into one until the last page. You won't be able to turn the pages fast enough as you go on another adventure with Jimmy while he searches for the one thing that he thinks can bring him closure."

-Lauren Guelig, author of the *Wish Me A Rainbow*

"Set in South Dakota in the seventies, *Remnants* is a fast-paced and fascinating blend of treasure hunting, mystery, and the spiritual journey of a young man discovering what is really important in his life. Through Jimmy's eyes, the reader is given a vivid and realistic look at small town life, set against a backdrop of Native American culture, even as he deals with life-changing events. This novel will seize your attention from the first page and hold it until the final sentence."

–Karen Stacey, author of *Feeding the Duke* and *The Risk of Love*

"The book is fantastic!"

–Mark S. Paget, executive director of Wisconsin Dental Association, Inc.

BOOK ONE

"*Bad Medicine* was a fast-paced story with a unique premise and a fresh take on the classic treasure hunter story."
-Amanda Waters, author of *You Again*

"...an adventurous, engaging page-turner."
-Lee Whittlesey, National Park Service Historian & author of eight books, including *Storytelling in Yellowstone*

"...this book grabs the reader and doesn't let go."
-Kim Suhr, author of *Nothing to Lose* (Cornerstone Press) and director of Red Oak Writing.

Dr. Colby Phillips, a professor of anthropology and archeology, sets out with his grandson Jimmy to dig in South Dakota Indian graves, searching for the Thomas Jefferson Peace Medal, the Holy Grail of artifact collecting. They quickly learn they are in a race with bandits and bureaucrats, a river is rising, and the whole enterprise may be damned, but with new friends and a revised sense of his own strength, Dr. Phillips stands up to everything that is in his way—including his own desires.

REMNANTS

A Novel

PETE SHEILD
Author of *Bad Medicine*

Pete Sheild

Ten|16
PRESS

www.ten16press.com - Waukesha, WI

Remnants
Copyrighted © 2023 by Pete Sheild
PB ISBN: 9781645387398
First Edition

Remnants
by Pete Sheild

All Rights Reserved. Written permission must be secured from the publisher to use or reproduce any part of this book, except for brief quotations in critical reviews or articles.

For information, please contact:

Ten|16
PRESS

www.ten16press.com
Waukesha, WI

Editor: (Check Trello Board to see editors wishes)
Art director & cover designer: Kaeley Dunteman
Interor designer: Ashton Smith & Kaeley Dunteman

This book is a work of fiction. Names, characters, places, and incidents are the product of the author's imagination or are used fictitiously. Characters in this book have no relation to anyone bearing the same name and are not based on anyone known or unknown to the author. Any resemblance to actual businesses or companies, events, locales, or persons, living or dead, is coincidental.

For Mom and Dad
Always

AUTHOR'S NOTE

Human history can, at times, be unflattering and reprehensible—even books of historical fiction that are based on facts. The reader should be aware that there are sensitive scenes contained in this book that could be deemed offensive. But they happened and were endorsed by private and public entities for decades. I have tried to deal with those scenes in the most dignified manner possible. In my writing, I have used the term *Indian*, as opposed to *Native American*, because it is historically correct for the time period in which the book takes place.

I have the utmost respect, admiration, and affinity for Native American people. Research for this book only deepened those feelings. With this book, I hope the reader will gain a better understanding of the challenges these proud people face.

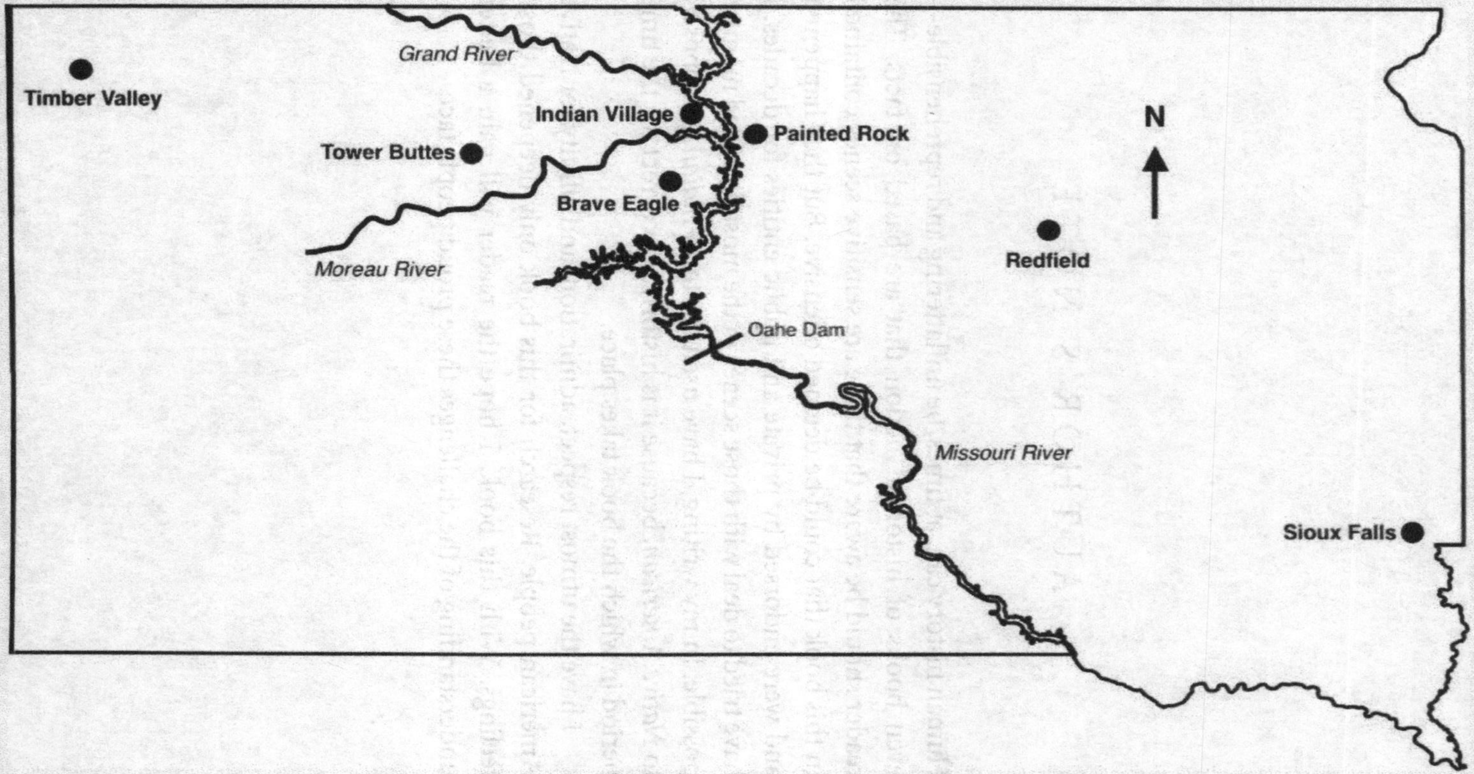
Timber Valley
Grand River
Indian Village
Painted Rock
Tower Buttes
Brave Eagle
Moreau River
N
Redfield
Oahe Dam
Missouri River
Sioux Falls

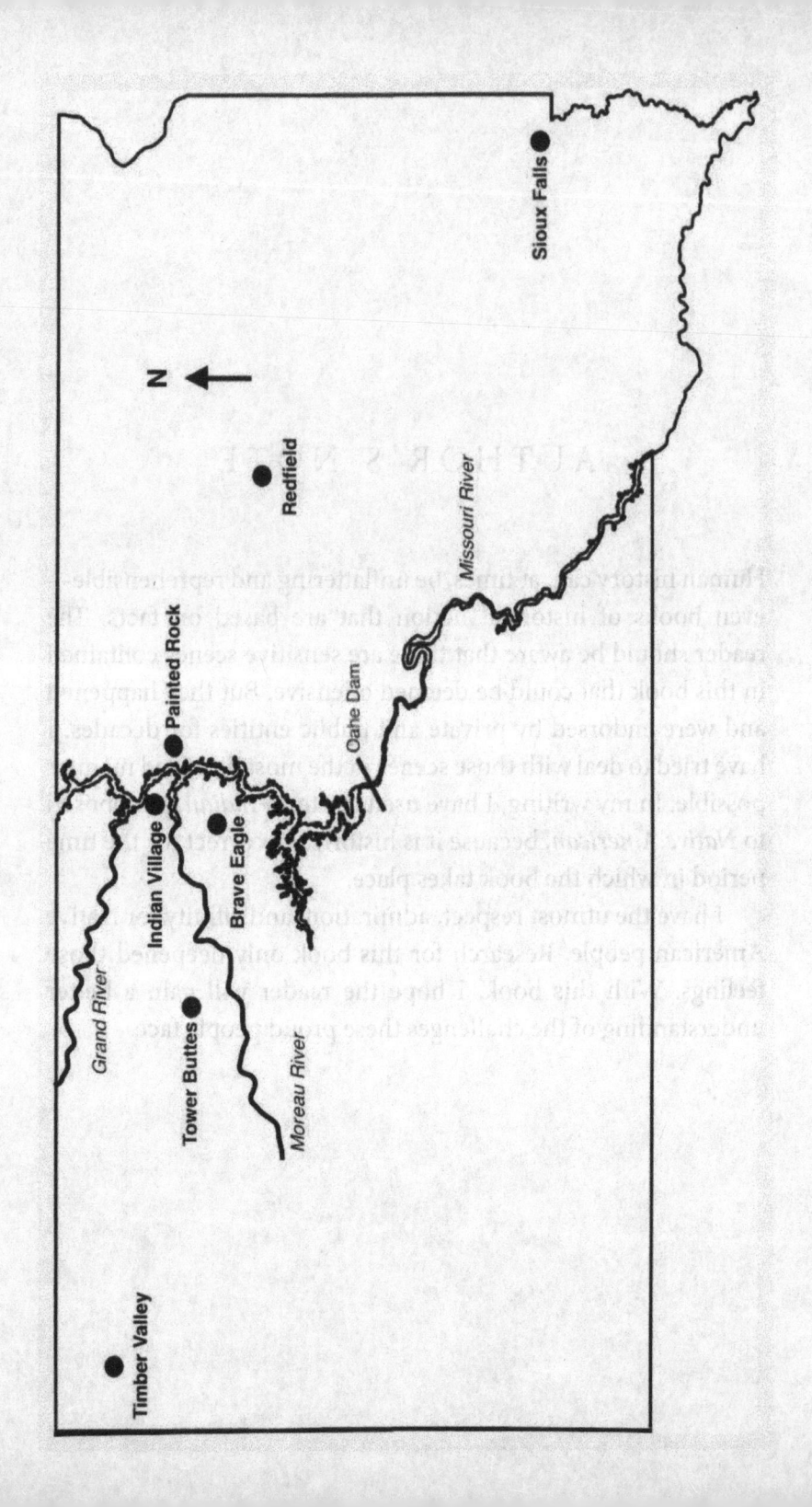

Grand River
Indian Village
Painted Rock
Tower Buttes
Brave Eagle
Moreau River
Oahe Dam

INTRODUCTION

South Dakota is a state of remnants. Abandoned farmhouses and grain elevators—remnants of a time when mom-and-pop farms dotted the landscape before the creep of corporate farming began to ooze its way into rural life. An empty orange and brown burger joint—a remnant of when frosty mugs of root beer and drive-ins graced every small town throughout the Midwest. Old cars from the fifties, forties, and earlier sitting cheerless in fallow fields—remnants of transportation no longer practical. Small towns reduced to boarded-up businesses and dilapidated houses—remnants of small-town America before the lure of the bright lights from the big city. The horizon sculpted by weathered hills and scoured flats—remnants of ancient uplifts, shallow seas, and leveling glaciers. Stacks of railroad ties no longer needed, with nowhere to go—remnants of the transition from steam to the heavier, more powerful diesel engines, requiring stronger railbeds and new rails. Empty liquor bottles on the shoulder of the road or bouncing along in the back of pickup trucks—remnants of broken promises and shattered families.

Time stops for no one. People move on. Well, most people.

1977

1977

1

"Jimmy!" Ruby's alarmed voice got my attention. "Something's burning!"

Preoccupied by an early-morning argument with Sarah, my mind took a second to register the warning. "Ugh, damn it!" I scrambled toward the kitchen, knocking a glass off the bar in the process. Behind me, there was a piercing shatter followed by a loud gasp.

I slammed through the saloon doors, greeted by climbing tentacles of acrid smoke obscuring the grill hood. Two sizzling hamburger patties sat scorched in the middle of the grill, surrounded by furious, saw-toothed flames erupting from the grease. I opened a box of baking soda and sprayed the white powder at the fire, which partially extinguished it. With another box, the fire was snuffed out. In the mayhem, I had painted the wall, grill, and floor a cloddy white. What a mess. In hopes of mitigating the lingering fatty-smoke smell, I placed the window fan at the screen door and leaned against the wall, bracing myself with my arm, head down. It was time to admit I couldn't run The Caboose by myself. Every day I was walking a tightrope, struggling with each step not to lose my balance. Something had to give.

I grabbed the red-handled broom from the kitchen closet and returned through the swinging doors. From the end of the bar, Ruby and Lee—a couple of regulars—blurted, "Jimmy!" in unison.

"Everything okay?" Ruby questioned.

"Not really," I grumbled.

Ruby's husband, Lee, waved an empty beer bottle. "No rush."

Ruby whirled and scowled at him. He returned the scowl. She was tall and leggy, without a gray hair of her beehive out of place, and always stood at the bar. Lee was short and compact, with thick-rimmed black glasses he struggled to keep from sliding down his pointy nose, and he always sat.

"You got it, Lee. Give me a sec. Let me get this glass swept up," I answered without lifting my head.

Swiiiiish swoosh swish. I began to sweep up the mosaic of glass scattered on the worn linoleum, my pity party continuing. Cat Stevens finished his time on the old Seeburg M100C, which led to a *hum, click, schlick,* and ended with a sound like crinkling paper vibrating from one of the cone speakers as the needle hit the next record. The opening riff of "I Only Have Eyes for You" pulled me right to Sarah's grandma, Katherine, who had died a short three months earlier. It was her favorite song by The Flamingos. A cloud of unhappiness enveloped me. I missed her kindness, her untamed nature, and her ability to make people feel welcome—including me and my grandpa when we needed it most—but right now I missed her help.

The first time we met her, she said we'd always have her as a friend if we needed one. More than once, she had proven to be true to her word. Although widowed, she owned and ran the bar, and she raised a wonderful granddaughter. Sarah had a number of her grandmother Katherine's attributes. The most prominent: they were both more lover than fighter. Katherine's frequent hugs had reminded us how much she loved us. Her regular customers became friends. At her funeral, Pastor Dawson called "Miss Kitty" a town treasure, and I guess that was true. I'd come to realize the bar had functioned as her pulpit, the patrons her parishioners.

Lost in longing for her comforts, all the colors of memory mixed together, transported my mind, and glazed my vision of the jukebox. My throat tightened. A single, warm tear stung my cheek. The day had just about broken me.

Angry hinges on the heavy oak door interrupted my thoughts. Golden beams of an early-fall setting sun cut a swath of light on the floor. A figure stepped forward through the doorway. His face came into focus, and our eyes met. He held my stare like he was trying to place me, and for a moment, neither of us flinched. The stranger's eyes darted about the room taking everything in before he lumbered up to the bar. His was a quiet entrance, one not too often seen in Painted Rock.

I leaned the broom against the wall under a glass-eyed, six-by-six mule deer mount, which had seen better days. I spun on my heels to serve my newest arrival. "What can I get ya?"

His perspiration-stained T-shirt had a picture of Bruce Lee on it. With strained effort, he unshouldered his filthy backpack and sleeping bag. The sizeable pack hit the floor with a heavy thud. He sported a red, white, and blue bandana over his greasy, shoulder-length hair. The bandana was undoubtably left over from last year's bicentennial celebration. He labored to slide onto the chrome and black vinyl barstool.

"I'll have a cold beer. Grain Belt, if ya got one," he said as his tired eyes circled back to meet mine. His demeanor was that of a man lost, without purpose or place.

I detected a bit of a Southern accent, but which area of the South escaped me. "You got it. You interested in seeing a menu?" I pulled back the pop top with a crack.

"No, sir. Um, can I let you know?" He took a long pull from his beer.

The phone's hollow ring interrupted. "The Caboose, Jimmy speaking," I said as I walked through the saloon doors into the kitchen for privacy.

"Jimmy, can you please talk to me for a minute?" Sarah begged.

I barked through gritted teeth into the receiver, "Sarah, I told you I don't want to talk about it anymore today," before slamming it down. I'd been stewing all morning after Sarah had pecked on me at breakfast about getting married. This was her third call to try to talk about it, and it was only lunchtime. Her constant yammering the last couple of weeks had given me a chronic headache. I'd already told her, I'll get married when I'm ready.

I returned to the bar from the kitchen, and a sharp crack similar to a rifle shot startled me. Had the fan tipped over? Perhaps my weak attempt at a repair job on the broken closer for the kitchen screen door hadn't held, causing it to slam shut. The remaining lunch couples looked at me wide-eyed. The stranger jerked his head in my direction. Was another transient off a boxcar sneaking in the backdoor of our bar? I grabbed Grandpa's old snub-nosed .38 from under the cash register, holding it behind my back. I had no intention of shooting if I found someone in the kitchen, but even the thought of scaring him with the pistol shot adrenaline through my veins. The back of my neck bristled as I pivoted, pushing hard through the swinging saloon doors into the kitchen disaster. A sickening feeling gurgled in my stomach.

Through the screen door, I could make out a cowered figure scampering away from The Caboose toward the railroad tracks. He hit his knees and scuttled under a parked box car.

I shook my head, readjusting the fan before locking the screen door. Then I made a note to fix the broken closer, which had probably caused the slam that sounded like a gunshot. Or maybe I would let it be, so it could serve as my warning alarm. I put the .38 away. When I turned back around, Officer Tittle—one of Painted Rock's finest—was at the bar. Starched khaki uniform, blond crew cut with a widow's peak above his triangular-shaped face, Stetson cowboy hat in hand, legs shoulder width apart. "You ought to consider locking the door."

"Didn't hear you come in," I said, throwing a cardboard coaster in front of him. "What can I get ya?"

Officer Tittle was familiar with Sarah and me. His parents had played bridge for years with Katherine and her husband. He had an uncle and cousin who were cops in Keogh, a town seven miles to the east. Over the years, Tittle had hauled more than a few drunken brawlers from our bar.

The lights above, which were muted by the diffusing smoke, produced a soft glint off his brass nameplate and badge. Officer Tittle's eyes pinched together as he glanced toward the stranger two seats down. He pushed the coaster back as if to say it wasn't a drinking visit. Tittle leaned forward. "I come from the rez," he said, dropping his voice. "The Corps of Engineers are dredging Lake Oahe on account of low river levels, right? Shallow water causing a bunch of trouble for boats, you know?" His eyes were eager.

I wiped my hands on a towel. "Yeah, I guess it was down a bunch for the year farther downstream in Kansas, so the dam at Pierre's been open, too."

"Right," his voice dropped to a focused whisper. "Well, anyway, the Corps dredged up a particular Department of Indian Properties car. The one Agents Gritzmacher and Calhoun were driving. You know what I'm talkin' about, right?"

I stiffened, forcing a slight head tilt.

The stranger's head snapped a look at Officer Tittle but rapidly went back to staring at the mirror behind the bar.

Officer Tittle checked right and left, leaning in closer. "It was all smashed to hell, of course. Corps tight-lipped on if them two Staties were still in the car. I'm tellin' ya because I thought you'd want to know. I know it shook you and your grandpa up pretty bad at the time."

My body tingled with the spirit of fear, producing light-headedness. "Boy, what a surprise," was all I could muster. My mind ran through the entire adventure kaleidoscope of finding the Thomas Jefferson Peace Medal with Grandpa, the subsequent confrontation with the D.I.P. agents, and their car narrowly missing a head-on with a combine before tumbling across the prairie and into Lake Oahe.

Multiple pairs of eyes from down the bar focused their attention on Tittle and me. With a head nod, he motioned toward the door. Coming out from behind the bar, I followed his lead. "D.I.P. and Corps might come askin' questions," he said, wide-eyed.

"Whatever." For the last eight years, I had been trying to put the whole incident behind me. Now it was resurfacing—literally. Having to fully explain to the authorities how the car with two bodies had gotten there was sure to give me more sleepless nights. What would the charge be if I were arrested?

"You feelin' okay, Jimmy? You look kinda pale." Silence. "Well, anyway, I'm givin' you the heads up." He cupped his hand to my ear and whispered, "Might set this town on fire if the lake drops enough to expose the medal." Officer Tittle gave me a man nod. "Give Sarah my best." He put his Stetson on and tipped it at me before walking to the door.

Paralyzed, I stared into the expanding space between Tittle and me. Grandpa and I had found the most sought-after artifact on the plains. We were sure to be included in the history books—a defining moment for both of us. Our special experience together had galvanized our already close relationship. Little did we know the serious danger our prized medal would put us in. So, Grandpa had tossed it into Lake Oahe—right in front of the agents.

"Jimmy? Jimmy!" The second time registered. I put away Officer Tittle's visit.

"Folks, can I get ya two more Hamm's?"

Ruby and Lee nodded in unison before Ruby spoke. "You all right?" They were smoking Lucky Strikes, eyeballing the stranger counting his change on the bar.

"Yeah, yeah, other than I forgot about your burgers. Your well-done burgers." I was so mad at myself. "I'm running around like a chicken with my head cut off. Hamm's are on me."

Ruby's waxen complexion melted into a frown. "I'm sorry, Jimmy." She sighed. "You know we got back into town not long ago from touring the Rockies in our Winnebago. We were sure sorry to hear of Miss Kitty's passing. She was a delightful lady." Her brown eyes welled as she tilted her head to Lee for support. Lee smoothed his comb-over and returned to peeling the label off his bottle. She took a drag from her cigarette. "You must have your hands full. Sarah should be helping you. Is she all right?"

I appreciated the concern, although Ruby's snide tone made me pause. "It's been rough on her. Pretty overwhelming for a while with lawyers, funeral arrangements, doing the books for The Caboose." I fumbled with the bar rag, reflecting on what Sarah had been through. My shoulders slumped as I let out a loud sigh.

"Please give her our sympathies," said Ruby, her head cocked to the side. She winked. "And I wish you would marry her." She took a deep drag, blowing the smoke to the ceiling. "Miss Kitty wished the same as me. She told me so."

"Thanks. Excuse me for a sec . . . " I left to check on the stranger, wanting to ignore her tongue wagging.

I cleared the bar, put the dirty dishes into a bus tray, and slid it under the counter. "Decide on some food?" I inquired to the newest arrival.

"A bag of chips. I'm low on dough, man," he said, curling his hair behind his ears. It was hard to tell where his bushy sideburns ended and his scraggly mop of hair started.

I grabbed the guy a bag of chips from the overhead rack. "Where ya from?"

"Georgia."

"Cool. So, what brings you to town?"

"Been here a couple of weeks campin'." He simultaneously flipped his thumb over his shoulder. " . . . East of town." He shoveled a handful of chips into his mouth and washed them down with a strong swig. "Funds is getting low. Hey, know anyone lookin' to hire?"

I met him eye to eye, sizing him up. Could he? "Nah, not off the top of my head. I'll keep my ears open though." I tilted my head. "What type of work you lookin' for?"

"Anything. I gotta get me some money." He extended his large hands, using them for emphasis. "I left Columbus over a month ago. Been thumbin' it ever since. Workin' through some things, you know. Gotta get my head right. Tryin' to make ends meet anyway I can, you know?"

"How long you going to be in town?"

"Can't say, unfortunately. A week more, a month more . . . " He shrugged. "Kinda depends."

"Depends on what?" I half chuckled. This guy intrigued me—his drawl, his free spirit, even his bushy facial hair. All things I was short on.

"Depends on a lot of stuff," he replied with squinted eyes accentuated by his crow's feet, head bobbing like I should have known what stuff he was talking about.

"You stop by from time to time, and I can let you know." He wore a dejected face, and I wanted to be a friend. What would Katherine do? I extended my hand as a token of friendship. "I'm Jimmy. Who should I say is lookin'?"

His calloused grip was strong. "Paul."

"Okay, Paul. Beer and chips on the house."

Excusing myself to the kitchen to clean up the mess, I contemplated if Paul might be a good fit here. We had tried high school and college kids, folks working for extra spending money, but they didn't last long. I was burned out, desperate, and out of options. What the heck? I returned through the saloon doors to hear Starland Vocal Band's provocative hit floating through the room. Lee and Ruby were shaking their heads as Paul waved an unlit cigarette in front of them.

He approached me, hand open, cigarette between his index and middle finger. "Hey, man, can I bum a light?"

I grabbed a book of matches from next to the cash register

and tossed them on the bar. "Were you serious about lookin' for work?"

"Sure am. I'm in a bad way," he said, curling his hair behind his ears. Despite youthful features, the premature furrows of his rawboned face suggested there had been a lot of upheaval in his past. He appeared older than my twenty-seven years, but something more than the sun and the road had beaten him down. I put him at twenty-one or twenty-two.

I leaned onto the bar with my arms extended. "We're closed tomorrow, but why don't you come by on Tuesday about this time. We can get to know you better. Discuss wage, job description, hours, those types of things."

"Thank you for your kindness." He smiled. "Peace out."

"Later, man."

He disappeared out the door into the bright sunshine.

I wiped off Paul's spot at the bar, revisiting Officer Tittle's speculation. Would the dropping water level of Lake Oahe potentially allow me to find the Thomas Jefferson Peace Medal again? Would it overshadow the happiness that I'd felt when we'd found the medal the first time? Would the recovery of the car open a chapter of my life that was better off closed?

2

Sarah stopped by The Caboose while I finished cleaning up the mess in the kitchen. I was sure she wouldn't be able to tell there had been a fire.

"Jimmy, have you calmed down?"

I kept wiping up the floor.

"Guess you can't hang up on me now, can ya?" she asked. Sarah wore a smug expression on her face, her hands anchored to her hips. She paused a beat, sniffing. "Wait . . . why does it smell smoky in here?"

Busted. "Don't ask. Yeah, sorry about earlier. Honestly, I was crazy busy, barely keeping my head above water," I replied with an edge in my voice.

Sarah moved closer with hands open. "What is wrong with you? Is there something you're not telling me?"

"Yep. You're never going to believe this, but Tittle told me the Corps dredged up a D.I.P. car. You know, the Staties."

"Oh, my God." She cupped her hand over her mouth. "Were the Staties still in there?" Her voice rose an octave.

"He didn't know. I'm sure we'll hear soon enough." The tingling of fear returned. "Next, it'll be the D.I.P. snooping around, asking questions. I'll bet since the Staties disappeared out of radio range on the reservation side of Lake Oahe, it didn't occur to the D.I.P. to question Sheriff Owl or Standing Bear." I shook my head at their stupidity. "There was no love lost from the Indian point of view with Gritzmacher or Calhoun. I know they had harassed Barking Coyote. Betcha Standing Bear buried Owl's report." I laughed at the irony. "And they got buried in thirty feet of water and thirty tons of shale."

"Ugh. Can you imagine?" She pulled back and sat down. "If I were you, I'd call Jay and tell him to let Robert and the combine driver . . . Stephen what's-his-name . . . know what happened. Make sure you all tell the authorities how vicious those agents were, you know?"

Jay's given name was Jay Red Feather, and Robert's given name was Robert Yellow Knife. They were friends of Sarah's from grade school, a year or two younger than me. Proud, full-blooded Sioux, they had married women from the Rosebud reservation near Rapid City. Jay's dad, Standing Bear, was the Tribal Chairman on the reservation on the other side of the river from Painted Rock, a position he'd held for many years. We treated each other like family. I considered Jay and Robert my best friends, my brothers. In fact, Sarah was godmother to Jay and Aiyana's daughter, Iris.

"Yeah, I will, but the story is the story, you know?" Anger began to tighten my jaw muscles at the prospect of reopening the case. "Jeez," I muttered and threw my blackened rag in the sink.

There were several beats of uncomfortable silence between us as the tension from this morning returned.

"Jimmy, we have to talk. I don't know what is going on. I'm so exhausted. Maybe I'm still depressed about Grandma, and I'm frustrated. I have another doctor's appointment, Tuesday at 3:30. I need answers."

She went on to remind me how pale she was, how she didn't feel like she had much of an appetite. Her symptoms mirrored those of my mom's breast cancer. I resisted letting my mind go there. Deflecting, I said, "I'm worried about you. You remember Pastor Dawson describing those five steps of grieving? He said it can take a while to go through them all."

"I know, but I feel like it's something else." She scratched her head. "I worry about you, too. You can't keep up this pace running the place all by yourself."

"Well, I might have someone who can help us out. This guy, Paul, came in here looking for work. Seems like an okay guy. Sure talks funny." I offered a job description off the top of my head. "Washing dishes would help. Possibly even working the grill. Sweep the floors. Stock the coolers. There are plenty of things he can help with."

"I'm sorry I'm not much help," she said, her lips pouty under soft eyes.

I offered a solution. "Next time he comes in, I'll arrange a time for the three of us to sit down and talk. You and I can discuss his specific job description before we meet." I cast a sympathetic eye. "I'd like to help the guy out. And, I'll admit, I need some help."

"You don't even know him," Sarah scoffed, hands returning to her hips. "We can't have some stranger working our business. You want him taking money? How's he going to treat the customers?"

I lowered my voice. "There were three things me and my grandpa told you when we first met. We were from Kansas, our Scout broke down, and we were hungry. Despite not knowing us, you and Katherine were so warm and inviting."

"Oh, come *on*. You're talkin' about something completely different."

"No, it wasn't, but we can talk more when I get home," I offered, kissing her on the cheek. "I'm shutting the grill off at eight, so I'll be home early."

Our brown Formica faux woodgrain kitchen table had seen better days but still matched up nicely with the six chairs upholstered in a brown and yellow vinyl floral pattern. Sarah said Katherine had bought the set shortly before I'd come to town. The spacious kitchen featured white appliances nestled between white metal cabinets, similar to the kitchen I'd grown up in. The kitchen light had one of the two bulbs burned out, but the dimness didn't stop us from enjoying the ribs I brought home. In fact, the low light added a touch of ambiance.

"Tittle half joked about the medal showing up if the water level keeps dropping," I said.

"It's possible, I guess. Would you look for it?" Sarah questioned.

"Hell, yeah, I would. I'd want you to come with me, though. I know where Grandpa tossed it off the bridge." I caught a flashback of the wind whipping his white hair as he tossed it. "Can you imagine?" I let the possibility hang in the air. "I wonder sometimes if Grandpa ever regrets throwing it off. Like, does he wish he would have kept it, you know?" I had never told Sarah I still harbored twinges of regret that he tossed it from the bridge. Perhaps there was a way he could have kept it.

"You should ask him sometime." There were a few beats of gnawing and smacking. "I don't know where you learned how to prepare these ribs, Jimmy, but damn, they are the best." Sarah's face showed rib sauce from cheek to cheek and from the mole above her upper lip to her chin.

I set a rib bone on the bone plate in the middle of the table. "I told you the last time. My mom's recipe. It was Dad's and my favorite." I paused to savor the memory. "Although we didn't eat dinner with him often," I lamented. "The farm work always took priority." I sucked the sauce off of the bone. "So, he wouldn't eat 'til eight or nine at night."

Sarah got up and washed her hands. "So, tell me what you think of this drifter guy. Why would you trust him?" The faucet squeaked as she turned it off and returned to the table.

I slid my plate under hers before casually tossing my napkin on top. "A gut feeling, I guess. I betcha nobody has ever given the guy a break. Remember what Pastor talked about last week in his sermon? It was something like, 'I was a stranger and you welcomed me.' Why did your grandma trust Grandpa and me the first time we met? When you know, you know." I raised my glass of milk and tilted it in her direction as a toast before taking a drink.

Sarah rolled her deep brown eyes and took our plates to the sink. She kept her back to me as she pulled out the dish rack, soap, and scouring pad. "Like I tried to say before you so rudely hung up on me . . . We have been together, like, over eight years you know, and honestly, don't you think it's time we get . . . Let me put it this way . . . We've said 'I love you' thousands of times over the years. I have needs and wants, Jimmy. I want to get married, because I love you and can't imagine my life with anyone else." She had put it out there. Turning, her eyes locked on mine. "I have to know . . . Where do you think our relationship is going?"

I inhaled deeply. "Don't start on me again, Sarah." I exhaled, pushing my chair away from the kitchen table. "You know I love you. It's... the pressure. Business is tough. There's plenty around here I should fix, but there's only so many hours in the day. The bills keep comin', you know?"

"So, you want me and love me, but you're insecure about our financial situation?" She half faced me; the delicate features of her face were pulled tight. "Oh, dream on, Jimmy. You know I'll be getting money from my grandma. More than enough to get us by." The banging of plates and silverware began to escalate. "Such *B.S.*"

I began to feel my stomach lurch, awash in acid and fear. She was right. Although Sarah had never once implied a financial hierarchy in our relationship, I put financial pressure to contribute on myself. My dad had been our family breadwinner, and I was convinced my role in our relationship should be the same. I'd finally found someone who could help take the stress off and keep the money coming in, until Sarah got better and she tried to change the subject to marriage. If I were being honest with myself, I'd have to admit the real issue wasn't financial. Long-term commitment, for whatever reason, scared the hell out of me.

I stood and rammed the chair in under the table with a thud. "I mean, we have a good thing going, don't you think? Why do we have to add pressure to our relationship by getting married? I certainly don't need a ring on my finger to show my love for you."

"Oh, the classic guy response. As long as the sex is good, right?" She shook her head.

I wanted to explain, because she didn't get what I meant. Instead, I bit my lip.

Turning around with a face older and menacing, she mocked me in an exaggerated deep voice. "There's no rush on forever." She paused. "Yes, I do want a ring . . . someday." Her face blossomed red. "And I need you to explain to me. What pressure are you talkin' about?" Her voice radiated heat.

Cornered, I extended my arms for a gentle plea. "C'mon, Sarah. I've got so much on my mind. One, tomorrow I have to get to the bar and clean. Both the men's and women's toilets clogged at different times today, so I have to get a plumber in there to take a look or we'll have to shut down. Two, do *your* job of ordering supplies. Three, there's a stack of bills to be paid. Four, Pastor Dawson called and said you volunteered me to come down and help him rake leaves at church." I extended my fingers one by one as points were made, which was ridiculous because she had her back to me the whole time while she finished the dishes and wiped off the counters. "Who knows if the D.I.P. is going to show up? And another thing! I have a beer delivery tomorrow, and I have to get the coolers stocked for the week." Her cleanup movements became herky-jerky. The tension was heavy. "I'd like you to at least come down on Tuesday and meet this guy. If he can help out, it would be a big relief for me. I can't think of anything else but work. I'm overwhelmed."

Still with her back to me, she replied in an angry voice, "Fine, I *will* meet this guy." She spun around, pointing a fork at me with one hand and her other at her hip. "Look, I want you in my life, Jimmy, because I love you. And getting married says you feel the same way. But in the end, even though I want you, I don't need you." Her face contorted and took on a deep shade of red. "You can run all you want, but at some point, you're going to need to grow up and be a man." I recognized her tone as the same one she used when kicking the belligerents out of The Caboose. At those times, despite her five-foot-six frame, her voice sounded like she was ten feet tall and bulletproof. "I'm not saying all this to hurt

21

you, but there are plenty of women these days who are content to live on their own, you know."

"Whatever, Sarah." Fear and panic washed over me as I stomped up the stairs. I tried to push my fear of commitment from my psyche. Sarah had become my anchor ever since I'd made my choice to stay in Painted Rock. At the time, it had been the best decision I ever made. I loved the life we'd built together. Was I afraid she would leave me in some form or fashion, like my mom had when she died of cancer? My head pounded with feelings of vulnerability.

I stripped down to shower before bed. I needed to wash the bar smoke, grease, and bar talk exaggerations out of my hair and off my body. As the warm water enveloped me, I questioned if her sudden low energy had caused this marriage talk to bubble to the surface. Was it depression? Was she sick? If she was, did she have cancer? Oh God, no. Was it me?

I dried off and climbed into bed but was awakened by her hostile rustling of the pillows and blankets. I remained motionless on my side, eyes wide open, waiting for her to say something. She tossed and turned and tossed some more. I had the feeling she wanted me to say something, but there was nothing I could have said to appease her current mood. Another thing my mom had taught me was that in certain situations, "The less said, the better." This was one of those situations.

Over the years, I'd asked myself why Mom had used that phrase so often when I was growing up. Did it have something to do with her and Dad? She was mostly nonconfrontational when Dad was hot-tempered after a long day in the field. Mom would shy away from butting heads, often going to a different room in the house when he would angrily raise his voice. By avoiding barking back, she kept the peace. I would follow her lead.

I lay on my back, searching the ceiling for the elusive answer to the question of why I couldn't commit to marriage. I knew I loved Sarah. I couldn't live without her, if I was totally honest with myself. What was wrong with me?

The conversation in my head was broken by the grandfather clock downstairs chiming twice. Sarah's soft breathing sounds filled the night's stillness. A drop in temperature snuck in through the open window, chilling my skin and raising goosebumps. I pulled the covers over my head, rolled onto my stomach, and tried to get comfortable. My insides had become a self-inflicted tangled knot, giving me a stomachache. I fell back asleep, but the tortured night of rest continued.

I couldn't lose Sarah.

3

Still in bed, I stared out at a Monday morning in shades of blue and gray. Clouds like brushstrokes interrupted a crystal blue sky. The curtains fluttered in a dance with no rhythm as my ears picked up a crow cawing in the distance. Hearing the toilet flush, I rolled out of bed as Sarah reentered our bedroom looking resplendent in my gray *Star Wars* X-Wing T-shirt.

She flopped down on the unmade bed and pulled the covers tight up around her neck. "I gotta go back to sleep. I'm beyond tired." Her voice contained a different pain than I'd heard the night before. The idea that she might be even more pissed at me flashed through my head.

"The flu's been going around. You think you caught it?" I navigated around our bed to shut the window. I rose up on the balls of my feet to get maximum leverage on the jammed double-hung window. "I don't know how your grandma ever got this window open or closed." It broke free and slammed shut.

Outside the window, farm fields stretched almost as far as the eye could see—some fallow, some corn, some alfalfa, some sunflower. The solitary old farmhouse, which predated the turn of the century, sat on the north edge of town surrounded by huge burr oak trees. Sarah and Katherine had lived there for years. It also happened to be where Sarah and I had first kissed. After Katherine passed, Sarah wanted us to use her bed and her bedroom. She'd said it made her feel close to Katherine.

"I think I'll be fine. I need to catch up on my sleep. I'll call you when I get up."

I finished getting dressed and kissed her on the forehead. Pulling back, I noticed tiny beads of sweat along her hairline.

"Do you want a glass of water or a washcloth for your forehead or something?"

"A glass of water would be nice. With a couple of ice cubes. Thank you."

I thundered down the wooden steps to retrieve the glass, ice, and water. I hustled back up the steps two at a time and placed the ice water on the nightstand. I hoped last night's dust-up was the result of her not feeling well, rather than my lack of marriage commitment. Gently brushing her jet-black hair away from her face, I hoped my water run would put some points on the positive side of the ledger. I returned to the kitchen to pound down a bowl of cereal. I put away the dishes and headed for the truck.

The shelves on the back porch, which were packed with Katherine's jams and pickles, reminded me of her love for others. The service door to the old garage opened with a groan. A musty, damp smell greeted me. I backed out my tired '70 C10 Chevy pickup, put my window down, and rested my arm in the open space. The air smelled fresh, filled with organic aromas from the earth.

On the drive down to The Caboose, streets and sidewalks were busy with kids in light jackets walking to school or riding their Schwinn bikes no-handed. The large windows of the businesses along Grand Avenue were painted up for Homecoming Week. While I waited at the stop light for the farm report to end and the weather report to begin on the radio, I reviewed a mental list of the things for Paul to do. It added up to between ten or fifteen hours a week, enough to take the edge off me.

As I bumped along the gravel alley approaching the back door of The Caboose, I noticed a darkened figure on the back steps. D.I.P.? No. It was Paul. He appeared to stuff a notebook into his backpack before awkwardly scrambling to his feet.

The crunch of crushed gravel and a trail of dust overcame me as I pulled in to park my truck. "Mornin', Paul. What brings you by this early in the morning?" I slammed the truck door.

"I got to thinkin' when I woke up this morning. I had talked to this guy at the campground a few days ago, and he started to tell me about these treasure hunters. Years ago, I guess, they were lookin' in these parts for a Thomas Jefferson Peace Medal." He tilted his head, and his eyes widened. "Sounds like if a guy found one, it'd be worth a lot of money."

His words caused the acid in my gut to kick into overdrive, producing a loud growl. Grandpa had told me of the medal's financial worth. Even worse, I had firsthand knowledge of the psychological power it could hold over someone.

Paul shifted his weight from left to right and curled his hair behind his ears. He went on to tell me what I already knew about Lewis and Clark's journey up the Missouri River and to the Pacific Northwest. They had passed right by Painted Rock in 1804. He tilted his head out of the wind to light a cigarette. "You bein' a bartender, I figured you might have overheard stories about them treasure hunters." His eyes softened. "You ever hear of anyone looking around here for the Jefferson Peace Medal?" His sincere tone and eye contact suggested his interest was genuine. But was he referring to me and Grandpa as the treasure hunters?

Looking over his shoulder at the dammed-up Missouri River, which had created Lake Oahe, I contemplated my response. A tremor crept up my spine. Grandpa Colby and I had almost lost our lives after finding the damn medal. I wasn't about to share my firsthand account surrounding the medal with a guy I barely knew.

"Oh, there's a story recycled every few years. I've never talked to anyone like a treasure hunter." I shrugged. "But they might be out there. Sorry I don't have more time, man. I'm running behind." I hopped up the couple of cement stairs to the landing and pivoted as I plucked the backdoor key from my key ring. "Hey, I'll see you tomorrow to talk about some hours, right?" The remains of a dead starling missing its head lay next to the door. I swept it into the bushes with my foot.

Paul stared at me, slowly rubbing his chin like he was either concentrating on my answer or doubting it. The call of a meadowlark in a nearby thicket of scrub trees interrupted the uncomfortable pause. He walked away, and with a tortured jerk of his head, he offered a mumbled retort. "Ten-four, good buddy."

I unlocked the door and hurried through the kitchen into the bar. Where was Paul headed? I fought the urge to feel on edge around him because I so desperately wanted help at the bar. Could it be that I wasn't used to someone with long hair who spoke different? I tried to rationalize it away, but our exchange struck me as odd.

Pulling back the smoke-gray shade, I couldn't see any movement at the rail yard to the south. Scanning the opposite direction, I caught a glimpse of the top of Paul's backpack as it disappeared over the embankment above the flats along Lake Oahe. I stepped away and allowed the shade to re-cover the window. I stared at the air between me and the window shade. No doubt, Paul had been fishing for information. Did he know something? Not possible. Our encounter with the medal had been eight years earlier and a thousand miles away from Georgia. There hadn't been talk of the medal in years. Was he familiar with Grandpa Colby? Doubtful, unless the guy from the campground was a local.

I told myself to quit being so paranoid but pulled back the shade again for one more look. His small figure was skirting a thicket of tangled buckthorn before weaving through the sagebrush. He was headed toward the sun-bleached cottonwood trees flanking the water's edge. "Yeah, he ought to take a bath in the river," I said under my breath.

Pushing Paul, the medal, D.I.P., and Sarah into the deep recesses of my mind, I got busy with the chores of the day. The two dollars I put in the jukebox made the work less tedious. I scrubbed counters, paid some bills, loaded the coolers, and inventoried supplies while listening to Elvis, The Stones, Lovin Spoonful, Cream, Johnny Cash, and even a favorite, Tom Jones.

I was locking up when the phone rang. I debated if I should pick it up. "The Caboose, Jimmy speaking."

"Jimmy?"

"Speaking."

"This is Officer Tittle. Need you to come down to the station. I have a couple of things to let you in on."

"Ah . . . yeah, sure," I said, thinking I wanted to get home and see how Sarah was doing. "Can't you tell me over the phone? I'm tight for time."

"Damn, I got another light blinking. No. It won't take long. C'mon into my office when you get here."

"I'm on my way."

The gravel popped under my tires as I backed into the alley. The police station was a few blocks south along Railroad Street. I parked at an angle on the street, and then I stopped at the foot of the cracking cement steps to eye the two massive cement columns flanking the intimidating eight-foot-tall oak doors. Iron griffins, painted black, sat stoically at each side of the steps.

Entering, I surveyed the foyer, expecting to be greeted. Pea green walls surrounded empty, institutional gray desks. A faint smell of mimeograph ink reminded me of my grade school principal's office. Overhead, the annoying buzz of fluorescent light fixtures irritated me like a relentless swarm of mosquitos at dusk. Mounted on the back wall were two mule deer heads—a six-by-six and a five-by-five—next to an antelope head. The call bell sat lonely on the yellow linoleum counter, so I tapped it and got the ding but no greeting.

Having been here before, I decided to let myself through the hollow core batwing door. I proceeded right and walked down the cavernous hallway to his office. The sound of my shoes on the polished gray marble floor, which reverberated off the walls, announced my approach. Stopping outside his door, I listened. A muffled voice became clearer. I gathered that he was on the phone, so I rapped on the gray metal door.

The door flew open, and the phone base slid off the desk with a clang. He picked up the base, set it back on the desk next to a can of Lysol spray, and reeled in the stretched-out handset cord. "Yeah, will do, Darlene." Officer Tittle swung around into his chair and motioned for me to close the door and take a seat. His shirttail was untucked, papers were scattered over his desk, and half a cheeseburger sat on top of manila folders. "Yes, I said we would keep an eye on it." He leaned forward with his elbows on the desk, rubbing his forehead. "Uh-huh. Yep, always our goal. Okay, you have yourself a good week. Bye."

He hung up the phone and tried to rub the tension off his face with both hands. Letting out a big exhalation, he steepled his fingers under his chin. "You know, Jimmy, sometimes I don't know why, but this old town seems damn hopeless."

"Oh, I don't know. The Lions put up new playground equipment at Acorn Park. There's even talk of the rodeo grounds being redone." I slowed, but another positive note popped up. "Canadian Club has committed to hosting another walleye tournament on the Oahe next summer." I pointed for emphasis to the plump Lake Oahe walleye mounted on driftwood behind his desk. "There's lots of good things happening if ya look for 'em, Officer."

"Yeah, I guess." He wriggled forward in his chair before folding his hands on his desk and looking at me with sincere concern in his eyes. "Anyway, the hippie guy from your bar was in here earlier today asking for public records about those two Staties and their car that went missing on the reservation in '69. Same one got pulled up dredging."

I shifted in my chair at the mention of the word "Staties". I tried not to look rattled as a wave of guilt passed through me.

Officer Tittle withdrew his notepad from his breast pocket, flipping it open. He continued, "Kid goes by Paul Van Brocklin. Asked him why he cares. He said folks at the bar were talking about it, and he got curious. Said he was aware of his rights regarding public records. I told him if we had anything it would be archived, and it would take some time to locate any information.

Told him we were short-staffed. Honestly, I don't think we ever got a report." He tilted his head and opened his palms, annoyed. "To top it off, I told the greasy pissant it's truly a tribal matter, the way I look at it. They disappeared on the rez side of the Oahe." He leaned back and clasped his hands behind his head. "I have no idea what a drifter of his kind is doing poking around my town, but I don't like it." He wagged his finger at me. "Nothin' to be gained by regurgitating a past episode. What happened, happened. Leave it lie, I say."

There was a dead space between us while I considered what Tittle had said. "Well, I appreciate the information, Officer Tittle, but—"

"Jesus, Jimmy, call me Don." He took an aggressive bite of his cheeseburger and chucked the remainder into the garbage can under his desk.

I smiled. "What I was about to say, Don, was with Sarah not right, I need help at the bar. So with all due respect, we are interviewing him tomorrow." I shrugged, extending my upturned palms as if to say, "What am I supposed to do?" I continued, "Not 'cause we want to, because we have to. I'm confident Sarah will be back to work in no time." I began to stand. "Speaking of which, I need to get home and see how she's doing." We shook hands. "Thanks for the heads up." Finally, I walked out.

He sat with a loud squeak. "Hey, Jimmy!" Tittle hollered.

From the hallway, I wrapped my long torso back through the doorway. "Yessir?"

"Has Corps or D.I.P. come by asking questions?"

I brushed it off. "Nope."

Tittle nodded. "Uh-huh. Say, Corps said they found one body still strapped in the seat belt, badly decomposed. Forensics are trying to get the dental records for both Gritzmacher and Calhoun."

"Was it the driver or passenger strapped in?" My heart thumped as I reentered his office.

"They're not sayin', but the other belt was unbuckled, and no body." Tittle cocked his head and shrugged.

"Huh. Keep me posted, okay?"

"Yep, and keep this between us," he said, sliding a thick folder into the filing cabinet behind him. "I . . . you know . . . shouldn't be telling you all this."

I promised to keep quiet, and by the time I passed by the creepy griffins, the conversation relating to Paul had been dismissed. My mind was preoccupied, racing in circles over mention of the Staties. One body?

I rolled down my window on the ride home, allowing the occasional perfume of pine to override the dry air. The radio blared "Hotel California." The streets were lined with bright, fluttering, multicolored foliage beaming in the late afternoon sun. It occurred to me that fall had suddenly burst forth overnight, painting the leaves with varying colors for emphasis. I melded the conversations with Paul and Officer Tittle together. Why was Paul asking those types of questions? Had he gone to Chief Standing Bear on the Reservation? Fortunately, people in Painted Rock didn't have any reason to discuss events from long ago. Was there a statute of limitations covering the events of eight years ago? How would jurisdiction be resolved? I reasoned there was nothing to worry about. At least, not yet.

Our farmhouse sat back from the road behind large, gnarly burr oaks, as if it were hiding from the newer homes across the street. Parking in front of our garage, I reached for the radio dial to turn it off, and a distinct voice from my past caused me to stop.

"And now, 'The Rest of the Story' . . . The Laramie Treaty of 1868 had been signed, giving the Sioux and the Cheyenne the right

to roam the unceded territory, areas of current-day Montana, Wyoming, and South Dakota. Additionally, the treaty granted the Sioux ownership of the Black Hills, their sacred hunting grounds. Fast forward five years—an economic depression was causing massive unemployment, banks failures, homelessness, and starvation. With the discovery of gold in the Black Hills in 1874, President Grant moved to try to buy back or lease the Black Hills from the Sioux, wanting to use the gold to stimulate the economy. The Indians said no deal, so the government broke the treaty, and war on the plains was certain to follow."

A commercial came on for Citracal. I stared west, in the direction of the reservation, thinking about the lives of those still living there—some by choice, some out of necessity. Not enough was being done to help them or for them to help themselves. I was proud of my best buddies, Jay and Robert, for striking a balance between their Indian heritage and gainful employment with the power company.

"It was late June 1876, and the western expansion across the plains was in full swing. Oh, but there was one problem . . . The settlers were immigrants to Indian Country—a country comprised of wide-open prairie, able to sustain a way of life for centuries. Its inhabitants, by and large, were tribal nomads roaming the land, following the bison herds. These bison provided food, clothing, tools . . . essentials for survival. A Civil War hero for the Union, Lieutenant Colonel George Armstrong Custer, had been assigned to Fort Abraham Lincoln, which was near Bismarck, North Dakota. His command had been tasked with herding the northern Great Plains Indians onto the reservation or exterminating them. A mission culminated in eastern Montana in a battle called "Custer's Last Stand," which is referred to today as "The Battle of the Little Bighorn." A gallant leader—flamboyant as he was brave—Custer died that twenty-fifth day in June 1876, along with over two hundred men from the 7th Calvary Regiment at the hands of over sixteen-hundred Northern Cheyenne, Arapaho, and Lakota Sioux warriors.

"After the battle, the two ivory-handled pistols Custer had holstered were never found . . . until a professor of archeology and anthropology was metal detecting along Little Bighorn River, where part of the fateful battle took place. He'd been there before, diligently done more research back at his third-floor office at the University of Kansas, and returned . . . This was his fourth year in a row. On this day in 1954, the autumn sun was positioned high in the sky, and the rippling river level was low as he worked the shallow waters of a ford below Medicine Tail Coulee. A ping for a shell casing, a ping for a belt buckle, and a loud ping for a black shape partially covered by river gravel. The water was cold as he reached below its surface to withdraw a pistol with ivory handles, the nickel-plated barrel pitted from time. He examined it and found the serial numbers, along with something else. Under the grips, the metal plate was marked with an inscription: . . . the name G. A. Custer.

"The pistol resides in the Smithsonian Institute, a remnant of the last Indian victory of the Plains Wars, of a battle lost, a pistol of a bold leader. As for the treasure hunter, the persistent professor who found General Custer's pistol? You've undoubtably heard of him. Why, . . . his name is Professor Colby Phillips . . . And now you know The Rest . . . of . . . the . . . Story. Paul Harvey, good day!"

Grandpa—featured on Paul Harvey. I chuckled, relieved his glory hound days were over. A life of self-importance had been replaced with a life of helping others—in his neighborhood, volunteering at the nursing home, tutoring kids at KU. I wanted to call him and catch up.

Bounding up the back steps, I had a lot to tell Sarah about my day. A flood of dread passed through me as I entered the kitchen. No one could survive a rollover and fall into the river off a shale cliff... Right?

4

"How was your day?" Sarah asked.
Over a dinner of Hamburger Helper, tater tots, and crescent rolls, I recounted my day, highlighting my interaction with "Hippie" Paul, the visit with Officer Tittle, and Grandpa's fame. Our tone and body language during dinner told me both of us had let the angst from last night go. Sarah was quiet as she listened, and soon it was time to clear the table.

"I already don't have a good feeling about this Paul guy. Don't you think it's weird he asked about the medal? We need to tell him it's not going to work out," she pleaded, running water into the sink. "He might be a rip-off artist or have a record. Did Don ever do a background check?"

I had to agree. It *was* odd he'd asked about the medal. On the other hand, Painted Rock was located on the Lewis and Clark Trail. His questions weren't completely random. "I'm sure Tittle checked.

He would have told me if anything had shown up from Paul's past. Like Paul told me," I paused until she spun around to face me, "he's a guy thumbing his way west on an adventure." We stood, facing each other in a comfortable pause. I held Sarah's eyes, remembering one of the first times she'd made me dinner, when we made out in this very spot before Katherine walked in. I leaned forward, pinning her against the porcelain farm sink. I planted soft kisses along the side of her neck, my hands resting on her hips.

She cooed as she laced her fingers behind my neck.

I tilted my head in a submissive manner, yet kept my eyes locked on hers. "You and I both know I can't keep doing this on my own. We lost our dishwasher when school started." I paused a second. "Plus, it's harvest time. We don't have any better options." I lowered my voice. "Okay?"

She stared at me blankly without saying a word. After hesitating a couple of seconds, she offered, "All right, I'll withhold judgement until I meet him. I have my appointment tomorrow, so let's make it a short interview."

"Yep, I remember." I shifted gears. "Oh, jeez, how did I forget? Tittle said they found a body in the car . . . Forensics had to get dental records before they could get a positive I.D."

"Gross. Wait, just one?"

"I guess one so far." I couldn't believe it myself.

"Okay, you're freakin' me out."

"What are the chances they'd dredge up a car? Unreal." I paused. "I'll dry if you finish washing."

Sarah nodded. "Deal."

We did the dishes and had the kitchen cleaned up when the phone rang.

"I'll get it," Sarah said. "Hello? Oh, hi, Colby. Yep, he's right here. I'll put him on." She handed me the phone.

"Hello?"

"Hi, Jimmy." I was barely able to hear him.

"Hi, Grandpa. Can you speak up? I can't hear you."

He cleared his throat before straining to talk louder. "Sorry, Jimmy. Been fighting a stomach bug. You and Sarah around the next few days? I've got someone special I'd like you to meet."

"Yeah, we're around. It'd be great to see you and meet . . . I'm guessing it's a female?"

Grandpa laughed. "Very funny. Her name's Joan."

I sensed Sarah's eyes burning a hole right through me. I looked over my shoulder to see her leaning against the sink, arms folded, face pinched with an unpleasant gaze. Once our eyes met, she unfolded her arms and softened her look.

"When will you get here?" I asked.

"I guess it'd be day after tomorrow."

"Okay, great. I've got a story about the car those Staties, Gritzmacher and Calhoun, were driving," I said.

"Oh, jeez, okay. Looking forward to hearing it. We'll see you day after tomorrow."

"Safe travels, Grandpa. Bye." I hung up the receiver. "Grandpa is bringing his new girlfriend up here for us to meet."

"Fantastic." Sarah brushed by me to wipe off the table.

"Are you being sarcastic?"

"It's so bogus, Jimmy. I know you are close to him, but what is this, the fourth or fifth girlfriend he's brought up here for us to meet? I'm not going to get too attached," she said, wringing out the dishcloth in the sink.

We settled into our comfy spots—me in the recliner, Sarah on our mushy teal couch—to watch our favorite show. *Little House on the Prairie* entertained us until Sarah abruptly said she was tired and needed to go to bed. She struggled to get off the couch.

"It's barely even eight o'clock," I objected.

She bent over to give me a kiss. "I know, but I'm feeling like I need some sleep."

"Well, all right. I'll come up with you and read in bed. Let me grab you a glass of water."

I put the water on her nightstand and stripped down to my T-shirt and underwear, needing to brush my teeth. With patient eyes, I stood outside the open bathroom door admiring her. I'd noticed in recent days she had begun carrying herself with a different posture. She had always been such a strong, independent woman. My rock. Never afraid of arduous work. Was the stress from the last few months beating her down? Hopefully, the appointment she had the next day would help us figure out what was ailing her.

My mind returned to my mother's cancer and how everything had changed with her body before she succumbed. Her hair color changed to snow white. She lost a lot of weight. The veins around her temples and in back of her hands became noticeable against her pale skin. I picked up the smell of her hospital room from the picture etched in my head; it nauseated me. The vision in my head jumped to the line at the funeral home, Pastor's empty words of comfort, and the last act of closing the casket. I knew I would never erase the vision of my dad sobbing as the pall bearers carried her out of the sanctuary.

I had witnessed how my dad reacted the death of his high school sweetheart. It hurt to watch. After she passed, he became withdrawn, including pulling away from me. He became void of emotion, unable to communicate with me. There were plenty of times when we should have talked about it—a father and son talk. "When you're older," he would say. But I'd needed to talk then. It was a matter of my heart. Dad never dated, never talked about it. He kept his head down plowing the fields, burying the pain. After I moved to Painted Rock, he'd gotten a couple of seasonal hired hands and worked another four or five years, before he sold the farm and moved into town.

For years, my grandpa had filled my emotional and companionship void. He had taken me fishing, to Kansas University activities, and we'd talked about the stuff a teenager coming of age should know. He spent time with me, helping me work through the cloud of confusing emotions surrounding Mom's death, but I wasn't sure if any of us had really come to terms with her loss.

On her last day, my dad and I had been with her in her hospital room. Lips dry—one hand holding Dad's, the other holding mine—she forced a smile. I'd never forget my mom's last words to me or the light in her crystal blue eyes fading. "Bear with one another in love, Jimmy."

Had it really been only, like, eleven years ago? Refocusing, I leaned my head beyond the door jamb of the bathroom as Sarah brushed her hair in the mirror. Her hands, which were red and raw from years spent in dishwater, appeared more swollen. Head down, I shook my head. Please God, not Sarah; I couldn't lose another.

I cleared the tightness from my throat. "Have I told you lately how much I love you?" The mirror reflected her smile. Moving a step closer, I planted an affectionate peck on her cheek, but my heart beat with worry.

5

The sun had positioned itself on a faded denim sky above the oak treetops by the time we finished breakfast.

"I'm going to take a run out to the bridge. I want to look from the spot where Grandpa threw the medal." I pictured the look of shock on the Staties' faces, which was permanently etched into my memory. "You want to come with?"

There was no hesitation in Sarah's voice. "Oh, for sure! You and me . . . treasure hunters." Her laugh was deep and rich. "Jimmy, I think I might . . . " She paused with a big smile. Sarah shook off whatever it was. "Let's go. I'll tell you when we get back."

Our movements were energized as we got dressed and hustled to my truck. We pulled to the side at the familiar spot under the iron superstructure, the midpoint of the mile-long bridge located west of town. South of us, the diesel engine of the barge moaned, with its massive dredging bucket straining to clear the original river channel. We both leaned over the silver painted beams to peer down at the light chocolate-colored water. The outline of an egg-shaped sandbar was visible below. It to be one to two feet under the cloudy water. Meringue-like white foam floated in swirls and eddies on either side of it.

On our way back to town, I opined, "I'm not wading out there. Too far from shore, and the current looks too strong. I'd need a canoe or rowboat."

"I don't want you going out there by yourself," she said in a stern voice. "I'm not sure I want you going out there at all."

"But if the river drops enough, I'm going to go for it," I said with confidence as we got to town. "We're talking forty or fifty grand." Dollar signs danced in my head. This could be my chance to contribute more financially. "It's a long shot with currents, silt, and all, but it'd be so cool if we found it, right?"

"I don't know, Jimmy." Sarah had a pained expression. "Don't you remember that the Indians believed it contained bad medicine and evil powers? For them, the medal was the start of the white man's takeover of their land, the attempt to assimilate their people and appropriate their culture. There are too many stories of bad things happening to those who came into contact with it." She swiveled in her seat to face me "Honestly, Jimmy, the medal scares me."

Her caution was too late. I was blinded with visions of grandeur, bitten by the medal's allure, and deaf to caution—like Grandpa had been. "If the sandbar gets exposed, we should get a metal detector!"

I had to mow the lawn before I went to work. Sarah stretched out on the couch to read *Love Story* by Erich Segal. She was trying to keep her mind occupied, and I was trying to keep busy while waiting for a call from her doctor with the test results from yesterday's appointment.

Mowing was a chore for me, sweetened by the smell of fresh-cut grass and the satisfaction of accomplishment. Grandpa had always said, "A job worth doing is worth doing well." Scuffling through the dry grass, I circled around the lilac bushes to the west side of the house. Far in the distance, hovering over the taupe buttes beyond the river, there were towering purple-black rain clouds, swollen with anger. The trees stirred softly with the smell of pre-rain air, as if bracing themselves for the inevitable violation of wind and rain. My '69 Lawn Scout riding lawn mower with an eight horsepower Briggs engine proved dependable to completion once again. Grandpa would be impressed with the manicure of the yard. The job had come with a filmy glaze of sweat, so I headed in to shower.

"Hey, Jimmy, can you come in here?" Sarah called as I chugged a glass of cold water in the kitchen.

"Coming!" A solitary bead of sweat inched down the side of my face.

She sat up on the couch as I entered the living room. Interrupted by the burr oak's web of branches and leaves, the sun's rays cascaded through the picture window, casting a bluish hue to her face and shoulder-length hair. "We have to talk." This was another way of saying I needed to listen. Unlike other, we-need-to-talk talks, her face held no expression. She patted the spot next to her for me to sit down.

"You know how yesterday I had an appointment?"

"Yeah." The word came out as *"yeahhhh."* I was uncertain if it would be good news or bad news. Please God, not cancer.

She surrendered to her own self-created attempt at suspense. Her serious expression transitioned to a giggle with both hands over her mouth as her eyes sparkled with excitement. "They ran some tests yesterday at my appointment. The doctor just called to tell me why I haven't been feeling good." She paused a beat to remove her hands. "I'm pregnant!" she blurted. As if shocked by 220 volts, she jolted forward, throwing her arms around my neck. She came close to knocking me off the couch.

A wave of queasiness rippled through my stomach. "How did that happen?" The words slipped out before I could stop them.

She loosened her embrace to straighten up. Stone-faced, her disbelieving eyes met mine. "Seriously? Are you kidding me? Did you ever take sex ed, Jimmy?"

"It's like . . . Well, you caught me off guard, you know . . . It's so fast," I babbled.

Having never been down this road before, I had to check my feelings. But of course, it made sense—wearing my T-shirts, sleeping more, the aversion to food, marriage talk.

Her eyes moved back and forth, searching mine. She tilted her head, waiting.

The Neanderthal portion of my brain began to process this life-altering news. My mouth felt drier by the second, opened, and stammered to a stall while my brain ratcheted up the right thing to say. My tongue wouldn't move.

"Well?" she said after an uncomfortable pause. "Say something."

I let the news settle in. I loved Sarah with every part of my being. Maybe we could do this. Like she'd said, it was time for me to man up.

"I am over the moon excited, Sarah." I said it like I believed it, before tipping forward into a tight embrace and long kiss. We reclined, so we were lying next to each other. "We are going to be the best parents ever." Internally, I began to flip out as a feeling of panic stirred. A *baby*.

"Yes, we are." Sarah pushed her hair away from her face. "Since my dad was never in the picture, it's important to me for you to be the best dad you can be." Her face was radiant, hopeful.

I balked. There was too much noise inside my head. "Of course. But not to put a damper on this moment, but I have to shower and get to work. You'll be there around one o'clock?"

She focused on the ceiling with tears beginning to well up. "Yeah, sure. I'll be there." She rotated toward me, forcing a smile.

Reciprocating with a mechanical smile, I removed myself from the escalating tension. I took the steps two at a time, stripped, and showered. The water cleansed me but did not clean me of the stain from my distress. Drying off, I caught a glimpse of my ashen face in the mirror. Apparently, my outsides reflected the turmoil thundering around my insides. I paused to stare at the man in the mirror. Was this what I wanted? Where was my life headed?

When I returned to our living room, I found Sarah flat on her back, eyes fixed on the ceiling, her face flushed. She lifted her head for an unenthusiastic, obligatory "have a nice day" kiss. Her bloodshot eyes were a red roadmap, letting me know where to go with my not-the-right-answer answer.

6

On my way to The Caboose, I stopped at Richard's Hardware, a remnant from the turn of the century. His store featured lofty ceilings, big glass windows facing the street, and the original tin ceiling tiles. I was there to pick up a repaired storm window for our house. The floor creaked under my feet as I proceeded down the worn maple floor of the center aisle toward the voices. Rick, the owner, was hunched over a glass display case. Behind him stood tall cabinets with shotguns of various gauges and rifles of various calibers. Like a carnival game, the iron gray colored hair atop his head would appear from behind one shelving unit, pass through my field of vision, and disappear behind another shelving unit, searching for something. I abruptly stopped to look at three different hobby-sized metal detectors, ranging in price from forty to one hundred dollars. Good to know if the river dropped even more.

"This one is popular with our mule deer hunters over in west river," Rick said as I breached the open space in front of the display case.

"Nice blade. Feels good in my hand, too. I'll take it."

I vaguely recognized that voice. I turned to my left. "Hey, Paul. Whatcha buyin'?" A hint of wonder laced my voice, since he claimed to be low on dough.

"Oh, hey, Jimmy. Uhm, yeah, I need a knife for campin'. Lost my other one yesterday somewhere. You know how it is." His mouth curled into a smile as if I should know he needed a knife for camping. The rest of his face showed no emotion.

"Oh, yeah. No, I get it. Major bummer to lose something like a knife." My impatience got the best of me. I still had to prep some food before I opened The Caboose. "Hey, Rick, mind if I go and get my window?"

Rick straightened up, his arms splayed on the top of the glass display case of knives. Peering over the black-rimmed cheaters resting atop his veiny nose, he instructed, "Yeah, go ahead, Jimmy. It's in back with a tag on it."

I hustled through the open doorway to the stock room and found the light switch. The bare bulb cast dull illumination on shelves of merchandise. A dehumidifier sat idle, leaving the room damp with a musty musk. Scanning beyond a workbench covered with hand tools, I found my red-tagged storm window along the back wall. Heavier than I remembered, I two-handed it back to the register, where Paul was checking out.

"See you a little after one o'clock, Paul?"

My eyes moved to the worn Formica counter. The box in front of Paul read, KA-BAR USMC, *The most famous fixed blade knife in the world*. He stared with furrowed brows at the knife, examining the leather handle carefully. I wasn't sure if he was admiring the power it possessed, the sheer size, or its lethal capabilities. He twirled it in his hand, making the sun's reflection off the seven-inch polished steel blade bounce around him, Rick's face, and the ceiling. Without making eye contact, he let out a satisfied giggle as he slowly slid it into its brown leather sheath. "Yeah, sure. Later . . . "

Rick and I exchanged glances. I nodded. "If you wouldn't mind, put the window on my tab," I directed.

"Okay, Jimmy. Hey, real sorry to hear about Miss Kitty." I was certain he meant it.

"Thanks, Rick." Stepping to the door, I said, "Later, Paul."

Rick smiled, graciously opening the door. "Have a wonderful day." I navigated between his outstretched arm and the door frame before sliding it with care into the bed of my truck. Before getting in, I glanced back through the hardware store window as Rick and Paul were consummating the sale with a handshake and smiles.

Driving the couple of blocks to The Caboose, I struggled with the fact that I should have a different mindset about Sarah's pregnancy. What was wrong with me? A surge of guilt came over me for not feeling supportive, enthused, elated—for not helping Sarah feel secure with my reassurances, feeling happy, or planning for our future. A flush of embarrassment filled my chest. Or was it shame?

The lunch crowd thinned out after one. Paul had shown up fifteen minutes early—his face shaved, hair combed, and wearing a clean T-shirt. What had he done with his ever-present backpack and new knife? He sat by himself at the end of the bar reading a MAD magazine.

I wiped the bar down as I headed in his direction. "Sarah's on her way. Shouldn't be long."

"Right on," he said without looking up.

Range Detective Ross Bradshaw got up to leave. He had washed his burger down with his scotch and without conversation. He was a thick-muscled man in his late forties or early fifties, six foot one, around two hundred and twenty pounds. He had an oversized square head with an aquiline nose. After college at the University of South Dakota in Vermillion, he'd joined the Marines and served with distinction, earning two Purple Hearts, a Silver Star, and the Navy Achievement medal. Some of those awards he had earned in Korean Conflict at the Chosin Reservoir, others in covert missions as an "advisor" in the early years of the Vietnam War. He'd told me after a late evening of a few too many scotches that his noticeable limp had been caused by shrapnel from a failed mission into Laos.

Detective Bradshaw slowed on his walk to the door and discreetly used his index finger to call me closer. He cocked his head over my shoulder, eyeballing in Paul's direction.

"Hey, Ross. How was lunch?" I asked. Well respected and reasonable, he was one of twelve Range Detectives in the state.

"Good." He tilted his head toward me, a no-nonsense air about him. "Got a report this morning of a mountain lion spotted north of the campground at Leon's S Bar Ranch." He spoke with a hushed tone, so I leaned in. He smelled of scotch and raw onion. "We think it might have come out of one of the draws along the river." He swung his arm, thumb extended, in the direction behind him. "Quarter mile south of the state line near Custerville. Took a calf there. Old man Cuff Leon said he was sure there was a calf crying for its mother around midnight, but he figured he must have been dreaming." He shook his head and scuffed at the linoleum. "Apparently, he didn't think enough to check it out. He figures the crying was the calf being hamstrung and getting disemboweled by the cat. Said it was like a talented butcher with a sharp knife had cut up the calf. I guess all they found was a trail of bits and pieces leading down toward the ash tree grove by the river." His confident demeanor, direct inflection, and rigid posture were serious. "Didn't mention any prints, though. Huh . . . " he mumbled under his breath. "Say, you don't have any small pets, do you?" He raised his right eyebrow.

I had my hands in the pockets of my blue jeans. "Sure don't." I shook my head. "Wow, been a while since anyone has reported a big cat in the area."

"Oh, they're out there." As he grabbed his dark blue South Dakota Range Detective jacket with white lettering and his ball cap from the coat rack, he halted to stare at Paul as if measuring him, assessing him. As a Range Detective, his authority was granted by State officials as a law enforcement officer. His job entailed enforcing livestock laws, chasing down modern-day cattle rustlers, and authenticating bills of sale for livestock, among other things.

He nodded in Paul's direction. "Who's the kid?"

"He's lookin' for a job, so we're going to interview him. I could use some help around here."

His eyes shifted to me, his volume returning to normal. "Oh. Anyway, I gotta go help the Tribal Sheriff over west river inspect some fencing along where the Corps is dredging for a property line dispute. Don't get paid enough at this job to go over to the rez, but I like Sheriff Owl. The river seems to be dropping pretty fast." He winked. "Who knows what Lake Oahe will give up next?" He paused a beat like he had more to say but shook it off. "Well, give a holler if you hear anything on the mountain lion deal." Ross hitched up his pants as he hobbled toward the door and nodded goodbye before the squeaky front door shut behind him.

The bar had emptied, save for the lingering grease smell, a light fog of cigarette smoke near the ceiling, and the beacons of color projected from the jukebox. Right as I finished clearing the bar of plates, silverware, and glasses, Sarah came through the swinging saloon doors and stuffed her purse under the bar. I greeted her with a kiss and whispered, "We never got to talk about Paul's . . ."

She cut me off. "Whose disgusting backpack and sleeping bag is in the kitchen?"

I crossed in front of her and pushed the double action hinged doors open. The pack resting against the butcher block appeared to be Paul's. I pivoted back through the doors. "Hey, Paul!" My voice had a sharp edge to it.

"What's up?" he asked, eyes like saucers, eyebrows arched. Clueless.

I opened one of the doors and pointed. "Your backpack?" My tone was incredulous.

"Well, yeah. Chill . . . sounds like you're not cool with it there. But see, what I did was come in the back door, and I left it there because I didn't want to bring it in the bar during my interview."

Sarah's mouth hung open in amazement.

Paul's eyes shifted from me to Sarah and back to me. "So, are we cool?"

"Ah, yeah," I mumbled.

An air of awkwardness hung over us. Paul nodded with his chin jutted toward the door. "What did he want?" He lit a cigarette, exhaling to the ceiling.

"Oh, he had a report of a mountain lion spotted north of the campground. We get them in the area from time to time," I responded plainly.

Sarah jumped right into the interview. "Have you any experience working in a bar or restaurant?" she said as she moseyed around and took a seat at the bar. Paul took the seat next to her but moved his bar stool back a bit. He pulled an ashtray closer to double tap the ashes off. I leaned against the counter in front of the liquor bottles, arms folded on my chest.

"I bartended in college at Jimmy's Double Tall and waited tables at the Cock-A-Doodle-Do. My dad split on my mom, and even though she worked two jobs she didn't have the money to pay for four years of college."

"Where did you go to college?" I chimed in.

"Columbus College, right there in Columbus. Majored in Ag Econ," Paul said, lighting another cigarette.

I leaned forward with a big smile. "Right on, man. My major, too." He smiled and extended his hand, which I slapped. I hadn't given anyone five in the longest time. It was invigorating.

Sarah rolled her eyes. She leaned her elbows onto the bar. "So where are you staying? Jimmy said you moved out of the campground."

"I'm at one of them little cabins towards the east edge of town. I think it's called the Waltz-On-Inn or something."

"It's called Waltson's Inn. Waltson family owns it." I felt obligated to correct him. "So, does like fifteen hours a week sound okay? I'm thinking you would help with dishes, stocking, some bartending, and you could work up to cooking, eventually opening and closing. You'd get minimum wage, $2.30 an hour, plus tips. We'll pay you *cash*."

Paul's eyes lit up, and his mouth opened to speak, but Sarah beat him to it. She snapped her head around toward me, her eyes cold and hard. "Jimmy, let's you and I talk first about how we'd set up the schedule. I'm still planning on working, you know." Darts pierced my eyeballs.

Given the rough road we had traveled that morning, I didn't push it. In fact, I wanted to crawl into a hole.

Paul lifted his arms, palms open. "No problem, man. I understand." He rubbed out his cigarette with force in the ashtray. "You guys want to talk about it, I'm cool, man." He stood; the stool scraped the floor as he pushed it in. "I'm lookin' for a working man's wages is all. This cat ain't afraid of hard work. No, sir. During high school I worked on a farm detasseling corn, mucking stalls, repairing fence line—all of it."

"No way! I grew up on a farm, too," I gushed, feeling an instant kinship. Our commonalities made me think Paul would fit in well. "Right on." I added a smile. "Why don't you check back in a couple of days to see if we've made a decision."

"Okay. Mind if I go out through the kitchen and grab my backpack?"

"Go ahead. Don't let the screen door slam when you close it, and pull the outside door closed behind you," Sarah said with specificity.

"Yes, ma'am. Y'all have yourself a good day."

Sarah and I were quiet as Paul let himself out. Fortunately for him, he followed the instructions.

"Okay. He creeps me out," Sarah sneered. "The whole backpack deal in the kitchen was completely inappropriate. I went through it. I didn't know whose it was." She shrugged. "But, Jimmy, inside there was a *Playboy*, dirty men's T-shirts, a can of Spam, a knife. Weird stuff."

Feeling like she wasn't going to want to hire him, I jumped to his defense. "I think you're overreacting," I scoffed, hands on hips.

"Wait. There was a white T-shirt I'd swear was a little girl's," she said. "I get the willies thinking about it."

"No way. C'mon, Sarah, *get real*." I shook my head, thinking about how ridiculous she was acting. "I'm sure it was a rag he picked up along the way. The rest was probably stuff he needed for hitchhiking survival," I reasoned in the hope we would hire him.

"Hmm, pretty sure I know what I saw."

"I'll give you, it was weird to put his backpack in the kitchen without asking," I said.

"What's next? We wake up to find him drinking coffee in our kitchen?" Sarah's tone contained in aggravation.

I needed to refocus the conversation. Folding my arms, I leaned against the inside of the bar.

Sarah maintained her hand on hip, the other arm braced against the back counter. Her head tilted with a "What are you going to do about it?" look on her face.

"How about this? He fills in until you are ready to come back. You make the call on hours, job description, all of it." I shifted to the other side of the bar, trying to read her expression. "I feel like we don't have any other option." I moved toward her in an attempt to melt the icy stare. "If you don't think it's working out, we'll let him go. Okay?"

Her posture softened. "I guess. But I'm not happy about it."

I pulled her close, and she reciprocated by patting me on the back like an obedient dog.

"Fifteen hours, no bartending unless absolutely necessary, minimum wage." Sarah pushed off of me. "I'll go back to my normal schedule, except I'm off on Saturdays and Sundays. With us being closed on Mondays, I'll have three days to recover." Her posture went rigid, and she wagged her finger at me. "And don't you dare invite him over to our house."

I forced a smile and nodded. Teasing her, I stiffened to attention and saluted. "Yes, ma'am. I hear you loud and clear."

Disgusted, she tossed a wet bar rag at me. "*Ugh.*" The sound she made came from deep within her throat like a prehistoric growl. Next came the out-of-patience yelp. "Jimmy!" With her upper front teeth pressuring her lower lip, she fought back a smile.

Sarah threw up her arms in frustration as she stomped off, nearly knocking the slats out of the louvered swinging saloon doors.

I might have gone too far with the salute.

Whoosh, bang! The screen door crashed shut. Sarah had not followed her own admonishment as she exited through the back door.

I danced a jig, relieved to have help.

7

I loved the snap of a fall morning. Long-sleeved shirts, the crispness of dried leaves, clear blue skies. Recognizing the seasons were transitioning, the Elders had called for a fall cleanup at our church. I passed Jay's house on my way and hit the brakes. The week had gotten away from me without a chance to call him.

My heavy footsteps bounded up the wooden steps and rang the doorbell. His face peeked from behind the drawn curtain, then withdrew. The oak door swung open. "What's goin' on?"

I took a deep breath. "Only have a sec. They dredged up a D.I.P. car. The car with the agents . . . "

Jay stepped outside. He put his hands in his pockets to ward off the frosty morning. "Yep. Heard about it. Crazy-city, man."

"I think you should get ahold of Robert, Mark, and the combine driver. Make sure everyone is aware of it. Corps may come by asking if they know anything about how it ended up in Lake Oahe. Tell them to be honest like when we were with Sheriff Owl."

Jay told me to relax, because there had been no tears shed by his people when the agents disappeared into the river. They had blackmailed his brother, Barking Coyote, for information, and there were others in Jay's tribe they'd harassed. He was confident any paperwork filled out by Sheriff Owl on their accident had been misfiled or lost.

Jay spoke with confidence. "What happened to those guys has always been a mystery to everybody. I think it will remain one."

I high fived Jay. "Right on. Catch ya later."

The dark red brick church was located at the corner of 7th Avenue and 2nd Street. Its bell tower dominated one whole corner, rising above arched wooden doors. Harsh northern winds had begun to undress the trees of their foliage overnight, leaving eerie shadows on the stained-glass windows. Leaves of blushed blaze red, faded yellow, and dull orange carpeted the grass and were ready for raking.

Pastor Thor Dawson divided us into six teams of two. "Many hands make light work," he said, flashing a warm smile, which revealed a small but noticeable chip in his front tooth.

Pastor Thor appeared to be in his early thirties. His wide, fleshy jowls were set on an alert face with bushy lamb chop sideburns. Thor was short for Thorlough. Despite being slight of build, he possessed more energy than the rest of us combined. He even taught a six-week self-defense course in the church basement, which Sarah and I had taken. Within his sermons, he had painted a clear picture of his background. He'd grown up in the northern Wisconsin town of Tomahawk, one of Edwin and Olga Dawson's twelve children. His grandparents were of German ancestry but had immigrated from Ukraine. He'd grown up in company housing along the Wisconsin River, close to his father's employer, the Owens-Illinois paper mill. He'd once described the smell carried by a northwest wind from the paper mill as, "three-week-old liverwurst hiding in the back of the refrigerator."

Pastor was dressed for work and weather in a flannel shirt under his jean jacket, tucked into faded, flared Levi's. He pulled me aside, handing me a rake as the others dispersed around the church property carrying hedge clippers, brooms, and metal garbage cans for the trimmings. "Let's you and I start on the north side, Jimmy," he started. "Bob and Amy, grab the other rakes and come with us. You'll go the opposite direction."

Once Pastor and I had separated from the other raking team, we each started making a pile in the middle of the side yard. After about ten minutes, he paused to lean on his rake. "You happen to catch *The Tonight Show* last night?"

"Nah. I was working."

"Always gives me a laugh. Carson's comedic timing is amazing." He removed his baseball cap to wipe his brow. "So, Jimmy, how are you and Sarah doing?" he asked with a gentle tone.

The workday had taken an unexpected twist. I stopped raking and leaned on my rake, too. My body was heating up under my Painted Rock Eagles sweatshirt. "Good. Some work challenges, but overall, I'd say good." I didn't know if I should tell him about Sarah's push for marriage ... or the fact that she was expecting. Plus, Sarah would want us to be on the same page with the timing of an announcement.

"So, I have to ask ... Are you and Sarah talking marriage yet?"

There it was. Sarah had "volunteered" me to do this job. Now I knew why. I cleared my throat loudly in an attempt to alleviate the tightness in my chest. "Yeah, we've talked some." I pulled a few stray leaves into my pile.

Pastor put his head down and started raking again, too. "I've been wondering. I imagine it can be tough to work together and live together, especially after Katherine's passing." The wind picked up, allowing a small portion of our multi-colored pile their momentary freedom. "When I visited her in the hospital, Katherine told me how much Sarah loved you, how much she had hoped to see you two birds get married before she died. I reassured her it would happen."

My face flushed while focused on corralling the escapees.

"You have a lot on your plate, but if you ever want to stop by and talk, don't hesitate to call, okay?"

My head was spinning. Visions of dropping my rake and running flashed before me. "Yeah, I appreciate the offer." My tone was sharper than I intended. I changed the subject to the football season and who was better—the Green Bay Packers, his favorite team, or my favorite, the Kansas City Chiefs. We agreed it had been a big win for our Eagles over the determined Redfield Pheasants in last night's homecoming game. To the west, the soft *flump, flump, flump* of an executive-type helicopter with the seal of South Dakota cruised toward the airport.

Cleanup went faster than I expected, creating extra time before I needed to be at The Caboose. Singing along with Rod Stewart's "Tonight's The Night" on KOLW, I used the time to stop at Gus Sinclair's to fill up.

The double ding of the welcome hose interrupted my singing. I turned off the car as Gus shuffled out of the big bay door singing Elvis's "Heartbeak Hotel." He wore his trademark blue overalls, today topped by a *Chubby's Drive-In* ballcap. "Can't believe the King is gone, Jimmy," Gus lamented as he reset the pump, then inserted the nozzle into my Chevy. Gus, who was pushing seventy, reminded me of a carved pumpkin when he smiled—spaces and remnants of his front teeth. His lower jaw over-closed like a turtle's when he shut his mouth. "It's been what, a month or two? He was a performer though, wasn't he? You see how he moved them hips?" The left side of Gus's lip raised up as the portly codger circled his hips inside an invisible Hula-Hoop.

"Easy, Gus." I pasted a wide smile on my face and pointed at his hips. "You're gonna break one of those if you're not careful." Gus had become a dear friend and someone trustworthy. Our initial meeting had happened when Grandpa and I first arrived in Painted Rock. Later on that trip, Grandpa's University of Kansas International Harvester Scout had had a radiator clamp come off in the middle of the prairie, miles from town. With many thanks from us, Gus had the Scout fixed in no time, and we returned to the dig site.

Gus returned the nozzle to the hanger with a bang.

"I can't believe gas has gone up to fifty-eight cents a gallon," I lamented, following Gus to the front of the truck.

Gus lifted the hood to check the oil. "I don't much care for it either." His flaccid lips made a smacking sound when he talked. "I gotta pay, same as you." He bent at the waist to check the dipstick. "Oil's good, but I wouldn't wait much longer for a change." He ducked from under the truck hood, slamming it shut.

On the way in to settle up, the noise from Grand Avenue had gotten busier, with combines and grain trucks covered in crop dust creating an irritating background hum. I figured some of the overarching buzz surrounding me came from last-minute prepping for the homecoming dinners and dance tonight, also.

Once inside, I noticed the once sea mist green walls of the waiting area had been repainted to a bright yellow color like the popular smiley faces. The cement floor had been painted gray, too, giving it a clean look. The station still carried the familiar smell of lubricant and oil. I got a ten spot out of my wallet and handed it to him. Muted but still charging, "Stairway to Heaven" burst from the radio sitting in the service bay. The cash register symphony played *click clack, ring, slosh*, and the drawer opened. Gus handed me my change before closing the drawer.

Wearing an apologetic veil on his face, he stepped from behind the counter to stand in front of the rack of neatly displayed candy, oil, road maps, and chips for sale. "Jimmy, you got a minute?"

I put my wallet in my back pocket and put my hands in my front pockets. "Yeah, sure, Gus. What's up?"

"None of my business, but there was this feller in here a couple of days ago lookin' for work. A stranger to town, long hair, south accent." Gus typically made a long story longer rather than shorter, so I sat down in one of the light blue tattered vinyl chairs. "I didn't have no need for an extra. I told him no." Gus had a worried look. "But he starts askin' about you, The Caboose, if you owned it, and if you were from Kansas. It didn't feel right to me. I got a real bad feelin' about him, you know. The guy was askin' too many questions."

South Dakotans, I had found, were of the "live and let live" type. To pry was to assault.

"We're slowly getting to know the guy you're talking about," I said. "He's a bit different, from Georgia, you know. Sarah has been struggling a bit with Katherine's passing. And honestly, I'm getting burned out. We needed help, and he was looking, so we hired him part-time."

"Well . . . okay." Relief replaced the fog of stress covering Gus's face. "Thought you'd want to know." He extended his permanently grease-stained hand. "But I still got a bad feelin' about him."

"Thanks for the heads up, Gus. Later." We exchanged a firm handshake before I left to enjoy the melody of a Saturday morning.

As I zipped up my windbreaker, I realized Gus was the third person to caution me about my soon-to-be assistant. Ironically, as I waited for the light to change, Paul came out of The Steer Horns Bar and Restaurant, followed by Range Detective Ross about ten seconds later.

A coincidence?

8

Homecoming night in Painted Rock was a festive scene. The bar reverberated with music and loud conversation as blotches of magnificent colors projected from the jukebox, circling overhead in a shroud of cigarette smoke. Our patrons were adorned in Painted Rock Eagles ball caps, sweatshirts, and long-sleeve T-shirts. The alcohol of assorted colors and concoctions I served was consumed between jovial conversations and music from the likes of Foghat, The Doobie Brothers, and Fleetwood Mac. Sarah brought Grandpa and his newest girlfriend over around seven. Her entrance, locked on Grandpa's arm, caused the heads of both the men and the women to turn. Girlfriend number five carried a presence about her as she surveyed the bar. Together, the couple bore a dignified air. I wasn't sure if the looks on their faces communicated condescension, excitement, or confusion at the patron heads swiveling for a look. Grandpa wore his white dress slacks and wide-collared blue shirt with white vertical stripes. His white hair covered the tops of his ears and shirt collar.

He moved forward with his arm wrapped around the waist of his "special someone" for introductions. Joan had a broad smile of perfect teeth, high cheekbones, and sparkling deep brown eyes. She wore a modest dress complementing her Dorothy Hamill hairstyle. We exchanged pleasantries. Grandpa didn't stop smiling. "Hey, Jimmy, can you get me a Hamm's? Joan will have a Chardonnay."

"You betcha, Grandpa." My chest swelled with admiration. He was still my hero for all he had taught me as a boy—along with the courage, tenacity, and smarts he'd used to find the Peace Medal. The advice he'd given me when I needed it the most.

I kept the customers happy by hustling from one end of the bar to the other, making small talk, refilling drinks, and cleaning up. Range Detective Ross Bradshaw showed up dressed casually in Wrangler jeans with a silver belt buckle the size of an Idaho potato. Despite being dressed in "civilian" clothes, he still wore his state-issued Smith and Wesson .357 Magnum. Curls of white chest hair sprouted from the open collar of his teal and brown checked shirt. He had been on full scholarship at USD for football and baseball and still kept in decent shape. Despite his age, he possessed a physique that intimidated the men and attracted the women. He got his usual—scotch—and limped to a spot along the back wall to survey like a hawk over the landscape. His demeanor suggested a strong internal current of wariness. Of what, I did not know. Was he watching for something or looking for someone?

From time to time, I'd hear snippets of Sarah and Paul talking in the kitchen, but I was unable to decipher the topic of conversation. Since the grill had closed and things at the bar were under control—at least for the time being—I snuck out to the kitchen to see how they were doing. Shared laughter greeted me.

"What's so funny?" A pang of jealousy ripped through me as I glanced back and forth between them.

"Paul was describing what his boss at the Cock-A-Doodle would do every time a hen burger got ordered. I told him about some of the characters we have in town—namely, Walter at Chubby's Drive-In. If I hear the story one more time about how his nephew led his team to the Wisconsin basketball championship last March, I'm going to throw up. He must have some serious forgetfulness. Something." She shook her head. "I mean, every time I'm in there, he asks if I want to see the scrapbook he put together of newspaper clippings." Sarah's voice ended an octave higher before transitioning into a giggle—eyes squinted, face stretched tight.

Paul burst out a chuckle. I still didn't get it. I waited for one of them to let me in on the joke. Paul cracked the uncomfortable silence. "She's killin' me with these stories. Man, she's funny." He smiled at Sarah.

I wasn't having it. "Paul, go grab the tubs of dirty dishes from under the bar and start washing."

He turned off the water before he wiped his hands on his apron, nodding through the swinging doors. "Yessir."

"So, Paul isn't such a bad guy after all?" I whispered with a tone of sarcastic told-you-so tinged with disgust.

"Don't misread one exchange as a coronation," Sarah snipped.

"Fair enough." I pivoted. "What do you think of Joan?"

"She seems nice. A little snooty, but she's probably nervous, ya know?" Sarah raised her arms with palms open, her shoulders scrunched to her ears.

"Can you help me for a bit before taking Grandpa and Joan home?"

"As you requested," she answered with a salute.

I laughed out loud. "Touché."

Rolling out of the kitchen, Paul had jumped into opening beers, pouring booze, collecting the money—all of it. Sarah and I exchanged glances. She wore a look of disapproval watching Paul service the bar. Without hesitation, she grabbed me by the elbow, ushering me back into the kitchen.

"What is he doing out there? He's not supposed to be bartending." Her voice was an angry whisper. "You told him to start washing dishes!"

"I think he wants to prove his value. You see it out there; there's a good crowd." I gently put my hands on her shoulders, meeting her eyes. "It's okay, he's fine. I got this."

"I don't like it." She folded her arms across her chest and brushed past me, looking disgusted. She stopped at the saloon doors to turn and point, her eyes narrowed. "You better keep an eye on him."

It was a night on the town for both parents and their high schoolers, who were attending the homecoming dance. It also happened to be a night out for a group of teachers. They were celebrating Connie Warner's thirty-second birthday. Rumor had it, she'd relocated from Bighorn after a divorce. Ringlets of blond hair surrounded brown eyes, her dimpled cheeks dotted with freckles. When she smiled, her bright-white teeth peeked out between full lips. Her outfit—a loose purple peasant top with embroidery over high-waisted bell bottoms—made her stand out in the crowded bar.

The rest of the night flew by. It was a festive night of excess consumption, bald-faced lies, painful truths, and blossoming romances. Grandpa and Paul were laughing, bantering back and forth, until Grandpa's demeanor changed dramatically. Out of nowhere, Grandpa's finger came up like a dagger about to stab Paul. Red-faced, Grandpa backed off his stool and nearly fell to the ground. I caught Grandpa's attention and shouted over "Paint It, Black" that Sarah would take Joan and him home. Beyond the conflict, Range Detective Ross smiled.

Paul's face constricted. He shook his head and laughed, saying something inaudible in my direction. Was he taunting me?

I responded by shrugging, thinking I'd try to sort out their heated discussion in the morning.

Out of the corner of my eye, I sensed Connie trying to catch my attention without being obvious about it. Before I could see if she needed another drink, she bid adieu with a covert wave and a slow strut toward the door. She reminded me of an exotic animal at the zoo—pacing, beautiful, cunning, and dangerous. Something inside me stirred.

9

Awakened by church bells, I crawled out of bed, my ears ringing from last night. Sarah asked me to shut the door as she pulled the covers up under her chin. Working with barely a few hours of sleep made me saunter clumsily downstairs to start breakfast. Soon, the smell of sizzling bacon competed with the freshly brewed coffee from our Mr. Coffee to capture my senses. Scrambled eggs were being kept warm in the oven, patiently waiting for the toast to toast and join them. Orange juice sat on the table.

Grandpa waddled through the doorway to take a seat at the kitchen table. He was dressed in brown and blue plaid slacks and a solid blue button-down shirt.

"Good morning, Grandpa," I said optimistically.

Grandpa reciprocated a dour expression. "Morning, Jimmy. What do I have to do to get a cup of coffee?" His sharp tongue caught me off guard. The subdued kitchen lighting accentuated the bags under his eyes.

I poured him a cup of coffee. "Hey, Grandpa . . . " A random need-to-know popped into my head. "You never told me you found Custer's pistol."

"I did. How did you find out?" He said it like it was supposed to be a secret.

I told him about Paul Harvey's radio vignette and suggested that a highly sought-after artifact like Custer's pistol might be something he should have shared with me.

He huffed with contempt. "What? You want me to recite all my legendary finds?" He took a sip of coffee. "If you must know, I also found his brother Tom's pistol a week before."

"Whoa, Grandpa. You feeling all right?" I was genuinely concerned. He'd never spoken to me so harshly before.

"Yeah, I guess. Why?" He dumped two packets of sugar into his cup and stirred. He bounced the spoon twice on the edge and took another sip.

"You don't seem too perky this morning—at least, not as perky as when you were at the Indian village reading to me about Lewis and Clark trading with Chief Kakawita for the medal." The start of a smile softened his face. I focused on flipping the bacon and managing the splatter. "You are one of one, Grandpa." My lips curled into a smile, remembering the intelligence and cunning he'd used to find the medal in the summer of '69.

His mood lightened as his smile grew. "Well, a blast from the past to start the morning. I'm glad we got to share a special time together. Wasn't a picnic though, was it?"

I faced him. "Not at all. Get this. The Corps was dredging on the west side of Oahe, and they dredged up Gritzmacher and Calhoun's D.I.P. car. With one body in it."

He stared at me as he set his coffee down. He paused like he was trying to understand words of a foreign language, then sighed. "Well, they got what they deserved." Grandpa gazed into his coffee cup. An uncomfortable quiet consumed the space around us.

"Officer Tittle warned me the D.I.P. might come asking questions. But Jay said he was pretty sure any report Sheriff Owl had written up would have been lost."

"Uh-huh. Gotcha." He bit off a piece of bacon. "Don't worry about it. They were bad men who were livin' a bad life. It was bound to catch up with them." He shrugged. "They can ask all the questions they want. Won't change what happened."

The quiet returned for a beat. "With the river level dropping, I was thinking the medal might surface."

His attention returned to me in a hurry.

"So," I started out slow, "Sarah and I took a drive to the spot on the bridge where you threw the medal off."

"You stay away from the river and trying to find the medal." He pointed a gnarled finger at me. "You know better. Either the currents or the medal are gonna get you killed." He took another sip of coffee. "Not to mention, it's covered by a foot of silt. Promise me, Jimmy, you won't go in the river."

"Okay, okay." I was taken aback by the stern tone and his directness. "I promise." His sharp rebuke reminded me of the night before. "Hey," I tried to sound casual. "Last night. What did you get so upset with Paul about?"

"Oh, you noticed. So . . . " Turning back around, he went into his professor-lecturing-a-class voice. "I introduced myself and Joan of course, and he says my reputation precedes me. And I'm thinking you told him I was your grandpa, you told him about us fishing when you were younger, living on the farm, going to KU football games . . . Those kinds of things."

The kitchen was filled with wholesome breakfast smells—coffee, eggs, and bacon. Joan made her entrance, looking ready for dinner at a fancy restaurant. Her makeup was flawlessly done, hairdo impeccable, tan blouse over a light blue skirt. "Good morning, honey." She bent over to meet his obligatory lips. As for me, I received a hug and the pungent smell of hair spray. "Good morning, Jimmy. Everything looks and smells wonderful." There was warmth in her smile.

"Thank you. Coffee?" I asked.

"Yes, please."

I brought the coffee and approximated the cream and sugar before setting the scrambled eggs and toast on the table. "Help yourself; bacon's coming."

Joan spoke up, "Shouldn't we wait for Sarah?"

I put the bacon on the table and sat down. "No, she's a late sleeper these days."

Joan had a twinkle in her eye and a sly smile on her face. Did she sense Sarah was pregnant?

"So, finish your story, Grandpa." I needed to find the underlying cause of his reaction, his anger.

He eyed Joan over his coffee cup, sans slurp. Politely, he said, "I was telling Jimmy about my displeasure with Paul asking so many questions."

Joan rolled her eyes as she nodded, affirming Grandpa had not been happy.

His eyes contained pinpointed pupils of seriousness. "I swear to God, Jimmy, if he woulda pressed me any further, I'd have punched him."

Stunned, I examined his face, accounting for every wrinkle and age spot. His lamb-chop sideburns had gotten whiter, the only part of him a lamb. The rest I'd still call wolf.

Joan shrieked mid-chew, leaving a bit of egg on the corner of her lower lip. "Colby Phillips, you most certainly would have not!" I wasn't sure whether Joan so vehemently objected to the threat of violence or Grandpa's language at the breakfast table.

"The hell I wouldn't have," Grandpa jabbed back, nostrils flared, violently tearing into his toast.

The conversation had begun unraveling rapidly. "Whoa, slow down, you two. Grandpa, what happened with you and Paul? C'mon, out with it," I pestered.

He leaned back in his chair a bit, wiping his mouth with his napkin. "We were getting to know each other, you know, where are you from, how long you been here, what did you do before you retired . . . Some back and forth in between him serving drinks, takin' money, keepin' the bar clean." He took a bite of a piece of bacon, swallowed, and crossed his legs. "Out of nowhere he goes, 'People told me they call you the Treasure Hunter because you dig in Indian villages.' Well, shit, I tell him, not me . . . You've got me mixed up with someone else. He puts a sly smile on his face and says, 'There's rumors about what you found around here.' What was it they said in the Watergate hearings? If those guys got caught, they said deny, deny, deny. So, I said he didn't know what he's talkin' about. Wasn't me." Grandpa took a sip of his coffee. "I sure as hell wasn't going to get into the whole story."

He used his arms to accentuate the expression in his voice and continued, "But he says it sounds like I'm an amoral person by digging at an Indian village. I have to admit, I'd had a couple of drinks over my limit, and I was about ready to explode. This punk is lecturing *me* about morality! Hell, I wanted to tell him I've got shelves in my rec room full of moral plaques, crystal, and certificates. Anyway, I stood up and told the long-haired hippie dirtbag he should go f—..." He stopped, catching himself before Joan's disdain could escalate.

The kitchen fell silent. "Well, I guess we know why you two were going at it." I nodded, seeing Sarah making her way down the stairs. "Paul's not a bad guy. I'd say he's different. Sorry his badgering and accusations upset you."

Grandpa stood when Sarah came into the kitchen. He cleared his throat and said, "Morning, Sarah."

"Morning, everybody," she said through a yawn. She wore her comfy pajama bottoms and one of my T-shirts with The Caboose logo on it.

"You can have my spot," I said.

She eased into my chair and started to pour herself a glass of orange juice when Grandpa let out an audible grimace.

"What's the matter?" I was concerned.

"Ah, nothing." Grandpa grabbed his stomach, his face strained with pain.

Joan jumped on the lie. "Colby has an appointment when we get back to have Doctor Waterfield check out his stomach. He's been having these attacks after he eats."

"Joan, honey," Grandpa spoke through gritted teeth. "Will you run into our bedroom and get me my pills?"

"Yes, of course." Her eyebrows dove toward each other, her eyes narrowed with concern. She moved efficiently to exit the kitchen.

"Hey, Grandpa," I whispered. "Does Joan know about the medal and, you know, all of it?"

"She knows most of it. Let's leave it there." His voice contained pain. "We didn't get into a lot of the—" He stopped mid-sentence.

Joan returned with a bottle of antacid pills. She dumped four of them into Grandpa's open palm. "And here's your pain pill. Doctor said to take one of these."

Cringing, Grandpa washed them all down with orange juice. He got up from the kitchen table to stagger—hunched over and clenching his midsection—into the living room.

Fear filled me as I followed, watching him collapse into the recliner. "Do I need to worry about your stomach problem, Grandpa?"

Grandpa waved it off. "No, Jimmy. I'm sure it's nothing more than a bug. Doc will figure it out."

10

Joan and Grandpa had gone to sleep, and we were close behind. "We have to leave by seven-thirty tomorrow for my appointment in Bismarck," Sarah said, standing in front of the bathroom mirror and taking off her makeup.

"Bismarck? You said your doctor was here in town," I responded, drying off after showering.

"He is, but Doctor Graham wanted me to get some tests done in Bismarck. I guess they don't have the right equipment or lab or something around here. He wants to make sure the baby is okay." Silence. "I think you should go with me," she suggested.

"Why not go to Pierre? It's so much closer," I questioned.

Sarah's face wore an impatient mask. "Because it's not where they told me to go." Her voice rose in volume. "I'm guessing the machine for the tests I need to have is in Bismarck."

My body tensed up, envisioning a bill of hundreds of dollars. "Sounds expensive. Can we afford to do it?" I was pretty sure these extra tests wouldn't be covered by our insurance.

She set down her makeup remover and washcloth, looking at me through a cloud of disappointment. She tilted her head like she was talking to a fourth grader. Slowly, she said, "Jimmy, we can't afford not to. This is *our* baby. I'll pay for the damn test or whatever they want to do." Her eyes started to bulge, and her lower lip quivered. "So . . . if you don't want to go, tell me. I am fully capable of driving to Bismarck."

"Yes, I absolutely want to go. Don't patronize me, Sarah. I know it's our baby, but it *is* a fair question." I spoke in a calm voice, hoping not to escalate the situation, while slipping on my white briefs. "Okay, so, . . . who is going to run the bar?"

"Have Paul do it. You liked how well he did with the Saturday night crowd." Her voice was full of confidence as she returned to doing her makeup, using the mirror to keep eye contact. "I don't trust him completely, but . . . " She must have read the hesitation in my voice. "If you're not comfortable with him, close for the lunch hour and open at four. People understand we have a life. Don't feel guilty. We hardly ever close for lunch."

"I should tell you the receipts and the cash didn't jibe last night. The cash register was forty-five dollars short. I'm going to have to ask Paul about it, I suppose," I confessed, knowing full well I was going to get an *I told you so.*

Sarah paused. "Shoot, I meant to tell you. I took it for groceries."

Relief. I didn't have to confront Paul after all. "Okay. So, when *are* we going to start telling people? I'm sure people will talk crap about us."

"People have been talking crap about us living together for years. People talking about our personal life is the least of my worries at the moment. *Anytime* is good with me." Her tone, her dark eyes, and her flat facial expression carried a coldness, a distance, that I'd rarely seen. "And by the way, I've seen how that Connie chick has been checking you out every time she's in our bar."

I recoiled, surprised she'd noticed. "C'mon. Connie knows we're living together. Your hormones are clouding your vision."

She shook her head. "You're being a jerk."

Quickly, I went for the redirect. "Are you going to want to stop and see your mom? She's still in Bismarck, right?"

She rolled her eyes with a scoff. "I wouldn't even know how to get ahold of her. She told me at Katherine's funeral she had moved. I never got her new number or address. Don't know if I would call her anyway."

I shrunk away and crawled into bed. In the distance, the yelping of coyotes pierced the quiet night.

Grandpa's note on the kitchen table said they would get breakfast at the café downtown before "taking Joan on a road trip to see west river country. Want to show her the village where we found the TJ Peace Medal." While Sarah had her breakfast and got ready for our trip to Bismarck, I scurried down to The Caboose. A heavy frost had painted areas white where the weak sunshine had yet to kiss. I spread out my AAA map on the bar. I estimated it to be about one hundred and thirty or so miles—more than a two-hour drive for sure. I taped a sheet of notebook paper to the front door. To account for travel and doctor time, in big red letters it read: *Closed for lunch. Open for dinner 5–8.*

We headed out of town, following a late-model Ford pickup with US government plates, likely Bureau of Land Management. In my rearview mirror, the peach-colored sky behind us contained slashes of red clouds above the horizon. Crossing the

77

bridge to the west side of the river, I snuck a peak at the shoreline for evidence of further retreat of the water level. The water had gone down enough to expose a narrow beach, but was it enough to expose the sand bar? The dredging of Lake Oahe to widen the main channel was still going strong.

Sarah asked, "Why do you think D.I.P. never followed up with Sheriff Owl or tried to dig the car up in '69?"

"I don't know. Either the D.I.P. had no idea where to look because they lost radio contact, or the good folks on the reservation stonewalled the authorities," I said with a matter-of-fact tone. "I'm with Jay. It's a mystery."

I headed the truck north, passing fields painted by an earthly palette of browns, yellows, creams, and tans. The fields spread for acres in every direction, void of grain and absent of corn. Rhythmic clacking of the tires on the tar-filled cracks in the highway kept time with Glen Campbell's "Wichita Lineman" on the eight track. Starlings and the occasional meadowlark zigzagged from pole to post ahead of our truck.

The silence grew more painful by the mile. Out of the corner of my eye, I caught Sarah sneaking a glance at me. She had something on her mind. Over the years we'd been together, I had learned she would talk when she was ready. I tapped the steering wheel to the music.

Finally, turning toward me, she spoke calmly. "Jimmy, I've been spotting and cramping."

"What does that mean?"

"C'mon, Jimmy. Seriously? At twelve weeks?" Her face twisted in disbelief. "It means there might be a problem with the baby." The tears had been patient, waiting for the dam to break.

I glanced in her direction. "*Ah*, the real reason we're going to Bismarck."

"Yes!" she screamed. The dam had burst, tears spilling down her cheeks. I drove a few miles without saying anything while she composed herself.

"The doctor *thinks* everything is okay. He used a fetal stethoscope at my last visit and was pretty sure he heard the baby's heartbeat." She wiped her tears.

I clicked off the eight track. "*Pretty sure?*"

Sniffling, she reached into her purse for a tissue. She dropped her head and cupped her bump. "My reaction, exactly. Which is why he referred me to Bismarck. The clinic up there has this thing called an ultrasound." Her face was wrenched with pain. "It will tell us for sure if the baby is okay."

Her last comment added a whole new dimension to our trip. "*If* the baby is okay"? Damn, I had just been starting to process the idea of being a dad. An urgent knock of disappointment crept into my psyche at the prospect of not being a father. If I were a dad, would I be a good dad? I thought so. Sarah would be a good mom, for sure. Our house would be more stressful if she lost the baby than if she'd had it. She would be crushed. I was certain I would be broken at the sight of her anguish. The range of emotions reminded me of being on a roller coaster.

I glanced at Sarah to gauge her mood. She had balled up, staring out the window with her head resting on her hand.

"You okay?" I put my hand on her thigh.

"I don't know..." Her voice trailed off. "You don't understand what it's like to be pregnant twenty-four seven..."

Continuing north, we crossed through sporadic patches of light and dark pavement as clouds crossed morning sunbeams. Below the heather clouds, Canadian geese were flying south, flocks varying in number and ability to fly in a V. Miles continued to spin the odometer as a pall fell over the truck cab. My teeth and jaw began to hurt from clenching, causing a dull pain to radiate toward the back of my head. I rubbed my cheeks and leaned toward the middle, hoping the pain would subside. There was no relief.

We crossed the muddy Missouri near the site of Fort Abraham Lincoln and arrived at the flat-roofed clinic attached to Bismarck Memorial Hospital, fifteen minutes before our appointment. We were directed down the hall to the Obstetrics and Gynecology wing. Nurses wearing smiles, professional-looking white pants suits, and white nurse's caps greeted us. Sarah was given a clipboard of paperwork by Phyllis, the head nurse.

Sarah finished the forms and handed them back. We followed Phyllis. "We'll be right down the hall in room three." I joined my sweaty hand to Sarah's sweaty hand from behind, but she didn't turn. Phyllis quartered over her shoulder as we walked down the hallway and said, "You found us okay?"

I waited for Sarah to answer. She didn't, so I did. "No problem. The directions were good."

Phyllis pushed through the door and said, "Okay." She motioned to me. "You can have a seat over there. Mom, you can hop up on the exam table. Doctor Young should be right with you." She winked before closing the door.

My heart leapt with excitement at the word *Mom*. I wanted her heart to be excited, too. "Your eyes look troubled." I'd opened my mouth without thinking.

"I guess they are, Jimmy. Did you not hear what I said about why we are here?" Her eyes were filled with contempt. She removed her jacket and tossed it at me.

"Yes. I'm sorry." My line of sight found the floor, embarrassed at my lack of sense. Why could I never find the right thing to say? I couldn't find the right words to tell her my heart's desire was for her pregnancy to be all right. My insides were bound up with excitement, yes, but also nervousness. Was Sarah about to lose the baby?

The door flew open. A tall, slender man with an athletic build, somewhere in his early sixties, and immaculately gowned in a white lab coat, greeted us. Phyllis followed in his contrail. Dr. Gary Young exuded red-hot energy to go along with his dazzling smile. He sat at his small desk and began writing something down in Sarah's chart while dispensing pleasantries. With sharp and intelligent eyes, he dug in. "I've talked to Doctor Graham down in Painted Rock, so I'm familiar with your case. Patrick is a fine doctor. I ran into him a couple of weeks ago at a continuing ed meeting. He doubtless told you his last day is February first."

"No, he didn't. Who will deliver my baby?"

"Oh, I'm sure one of his partners. Not to worry." He tossed a reassuring wave to go with a comforting smile.

Sarah looked at me with a concerned expression on her face.

"I have reviewed your chart notes but do have a few questions." He looked up from his notes. "I want to hear from *you*, how things are, okay?"

"Sure." Sarah's body language softened. I had to admit, there was a calming presence about him.

"It looks like from Doctor Graham's notes you are twelve weeks, correct? Due early April?"

"Yes."

Doctor Young set his pen down to read Dr. Graham's notes. "Your chief concern is that you have been spotting, and things feel different than earlier in your pregnancy?" He picked up his pen again, intent.

"Well," she started, "Doctor Graham said he was *pretty sure* he heard the baby's heartbeat. So, he scared me." She wriggled on the table, crunching the paper underneath her. "The nausea I had early on is gone. I think I had a few times where I spotted. My breasts aren't as tender anymore. I don't . . . " Sarah picked at the hem on her shirt.

Silence. Doctor Young diverted his attention from his furious charting to Sarah. His eyebrows raised, asking with a gentle tone, "You don't *what*?"

Sarah's hair fell around her face as her head dropped. She tugged at her shirt, opened her mouth, and closed it. Her shoulders rose and fell with a deep breath. "I don't feel pregnant anymore." She lifted her head, eyes brimming with tears. "I'm afraid I'm going to lose the baby."

Doctor Young dropped his pen, springing to his feet. He grabbed a couple of tissues and handed them to her, placing his hand on her shoulder in a fatherly way. "What you are experiencing is not unusual at the three-month mark." He tilted his head to meet her eyes. "This is okay. Let me do an exam, and we can go from there, okay?"

Sarah leaned back, and Phyllis handed Doctor Young his fetal stethoscope. He moved his stethoscope smoothly, pausing at five places.

His face wore a confident expression borne from experience. "I can hear it perfectly. Congratulations, you're pregnant." He chuckled at his own humor.

Sarah smiled. "Thank God." She hesitated before releasing a giggle, relieving the tension she must have been carrying since her last appointment with Doctor Graham.

"This is common. Sometimes it's simply the way the baby is positioned." He backed off a bit and took command. "I still want the ultrasound for confirmation, so Phyllis is going to do it today."

My first thought was to question whether the test was really necessary since he could hear the heartbeat, but I decided not to say anything. Sarah had been so upset on the drive to Bismarck. The last thing I wanted to do was give her one more reason to think I wasn't taking the pregnancy as seriously as she was.

"Since this is a referral case, we will have to review it with my partners. Our group feels it's always good to get another set of eyes on these types of cases."

"What do you mean . . . 'these types of cases'?" Sarah asked.

"Any time there is a question of heartbeat. Our group will review your ultrasound for potential birth defects, confirm fetal development is right on track, evaluate the head and spine . . . those types of things. We have to be positive baby is okay." He swiveled his head toward me with an assuring nod, then returned to Sarah. "Either I will call you, or I'll have Phyllis call you in a day or two with the results."

Sarah wrinkled her nose in puzzlement. "Oh, not any sooner, huh?"

He smiled. "Yeah, unfortunately. These new gizmos are great, but we don't have the ones out here yet with real-time scanning. They're on the east coast but not in our area yet. I'm certain everything will be okay." He wrapped up his time, reminding Sarah to call if she had any questions.

Phyllis jumped in. "I'll get the cart and be right back. This won't take long at all." Her face was a blend of empathy and efficiency.

With a click, the door closed, and we were alone. A weird sensation ran through me; with this visit, things had gotten real. Until the door closed, the whole baby thing had been an abstract concept for me. Suddenly the room was uncomfortably warm, forcing me to take my jacket off. "You feeling any better?" I asked with trepidation.

"Yeah, a little. I'll feel better once we get the results." She chewed on what fingernails she had left.

The door swung open with a clunk as Phyllis wheeled the ultrasound in on a cart. She proceeded to set up the unit, instructing Sarah to pull her shirt up above her stomach. Phyllis squirted a clear jelly onto Sarah's belly.

Sarah flinched. "Oh, I wasn't expecting the cold."

"I'm sorry, hon," Phyllis responded with softness.

The control module whirred, followed by a high-pitched beep letting us know it had powered up. She unwound the cord of the wand attached to the module and stepped on the rheostat control, making the wand hum. My nose picked up a caustic smell. Phyllis passed the wand over Sarah's lower abdomen, creating a grid pattern and collecting the information the doctor wanted.

Sarah stared at the ceiling. "When can we find out if it's a boy or girl?"

Phyllis's face of determination softened as a smile formed. "Oh, not 'til around eighteen to twenty-one weeks." She clicked off the machine. "Okay, you're done." Phyllis efficiently handed Sarah a handful of tissues for the jelly cleanup, wished us a pleasant drive home, and excused herself.

The tension in my jaw began to dissipate as I walked out the door of the clinic. On our walk to the truck, Sarah took my hand, squeezing it tight in an affirmation of her relief. We pulled out of the clinic and passed a Dairy Queen four blocks down. She smiled and pointed. I pulled a U-turn. She ordered her favorite: a hot fudge malt with extra malt powder. Obliging her need for comfort food made me feel better, too.

The strip mall next door had a shoe store, a Ben Franklin, a public library, and a maternity store. Sarah had a mouthful of malt when her eyes widened, and she began simultaneously squealing and pointing. How could I say no? An hour later, we left with clothes, blankets, and decorations for the nursery. Retracing our route back to Painted Rock, our mood contained laughter, reminiscing, and hand holding. I was happy we had reconnected the frayed bonds that had been weakened by fear.

A pang of worry spread through me, questioning how long it would last.

11

Her full stomach, a sugar crash, and the warm cab put Sarah to sleep well before we crossed back into South Dakota. Looking at her resting so peacefully, it dawned on me... The waiting is the hardest part. Two days would be an eternity. I wished they'd been able to tell us the results right away. I knew how waiting could cause all kinds of issues—it could strangle matters of the heart, make a person's insides get tied up in knots, spawn circular internal conversations in the middle of the night. In the end, though, it'd be what it'd be.

Coming back into town, we had to stop at the crossing for a train. Sarah woke up, slow to shake off the grogginess. The locomotive thundered past, causing the ground beneath us to quake. The train cars generated a forceful current of wind to shake the truck. We exchanged startled glances. In the silence between us, it occurred to me the freight cars all looked the same. *Click clack, click clack* filled the cab of the truck—Milwaukee Road rolled on, rolled on down the line. I traced my infatuation with trains back to my first train ride from Kansas City to Philadelphia when I was eight or nine. Me and my mom had traveled to see the heart of the American Revolution. I warmed to think of doing the same thing with our child one day.

When we got back home, Grandpa's car wasn't there. As I checked my Timex, a stitch of worry circulated in my gut. They should have been back already.

Sarah tried on her new clothes, reminding me on which occasion she would wear them. She showed me her vision of the nursery we'd set up in the northeast bedroom. With undisguised forethought, she described how the mahogany paneling would have to go, the room would get painted a light yellow, the disgusting carpet would be torn up, and the hardwood floor underneath would have to be refinished. The weight of all the overwhelming tasks crushed me. Forcing smiles, nods of approval, and tepid suggestions, I yielded, void of enthusiasm.

We went down to The Caboose to prep for the night. Katherine had passed on to Sarah her recipe for "Ma's Sauce." We liked to feature it with different pasta. Tonight, the menu offered all-you-can-eat spaghetti and meatballs. Our customers loved it, and we paid homage to Katherine each time we made it. Soon, the regulars began to filter in—Rancher John, his wife Jean, Range Detective Ross, Lee, Ruby, Connie, our close friends Jay and Robert, and their wives.

Sarah kept the sauce bubbling like the mud pots at Yellowstone. She had become, like her grandma, an expert at keeping the sauce at the correct temperature with the pot uncovered. Katherine always said it was a mortal sin to cover the sauce—uncovering allows a permeating aroma of garlic to fill the air, famously clinging to your clothes. Ultimately, the smell sparked a memory of coming home and seeing Katherine in the kitchen. One time, I had told Katherine I wanted it to be the last thing I smelled before I died.

A harmony, perhaps due to the aroma of "Ma's Sauce," pervaded through the bar. Chain-smoking the entire night, Ruby swayed to the crooners serenading out of the jukebox. Pastor Dawson and his wife, Melissa, sipped their Tab sodas as they enjoyed polite conversation with a couple from church. Connie, wearing bell bottom jeans and a floral blouse, ate with one of her teacher girlfriends, smiling at me each time I came out of the kitchen. Robert played our new video arcade game, Pong, while his wife, Beth, shouted encouragement. John and Jean from the Circle J ranch bought a round to celebrate their nineteenth wedding anniversary. In contrast, Ross ate and sipped his scotch while talking to no one. Like a predator, he never stopped taking inventory of his surroundings.

The night wound down without our energy level waning. The crowd had thinned out, so I sent Paul home. Jay poked his head in the kitchen while Sarah and I ate our dinners. "You guys up for a nightcap? Robert and Beth are stopping by."

Sarah and I were silent.

"Both Robert and I have an early morning, so it won't be late. C'mon. What else you gotta do?"

Sarah nodded her head. "Yeah. Sure. You going to help us clean up?" She smiled a sassy smile at Jay.

His laugh contained the chemistry of familiarity. "Of course, we will."

Stepping out the back door to get into the truck after we had cleaned up, the night smelled of wood smoke. Overhead was a canopy of blue-black velvet, perforated by thousands of bright pinpricks set around a thin slit of moon. Windblown leaves somersaulted at our feet, racing uncontained down the alley. Sarah and I headed over to Jay and Aiyana's place near the high school. Streetlights accented by storefront orange, pink, and green neon guided our path along Grand Avenue. Upon our arrival, I sneaked a peek at the window of their nosy neighbor, Mrs. Spielbauer, and caught a glimpse of her peeled-back window shade. Blocks away, a police siren awakened but gradually faded into the night.

On our way up the noisy front steps, a babysitter clutching textbooks to her chest passed us baring a wide smile full of braces. The smell of baby powder greeted us as we entered the foyer. Jay had Iris by the hand, about to head up the stairs for bed. Sarah rushed to intercept her godchild, who let out an impish "tee-hee" when hugged.

Peeking up at Jay, Sarah kissed Iris on the cheek and said, "Do you want me to tuck her in? I'll read her a story." Hope sprung from her voice.

"Thanks, Sarah, but I'll do it. She's in a daddy phase where she wants me to do it."

Sarah's face was a mask of reluctant acceptance. "Good night, my little angel."

Iris, already in her booty jammies, waved goodnight to Sarah. She paused on the landing to peer through the railing spindles and say goodnight to everyone else. Jay's face beamed, exchanging glances between Sarah and Iris. Such a good dad. Would I be one?

We adjourned to the front room to get comfortable. Robert said until Jay came down, his beers weren't going to drink themselves, so we helped ourselves to his refrigerator. I asked Robert if Jay had talked to him about the dredging and the potential of unwelcome visitors. All he offered was, "Yeah. We talked. I'm cool."

Two hours later, Sarah's facial expression said I had had more than enough to drink, and it was time to go home.

I had a hard time keeping up with her march to the truck. "I don't know what happened. I had four or five beers." Five came out *fahh-ive*, because I hiccupped.

"Well, Jimmy." Sarah tilted her head as if to say we'd been down this road before. "By my math, you had closer to eight or nine." She stared straight ahead, her body rigid. "As soon as you and Robert started playing dice, it was sure to be trouble. Jimmy," she spoke with a matter-of-fact tone, "you gotta pull it together. You're going to be a father."

"You sound like you're mad at me or something." The truck bounced, jarred by a pothole.

"Watch where you're going!" she exclaimed, looking at me with eyes like talons, her hands braced against the dashboard. "I'm not mad. I'm disappointed after the good day we had." Her eyes told me I was inadequate. Maybe I was.

Sinking fast with no comeback other than to switch gears, I uttered, "So what happened to Jay?"

"Ah, duh. He fell asleep with Iris." The disdain in her voice was evident.

She was right. Things were fuzzy—vision and memory.

We bumped down the two ruts of the driveway. The kitchen and living room lights lit the farmhouse front to back. Sarah commented that Colby and Joan must have gotten home. I got out to open the garage door, a cloud of exhaust vapors drifting by me. The cool bite of the night ran up my back, my gait heavy to the garage door. The neighbor's basset hound bellowed hello while unseen crickets chirped their greeting.

"Where have you been?" Grandpa met us in the kitchen.

"We stopped over at Jay and Aiyana's after work." I hiccupped again.

Sarah walked right by. "'Night, Colby."

"'Night, Sarah," Grandpa said in a perplexed tone. He pointed at her and mouthed the words, "What's going on with her?"

I shrugged back. "So, how was your trip to the Indian village?"

"It was a lovely day for a drive, but turns out parts of Chief Kakawita's village and burial grounds are under a foot of water." Looking tired, Grandpa leaned against the counter. "Hell, the water was comin' up fast when we were there in '69, but with the lake dropping, I was shocked most of the village is still under water. The terrain was barely recognizable."

"We drove by the turn-off on our way to Bismarck."

"Bismarck?" Grandpa snorted.

"Sarah had a doctor's appointment." I immediately wished I hadn't started down this road, gassed by the alcohol. I rubbed my forehead to hide the grimace.

"Everything okay?" The corners of his mouth drooped, and concern rode his furrowed brow.

"Oh, yeah, all good." I started toward the back door to lock it and turn off the lights.

"Ah, by the way..." Grandpa had started to leave the kitchen but quartered back to get my attention. He spoke with an even, deeply graveled voice. "We stopped over to see Standing Bear. He said to say hi to you and Sarah." The remaining ambient light deepened the lines on Grandpa's face as he stepped toward me. "Sheriff Owl reported to Standing Bear it was Calhoun in the car, and they haven't found Gritzmacher, at least not yet."

"They must have gotten dental records," I said, getting a glass of water from the sink.

"Anyway, we talked a while about our families, issues with his tribe, my retirement . . . you know." After a sideways glance, he went on, "Stopped in at Barking Coyote's jewelry shop, too. By the looks of things, he's done okay for himself. We had a nice talk. I guess he's had some health issues for a number of years. He lives with Standing Bear."

"Yeah, Jay said something about his brother having issues."

"Took Joan by Tower Buttes, too. Didn't stay long. We were runnin' out of daylight."

"Tower Buttes? Why did you take her there?" I asked.

"Ah . . . a discussion for another day. It's way past my bedtime."

"Man, you had a busy day," I said as we exited the kitchen.

He paused in front of the downstairs bathroom as I walked to the stairs. He said, "We'll be getting an early start tomorrow morning. Doubt if we'll see you." The light from the bathroom illuminated his front half. "I gotta get this gut thing checked out. Something's not right." His voice dropped with resignation. He opened his mouth like he had more to say, caught himself, and averted eye contact.

"What? What were you going to say, Grandpa?"

"It's nothing, . . . really." He smiled as he shook his head. "When we have more time." He wrapped his arms around me, then broke away but held his gaze.

"Okay, sounds good," I said with hesitation. Did he know something was going on with his health that he wasn't telling me? Or did he want to remind me of the addictive allure of the medal? "Have a safe trip home, Grandpa," I said in a solemn tone. "Let me know what the doctor says. I'm sure he'll give you some medicine to fix it." The wooden steps creaked despite my efforts to be quiet.

I stepped onto the landing as Sarah flicked off the light switch in the bathroom. On lithe and powerful legs, she padded barefoot past me to our bedroom without a word or eye contact, her new nightgown flowing behind her.

A cascade of rolling thunder in my head told me all I needed to know.

12

Jay stopped into the bar after I opened for lunch. He was all decked out in his Dakota Plains Power Company jacket and hat, his name and title—Head Linesman—stitched over his left breast pocket. Scattered, potbellied gray clouds had drizzled around the area, leaving Jay's jacket damp. He shook off the moisture and hung it up. Jay took his job and responsibility seriously, so I figured the constricted expression on his face was due to the weather messing with his schedule. He had his hair pulled back tight into a ponytail ending below his collar. He asked for a Hamm's and apologized for falling asleep with Iris.

"No biggie," I told him.

We bantered back and forth until Jay got choked up filling me in on his brother, Barking Coyote. The doctors thought a gum infection had traveled to his heart. He had been battling a high temperature, headaches, fatigue, and a persistent cough.

According to Jay, he'd been battling it for several weeks and was getting worse. They'd tried different antibiotics, but he had continued to have a rapid decline.

Our conversation was interrupted by a couple of the dredge operators entering and seating themselves at the opposite end of the bar. Their ball caps were grease stained, their faces deeply tanned and unshaven. I got them the water they requested along with menus. When I returned to Jay, he brought up the Corps finding the D. I. P. car. I leaned forward using a low voice and told him they'd identified Calhoun. Jay was confident they'd never find Calhoun's partner, Gritzmacher, after all the shale had cascaded on top of them . . . unless he'd flown out of the car and floated away. He told me he had spoken to Running Dog, the combine driver. Running Dog remembered the incident like it was yesterday and said not to worry if he got questioned.

Eventually, the conversation turned to Paul. Jay bristled when I brought him up. "I gotta tell you . . . Paul told me he came here to look for his dad, who apparently went missing while on some assignment somewhere around here."

I stood with my mouth agape, eyes dancing back and forth, trying to register what Jay had said. I exhaled. "What the hell? He never said a word of any of this to me or to Sarah." I opened a case of Schlitz and started stocking bottles in the cooler. "What else did he say?"

Bob and Mick came in, waved, and grabbed stools at the bar. They worked for the county highway department. The smell of crack sealing tar emanating from them confirmed it.

"Hang on a sec." I excused myself to get the guys each a Hamm's. Returning, I met Jay's eyes. "Did he say anything about the medal?"

"The medal? Yeah, y'know, he did. He said he'd studied its history. Asked if someone around here found it. I told him it's one of those urban legends. Never happened." His head flew back as he took a swig. "He had this suspicious look on his face. I feel bad for the guy searching for his dad, you know, but he asks too many questions, if ya ask me."

"Paul is curious, I'll give him credit . . . " I shrugged. There was a tingle through my scalp. I told Jay about the verbal spat Paul and Grandpa'd had. I told him about Grandpa wanting to punch Paul. I didn't share the fact that this new information about Paul was confusing to me.

"I wouldn't get too wound up about him. Might be the guy's a dork and full of it," Jay offered and finished his beer. "He seems pretty harmless. And by the way, if the river drops much more you might be able to find the medal again."

"Yeah, Sarah and I have talked about it, but it's not a priority," I offered without emotion. I was preoccupied with Paul. "I think I need to talk to Paul. Get the honest truth about what he's doing here." I meticulously folded the white flour sack towel and tucked it into my waistband. Maybe Sarah had been right about him.

Jay stood and extended his hand. "Gotta run. Duty calls."

I shook it. "Do me a solid and keep this between us, okay?" Paul didn't start until four in the afternoon, and I wanted as much time as possible to figure out how to deal with him.

"For sure, man. Anyway, sorry again about last night." Jay dropped a couple of quarters on the bar. "And by the way, Aiyana told me she and Sarah talked last night."

"Oh, yeah?"

"Sarah was on a roll." Jay smirked. "Alls I gotta say is, she's getting impatient. You better marry her."

"Yeah. Yeah. So I've been told."

"Later, Jimmy."

"Right on," I said, wiping off the bar.

Jay threw on his jacket, giving me a heads up as he flew out the door.

Without a care in the world, Paul sauntered in twenty minutes late. He immediately went through his routine of checking the beer coolers and liquor bottles to make sure we were fully stocked for the evening. He circled the bar, turning on the Hamm's and Schlitz neon signs, along with the Canadian Club light over the pool table. While he did his thing, I alternated between serving, reconciling the money from the day before, filling out the bank deposit, and counting the money in the till. We weren't busy, so after my financials were completed, I went into the kitchen.

I stopped in my tracks. He was using his hunting knife—the KA-BAR he'd bought at Richard's—to cut up the fruit. I let out a nervous laugh. "Couldn't find a serrated knife, or what?"

He didn't look up. "Nah, man. I love the work this blade does. So sharp. Cuts like no other."

I went to the sharps drawer and pulled out a serrated knife. "Here, use this. Put your knife away," I demanded and slid the knife across the wood chopping block.

Paul face was gnarled in anger. "What's your problem, man?" His voice carried an air of self-importance.

"I have no problem. I don't want to see your knife in my bar again." My voice had risen an octave.

"Chill out, man." He laughed. "I'm playing with my new toy. It ain't hurtin' nobody." He put it back in its sheath and left it on the block. He picked up the serrated knife and resumed slicing. I didn't care for this streak of belligerence. He and I were going to have it out at some point. It was just a matter of time.

"Paul, we need to talk." I tipped my head until our eyes met.

"What about?" His answer was filled with impatience.

"I appreciate the work you have put in at The Caboose." I stood with my hands in my pockets, wanting to appear nonthreatening. "You've been a great help. But what brings you to Painted Rock, exactly?" I needed to hear it for myself.

His taut face relaxed as his obstinate demeanor began to melt. He stopped slicing, his voice a whisper of embarrassment. "Like I told you, I'm trying to work through some things." He paused a couple of beats. "If you must know . . . I'm trying to find the dad I have never known."

Finally, there was a glimmer of truth corroborating what Jay had told me earlier. "So, why do you think he's here?"

"I don't know if he is or not. I'm kinda following a trail of breadcrumbs." His voice carried a forlorn mood, his palms open seemingly in hopes of gaining my sympathy. He put an unlit cigarette in his mouth and withdrew his wallet from his back pocket, handing me a worn picture of a young man in an Army uniform. A typical young conscript, clean cut and full of promise.

"How long you been lookin'?" The unmistakable sound of Simon and Garfunkel eased out of the jukebox.

"I've been lookin' ever since I left Georgia," he said, back in the midst of slicing fruit. He'd slipped the knife back into his backpack. "So, let me back up." He paused, looking me in the eye, evaluating.

Whatever he said next felt like it would be personal.

"We never had any money growing up. My mom was a waitress. He was in the Army, stationed at Fort Benning, Georgia. Korea was winding down, I guess. Columbus is the town next to it. From what I've been told, Dad was a regular at Brett's Freedom Diner, where she worked." He stopped cutting and grabbed a dish towel for his sticky hands. "The way Mom tells the story, one thing led to another, and she gets pregnant. He gets shipped out or left town—she never found out which—and she never hears from him again."

"Did your dad know he got your mom pregnant?"

"I asked her the same thing. She said by the time she realized she was pregnant, he was gone."

Paul had stripped himself naked, laying bare his soul. It made me uncomfortable, oddly voyeuristic. "Huh." The similarities and differences with our dads had unexpectantly come into focus. My dad had been physically there when I was growing up, but he sure wasn't "present" emotionally. He'd been too consumed with the work on the farm and Mom's illness—overwhelmed with life in general.

I hopped up to sit on the counter. The tension of confrontation had been replaced by the tension of sharing one's deepest wounds. He had put it out there, so I ran with it. "Your mom never married him and . . . One day, you all of a sudden decide to leave Georgia to find him?"

"Sort of. I was at a point in my life when it was time for me to get some answers. I talked to my mom about it. Told her I had struggled with this for a long time. It took a while, but she finally tracked down his mom, my grandma. She said, to the best of her knowledge, he worked for the State of South Dakota in Pierre." He started to scoop the fruit into individual Tupperware containers.

I smiled in an effort to bring a touch of levity. "This sounds like a made-for-TV movie or something."

His facial expression remained blank, the pain still present in his voice. "Yeah, so I quit my job, dumped my girlfriend, and made it to Pierre." The cigarette in his mouth bobbed up and down, distracting me as he spoke.

I still didn't get how he'd wound up in little ol' Painted Rock. Something was missing. "What happened in Pierre?"

"It took some digging, but I found out he worked at the Department of Indian Properties," Paul said. "Unfortunately, the guy who replaced my dad's boss said the word was that my dad went AWOL. Said my dad's last radio communication that he was 'crossing the river' was transmitted somewhere north of Pierre. The Bureau had a record of him working for them, but his file got lost when their storage building burned." His shoulders slumped.

At the mention of the Department of Indian Properties, my skin went clammy. My stomach churned acid. Fear ran up my spine. I knew all too well those folks were crooked operators. Eight years earlier, the same two D.I.P. agents, Gritzmacher and Calhoun, driving the dredged car had tried to steal from us and kill us. And a few years prior to that incident, they'd tried to steal a bunch of artifacts from Grandpa to sell on the black market. Wouldn't surprise me if those two had something to do with Paul's dad's disappearance. It could have been that Paul's dad discovered their thuggery and threatened to expose them. Or perhaps they were trying to extort Paul's dad, and he'd resisted. In either case, I'm thinking Paul's dad was a dead man.

Paul continued, "I hit a dead end, so figured I'd head up here and see if he showed up or had been here." He went silent.

We were joined by an increased buzz from the bar. "Man, I'm sorry to hear about your dad," I said, shaking my head. "I'll be sure to let you know if I hear anything." I hopped down, appeased by his answers, anxious to get to work. "Well, we should get to it. Best of luck finding him."

"I have no doubt I'll get the satisfaction I need . . . one way or another," he deadpanned.

A dozen boisterous, thirsty, and hungry townsfolk greeted us. Out of the crowd, I spotted Range Detective Ross leaning against the wall in the far corner of the bar, resting his right hand on the butt of his gun. I waved acknowledgement, curious about why he was hanging out in the shadows. He half waved to me and man-nodded to Paul. Paul raised the bottle of Scotch at Ross, which drew a smile. There didn't appear to be any current or potential threat. According to him, he'd had to pull his .357 Magnum only a handful of times in his lengthy career. He projected raw physical power and had gained a formidable reputation for being able to settle disputes with reason, compromise, and on occasion, brute strength. I respected him. Come to think of it, he'd been showing up more than usual, which wasn't a bad thing.

The space before me was alive with colors flashing, a layer of cigarette smoke forming, disjointed conversations, and laughter. I caught myself singing along with Jackson Browne's "Doctor my Eyes." It was bound to be a good night.

13

I decided to close The Caboose from two to four. My shirt had a coffee-ketchup-flour issue, which wouldn't have gone over well with the after-work crowd. Plus, I wanted to see Sarah. Passing through the farmhouse kitchen, I stopped in my tracks. She had gone to the library and left various books on the kitchen table: books about pregnancy and a baby's first year, a book of names for boys and girls, and parenting tips for new parents.

The ringer on the phone startled my survey of titles. "I'll get it!" I yelled, thinking she might be upstairs. "Hello?"

"Hi, this is Phyllis from Doctor Young's office. Is Sarah home?" Her voice was pleasant.

"Let me check," I responded as I set the phone on the counter. "Sarah!" The house was silent. I called louder, "It's Doctor Young's office!"

"I'm right here," she snapped, rounding off the steps. She wore a determined expression, moving with purpose to grab the phone. "Hello?"

I leaned in as she butterflied the phone on her shoulder. "Hi, Sarah, this is Phyllis from Doctor Young's office. Your ultrasound read normal."

Sarah exhaled audibly, and her body softened against mine. "Oh, thank God."

I put my arm around her shoulder and pulled her tight.

Phyllis went on. "Doctor Young said he would like to redo the ultrasound in three months."

"Why? Is something not clear or . . . " There was worry in Sarah's voice, which made me anxious.

"No, not at all. Dr. Young is thorough and wants the best for you and the baby. Let me put you on hold, and the receptionist can get you scheduled, okay?"

"Okay, thanks for calling."

Sarah made the appointment, and I got a Hamm's out of the refrigerator. She hung up, collapsing in a heap on a kitchen chair, and grabbed a tissue to wipe tears from her cheeks. She reached for me, and we embraced as sniffles transitioned to giggles. I offered to run back to the DQ for a celebratory hot fudge malt. Joy filled the kitchen.

I quickly changed clothes and returned to find Sarah still seated at the kitchen table, staring straight ahead. "You okay?"

"Relieved. I haven't slept well in two days."

"You're still up for working dinner with me 'til eight, right?"

She nodded, simultaneously blowing her nose. "Yes, of course."

As I drove to The Caboose in the soft light of dusk with Sarah following, the removal of the thousand-pound boulder off my shoulders infused me with energy. I hadn't appreciated how much the stress of potentially losing the baby had weighed on me. At last, it was starting to look like I would get to play catch with my son or daughter after all. My face broke into a satisfied grin. I realized I wanted to be a dad more than I'd admitted to myself. Grandpa would be so excited to become a great-grandpa. I hoped I could be a loving dad like Grandpa had always been. He was such a loving father figure to me.

I cruised through the green light before arriving at The Caboose, poised for a good night. I picked up *The Independent*, Painted Rock's weekly newspaper, lying by the back door. The headline above the fold read, "Inflation Rate Continues Climb, Now 6.5%," and in smaller print, "Federal Reserve Policies Questioned by President Carter." Below the fold was a picture and story of the D.I.P. car being dredged up. Scanning the article, I found no mention of bodies. The last paragraph said the river had dropped another foot to 1,568—a good prompt for Sarah and me to see if the sandbar was out of the water yet. Grandpa's plea for me to not go looking for the medal replayed in my head. It made me feel queasy. I'd never broken a promise to him. I threw the newspaper away as the screen door wheezed, slamming shut. I needed to fix that closer.

"Evening, folks," I said to the night's first patrons, Lee and Ruby, with sincere happiness as I placed two cardboard coasters on the bar. "What can I get ya?" From the moment of their arrival, time flew by. My mood bordered on euphoric as I darted around the bar serving, clearing, and hustling—drinking a celebratory beer every chance I got.

The younger, after-five crowd primarily opted for the bucking bronco burger with fries before settling in for the evening. The meatloaf dinner with mashed potatoes and a helping of peas with sliced carrots best suited the fancy of the older crowd. When dinner was completed, Sarah poked her head through the saloon doors to get my attention.

I scooted behind her into the kitchen. "You heading out?"

She had her jacket on with her purse slung over her shoulder. The light made her face look puffy. Her posture slumped to match her tired eyes. "Kitchen's cleaned up, and burners are off. I'm going home to take a bath, maybe watch some Carson, and go to bed." She paused, examining me. I tried to stiffen, to look sober. She shook her head and walked to the door, her bow-legged gait becoming more pronounced. Without turning back, she admonished, "Go easy on the beer, Jimmy. Looks like you've had enough already."

The door closed, and I felt free. The night was young, and already the tempo at the bar was being ratcheted up. After what I had been through the past few days, damn it, I had earned a night of fun. I went to the cooler and opened a beer—again.

Paul stopped by long after dark. The screen door slammed. I winced. "What's happenin', Paul?"

He leaned against the wall to take his muddy boots off. "I took a walk down along the river," he said through tight lips, holding his half-smoked cigarette. "The sunset had these slivers of purple and blue. Pretty damn amazing, man." He pushed his hair behind his ears as he approached. "Anyway, I found these." He opened his fist, revealing two stones and a bone. "I didn't know what I was lookin' for exactly but hoped these might be something."

I took a swig of my fifth beer. Or my sixth. I picked up the bone first. "Oh yeah, you got something here. It's a broken end of a bone awl. See the point there? The Indians used it to punch through hides for sewing clothing."

Paul pointed with his cigarette notched between his index and middle finger at the other stone, midnight brown in color, the size of a cherry tomato. "What about this?"

I spun it in my hand to examine it from every angle. "Looks like knife river flint. I'd say it's a spall core."

Our eyes met. "What the hell is a spall core?"

My chest swelled a bit. I was excited to share some of my Indian artifact knowledge with my junior treasure hunter. "A spall is a bigger stone that they would chip pieces off of to make arrowheads, thumb scrapers, and pottery markers. When they had chipped as much as they could, the Indians were left with the core." I smiled at Paul. "A spall core." His face showed disappointment as he exhaled. He wanted it to be more. "Sorry, man, it's a leftover."

He tilted his head like a dog, eyes wide with curiosity. "How do you know so much about this stuff? Your grandpa?"

I played it coy. "Not him so much." I stammered, "Living here, you learn stuff. Friends of mine, Jay and Robert, have taught me some." Paul's eyes were doubting me. "I'm serious. And I walk the river from time to time. Learned from the old-timers around town." I shrugged before taking the sausage and onion pizza out of the oven.

Paul stared at me with narrowed eyes, his forehead furrowed. "What ya got there?" I said, pointing.

He handed me a grayish-white stone about three inches long and an inch and a half wide with a squared-off fracture on one side and a finely serrated edge on the other.

"Okay, this is a broken knife made of plate chalcedony. It's a quartz." I spun it in my hand, feeling the rough edge and the warmth of the stone leftover from Paul's hand. "A nice piece. Congrats."

His face softened into a proud smile. "We should walk the river together sometime. I can show you where I found these. It's not far.

You'd be a good teacher." His eyes were begging like a puppy dog. "We might even find a Thomas Jefferson Peace Medal."

I sensed a tinge of sarcasm but let it pass. "Yeah, sounds good, man," I said and slapped him some skin. Because no one around here liked their pizza in triangles, I made a grid work of squares. "I'm swamped. I'll catcha ya later."

He yelled after me, "You want me to stay and help?"

"Sure!" I yelled over my shoulder without breaking stride through the saloon doors. I returned to the music, the crack of pool balls, and an inviting gaze from Connie. Placing the pizza in front of Tony, I grabbed the napkin and silverware carrier from under the bar and put it in front of him. I got him another vodka tonic with no lime, and he bought me a beer. Such a reliable regular.

I had a good buzz going, so singing along to Don McLean's "American Pie" took the night to a higher level. The pulse of the night beat strong. My song was interrupted by the crack of glass breaking and a voice above all the others yelling, "What the hell?"

I pivoted to my right as Bart "Rooster" Moon was swinging an empty glass pitcher at Jesse Griese, who deflected the pitcher with his pool cue. The sound of pool cue shattering rivaled the sound of a .44 Magnum being fired. Some guys ran out of the bar, while some backed away one big step at a time. A couple of brave souls attempted to intercede, knowing something real bad was about to happen.

They were unsuccessful. Bart's red face contained a formidable snarl. His bloodshot eyes bored through Jesse. Jesse's blue eyes were big and alert and set on a bleached face, his torso crouched in a protective posture. The two were in a standoff on the other side of the pool table with Connie trapped in the corner. Bart took another swing; Jesse took a jab at Bart with what was left of the cue. The music became more distinct as the clamor waned.

I yelled for Paul to turn on the overhead lights. Hustling from behind the bar, I motioned the way out to Connie. She crouched along the wall behind a high top, throwing her rounded contours right into my arms. The softness of her sweater and the sweet aroma of her perfume infused my senses. Her hand ran over my butt as she shuffled behind me.

Full of liquid courage, I yelled at the top of my lungs, "You both have ten seconds to get the hell outta here before I call the cops!" My head pulsed like it would explode. The loud current of the bar stopped except for the blinking lights of the pinball machine jousting with the colored lights of the jukebox.

Flying in from the retreated gawkers, Paul blindsided Bart with a right cross, which wobbled his legs. Bart swung the pitcher wildly, stumbling toward Paul. In rapid succession, Paul followed up with a left uppercut and grabbed him by the hair, slamming his head on the edge of the pool table. Bart tottered and fell to the floor, the pitcher skidding to a stop under the table. Those who hadn't left were aghast. I was stunned. Bart's wingman, Chuck, grabbed Bart immediately and got him out of The Caboose. I watched cautiously as Paul walked back behind the bar with a smirk like he'd enjoyed beating the crap out of Bart. He resumed bartending as if nothing out of the ordinary had just happened.

Once the disorder settled down, Paul and I discreetly made eye contact, followed by a nod of respect from me. I had to give the guy credit for protecting our turf. The hum of people enjoying their drinks, cigarettes, and conversation returned. Jesse wisely hung around until the coast was clear. He was a good guy who happened to be in the wrong place at the wrong time. Officer Tittle stepped into the bar, bobbing his head over and around people, searching. He quit after a quick looksee, vanishing back into the night.

Jay called for me from the other end of the bar. He and Robert were drunk and happy. "Jimmy, Jimmy . . . " His eyes were unfocused.

"Yeah, Jay. I heard ya the first time. What's happenin'?" I laughed, shifting my gaze from Jay to Robert. Robert was giggling like an excited little girl.

Jay focused on my shoulder, his lips pursed, dark eyes narrowed. For a second, he got serious, like he had something important he wanted to say. "Marianne or Ginger?" He slapped the bar and let out the loudest belly laugh of the night. Robert laughed so hard he snorted.

"Mrs. Howell," I deadpanned, giving them both a high five, which threw them both into an even deeper rush of laughter. I backed away with a disco shuffle, laughing and pointing in their direction.

Connie found a seat at the bar with Darcy, the flower shop owner, plus a couple of her girlfriends. They kept me busy pouring all night. I might as well have put a bottle of gin and another of tonic on the bar. Connie's eyes made sure *she* got my attention with each round I poured for them. She wasn't shy about touching my hand when I delivered her drink. I enjoyed her flirting and didn't try to hide it. Connie had put me adrift in a current, which I was powerless to stem.

With a crack, I pulled back the tab of another beer as a shortish, olive-skinned customer emerged out of the crowd, timidly approaching the bar. He was about my age, hunched over, and wearing a stained green Army jacket with a ripped front pocket. Wisps of dark hair poked out from under his black stocking cap. His eyes were blue and soft, shifting with uncertainty.

Paul stepped in. "Yessir. What can I get ya?" He put his cigarette in the ashtray on the ledge behind him.

The stranger rubbed his stubbled face. Barely audible, he said, "Hi." With trembling hands, he placed the menu on the bar and pointed to the chicken cluck sandwich.

"Sorry, buddy. Kitchen's closed," Paul said with an edge of annoyance in his voice.

Studying the interaction, I shifted my gaze back and forth between Paul and the stranger.

The stranger shifted his weight from one leg to the other like he wasn't sure what to say. His head jerked from a spastic tic. Another stronger tic followed. A mask of desperation covered his face. "What can I eat?" he pleaded.

A voice from the space behind him shouted, "Two Schlitz and two house whites!" I glanced to my right with two guys holding tens in their hands, while another was waving his empty glass at me, ready for another round.

"Look, I can get you a bag of chips but nothing else," Paul said as I passed behind him toward the waving money. A twinge of sympathy passed through me. "Well?" Paul's impatient voice was grating.

The guy stood there with his mouth slightly open, unable to speak. His brow wrinkled like he was thinking hard.

Paul waited a beat. With a face full of disgust, he walked away. "Let me know when you make up your mind."

I grabbed a couple of Schlitz bottles from the cooler and poured a couple of white wines called Blue Nun. As I exchanged the drinks for money, the quiet stranger stopped at the door and eyeballed Paul in disbelief. I stared down the bar at Paul. He stood, hands on hips, an amused smirk on his face, and mouthed to the stranger, "What?"

I shifted my thinking to counting the money, opening the cash register and parsing the bills into it. "Hey, I need another buck-fifty!" I barked, turning and locating the guy with the Schlitz.

"Relax. Here ya go," the voice out of the crowd said. "Keep the change."

I started to recount and abruptly stopped. Resting my hands on the cash drawer, I stared at myself in the mirror behind the liquor bottles. I shook my head, disgusted with myself. Turning, "Paul!" I yelled down the bar.

"What's up?"

I had to bark over the music. "I appreciate what you did earlier tonight, but that guy didn't deserve your attitude."

"What?" He pointed to the door. "C'mon, the guy was a bum."

Stunned by his callousness, my blood began to boil as I recalled helping Paul when he showed up dirty with no money, looking for a job. I'd offered kindness and employment to him. Replaying Paul's tone and the look of disgust on his face toward the stranger ratcheted up my anger. My displeasure with his attitude boiled over. "Why don't you call it a night? You need to chill out, man. I can handle it from here."

"You tellin' me to leave?" He put his hands on his hips.

"I think it's best." I wanted to extinguish the potential for confrontation.

His face blanked with shock. After a beat, he walked past me, slamming the saloon doors against the wall on his way out.

Returning to the packed bar rail, I grabbed more drinks and more money. The Caboose had reached a crescendo. Someone put on The Outlaws' "There Goes Another Love Song" and the joint was rocking—people dancing, drinking, laughing, having a good ol' time.

It was one of those nights when you wanted time to stand still.

14

The music stopped, leaving me with the sound of ringing in my ears. A great beer buzz had begun to wane, replaced by a dry mouth. My eyes burned from the night's fog of smoke. Overhead lights cast a filtered glare, giving the bar a mystical look. It had been a rousing evening, and the bar showed it. Glasses sat half-filled, empty bottles on the pinball machines, stools askew, piles of cigarette butts in ashtrays on the bar.

People filtered out the door as I said my goodnights and began my systematic cleanup. I started to sweep the floor, reliving what I remembered of the night. Jay, Robert, Jesse, Bart, Paul. Paul—the night's fireworks had started and ended with him. Had he been walking the river hoping to find the medal? Nah, not a chance. I was glad Paul had left without confrontation, so we didn't get into a shouting match—or worse. Something bubbled below the surface of his otherwise amicable demeanor. Was it frustration with the search for his dad?

The intuitive part of my brain rang an alarm. Raising my line of sight, I saw Connie was standing inside the door, staring at me. Alone. "Hey," I said. Seeing her with the lights on reinforced her natural beauty. "Are you okay?" I questioned.

"My car won't start." Her pouty lips projected a tease. She wore her red down jacket off her shoulders, accentuating her contours. "Can you help me? I don't know what happened to Darcy," she said, thick tongued. "Joanna and Lynn left an hour ago 'cause they had to drive to Silvertown." She tilted her head in a submissive manner and braced her arm against the wall next to the door frame.

"Yeah, sure." I nodded, leaning the broom against the cigarette machine. "Not sure how much help I'll be, but . . . "

She cut me off. "I'd appreciate any help you can give me. There's no one around. It's like the town suddenly went . . . poof." Her clenched hands exploded in the space between us as she forced an awkward laugh.

Parked in front of the foreclosed brownstone hotel next door, her tan Dodge Dart sat lonely on the vacant street. The soft amber streetlights cast overlapping circular patches of light, unable to warm the late fall nip. A breeze puffed up from the river, passing between buildings with a muffled whistle and carrying the diesel smell of the railyard.

The heavy car door opened with a screech and a clunk. The dome light didn't come on as it should have. I turned the ignition to "on" and heard a miserable groan from the engine. I located the knob for the headlights and pushed it in. "Connie, you left your lights on."

"I did? No way."

"I would say your battery is dead."

"Can't you jump me?"

"You got cables? 'Cause I don't," I said emphatically. The fall's rawness was making me impatient.

"No." She glared down the street, hands deep inside her coat pockets, shivering. "Damn it. Who am I going to call at this hour?" Her face was genuinely concerned, and she crossed her arms. "*Harrumph.*"

I had a feeling I knew what was coming next.

"Is there any way, um, I can get a ride home from you? I live three blocks east of the high school," she pleaded.

What should I do? Was there a choice? "Sure. You can get Gus to jump it in the morning." The clack of the key turning locked the Dart while we were serenaded by the deep-throated rumbling of a westbound train approaching the silent town.

I held the heavy wooden front door of The Caboose for her and locked it behind me. "Let me put the stools up, unplug some stuff, and we can go," I said, compressing the closing list in my head to the essentials.

"Wow, this is so cool. It feels so much bigger when there aren't any other people in here," she opined as she flitted and sashayed from one end of the bar to the other, her shoes nimbly scuffing on the linoleum. "Did you know I used to be a dancer?"

I stopped, forgetting about unplugging anything else, to watch. She took off her jacket and fluffed her blond locks. Meticulously, she picked a couple of down feathers off her sweater before hiking up her button-front jeans. She raised her head with a smile. "You want to dance?"

The combination of her beauty and opportunity stirred arousal. For some unknown reason, I blurted, "Nah, we should get going."

Her posture tightened as her head jerked back. She crossed her arms. "Oh." It was as if her voice had dropped into a hole to the center of the earth. "Well, yeah, okay." She put on her jacket and threw her purse over her shoulder. "Let's go," she said, wobbling in place.

I locked the back door, and we pulled out of the alley onto Grand Ave. She turned on the radio, spun through the late-night static until finding America's "Sister Golden Hair" on KELO out of Sioux Falls. She sat up, turning toward me and singing along, her eyes begging for my attention. The truck cab warmed, although I wasn't sure if the cause was the heater or her unbridled magnetism.

She deftly unzipped her jacket and slid a bit closer to me. "Take the next left," she instructed. She placed her hand on my thigh.

I became uneasy. "I can't . . . Sarah . . . "

She placed a finger on my lips to hush me. "Take the next right. Mine's the yellow ranch with the yard light on." She spoke barely above a whisper, her eyes inviting. "Love to give you a night cap . . . " She leaned over and started kissing my neck, her tongue darting in and around my ear. Her warm breaths on my face increased, and her hand slid toward my erection.

With my mind preoccupied, we came to a jarring stop just inches short of her garage door. The line had been crossed. "No, Connie. You're nice and beautiful and all, but I'm not your guy." My head swiveled to meet her disappointed gaze. "I've got a special girl waiting for me at home." I paused a beat. "Good luck with your car."

She exhaled through her mouth with emphasis, her shoulders slumping. Her hand left my leg to cover her eyes before she pulled away. "*Harrumph*. Well, ya can't blame a girl for trying. It's not like you're married or anything."

I wanted to come back at her with a zinger, but there was nothing to say. She was right.

"I'm here if you change your mind." She opened the car door. "Thanks for the ride, Jimmy."

I eased into our driveway, relieved. I could so easily have thrown it all away with Sarah for one night of empty sex with Connie. I tried to close my door without a sound, then breathed in the sharp prick of the night air. Gray-black clouds hung as a close ceiling spit an occasional flake of snow. An owl hooted softly from the front yard. Beyond the backyard clothesline, I spied a pair of eyes from the three-hundred-year-old oak monitoring my steps. My mind went to the mountain lion. I froze. Squinting for acuity, my nighttime eyesight wasn't good enough to detect shape or color, so I dismissed my paranoia. Maybe it was a raccoon.

When I stepped into the kitchen, the smell of lemons welcomed me, as did the clean dishes in the drying rack. I clicked off the kitchen light before tiptoeing upstairs, accompanied by the sound of water splashing. A light from our bathroom poured onto the landing. Sarah stood at the sink, her back to me.

"Hey," I said quietly, trying not to startle her. She turned off the water but wouldn't meet my eye in the mirror. "You okay?"

"Yeah" She swiveled away from the sink, staring, appraising. Two vertical creases between her eyes paired with her tense lips. "You start wearing perfume?" She faced me, wiping her hands on a towel. "What the hell, Jimmy? Where have you been?"

I diverted my eyes. "Connie Warner's car wouldn't start, so I gave her a ride home. Dropped her off and came home."

"Did you fix her car?" she snipped.

"No." I was starting to smolder. She wasn't going to make me feel bad for helping Connie, and definitely not for resisting her come-on. I stripped down for a quick shower, the tile floor as cold as Sarah. I ran the water and pulled the diverter valve on the tub spout to start the shower.

"Anything happen? Did she invite you in?" She crossed her arms below eyes shooting darts.

A jolt of anger surged through me. "Yeah, but I told her no." I pulled back the reins to diffuse an escalation. "Look, neither of us had jumper cables, so we left her car downtown. What's with the third degree anyway?"

Sarah held her reserve. "I know, but I told you I've seen her in action around you. And women talk, Jimmy. She's a big flirt." She paused, one hand on her forehead, one hand on her belly. "Be honest with me. Do you have a thing for her or what? Aren't I attractive to you anymore, Jimmy? Huh?"

"I don't have a thing for her!" So much for not escalating. I took a breath. Softer, I appealed to her, "C'mon, Sarah. You're being ridiculous. You have no reason not to trust me. Does this have something to do with your dad cheating on your mom?"

She narrowed her eyes. "Oh, don't you go there." Her slumped shoulders told me she wanted sympathy. There was a brief stare down. "I'm sorry. I'm feeling a little maternal and protective of you. I know how women can be."

"No problem. After all, I am going to be a dad—of our baby," I said, full of pride, touching her stomach. She welcomed my attention with a kiss. "And you look beautiful being maternal!" I shouted from behind the shower curtain.

For an unexplained reason, my high school sweetheart, Jenny, popped into my head. There was someone who was less quick to anger and not the jealous type. I wished Sarah were more like Jenny and could let it go for once.

The warm water spray continued to cleanse the temptation of Connie away.

15

I was awakened by a muffled voice from the kitchen mixed with silverware scraping on dishes under running water. The warmth the blankets provided was a comfortable refuge from the freezing rain mixed with snow plastered on the bottom half of the window. The monochromatic heather gray clouds were acting like a tight lid on the area. Rolling away from the window, I closed my eyes, revisiting last night's interaction with Connie.

I remembered her scent, her bedroom eyes, the softness of her sweater, and what might have been. A dollop of guilt dropped on my consciousness, and I stared at the ceiling with eyes wide open, wondering. What did I think was going to happen? Small town gossip traveled like a prairie fire. Had she been playing me the whole time, testing me to see if I would take the bait? A riptide of guilt towed the fool of me under.

The faucet squeaked. The background noise stopped, and a voice remained. Sarah's absence from our bed refocused my attention. I threw on some clothes and made my way to the kitchen. She moved in slow motion to hang up the phone.

"Who called?" I said on my way to get Frosted Flakes out of the cupboard. No response. I poked my head from behind the cupboard door to see Sarah red-faced with frightened eyes. Oh no. She had lost the baby. "What? Sarah?" My chest tightened as everything shifted to neutral. "Tell me."

"Jimmy, it was Joan," she said, stammering to get the words out. "They had to rush Colby to the hospital. He's been diagnosed with pancreatic cancer."

Cancer. My stomach dropped. My head began spinning like a blender with the fear of death. First my mom, now Grandpa. The two most important people in my world.

Sarah's dam of tears broke as her shoulders shuddered. "Joan said the doctor had run some tests." She gasped for air and reached for tissues while she pulled out a kitchen chair. "The doctor said the cancer was pretty advanced, based on the results and how much pain he was in." Her eyes were filled with pain. "Joan said there's no cure."

The room got dark for a second, my thinking disjointed. A fog descended on my brain, making it hard to fathom what was happening. *Pancreatic cancer... There is no cure...* Shaky hands set the cereal box down on the counter. I centered my vision on Sarah. "I have to go to Kansas today. I need to leave ASAP."

"Do you want to sit down?" she asked. "You look white as a ghost."

"No, I'm fine," I said, rubbing my eyes as things came back into focus.

She sprang into action. "Okay. Let me help you pack your things." She sounded like Katherine, staying calm, taking charge. "I'll ask Jay and Robert to manage the bar ... you know, keep an eye on Paul, too. I don't want him to think he can take over the bar with you gone." She led the way up the stairs, two steps ahead of me both in space and planning.

"Not going to happen with those guys there. They got our back," I said with confidence. "Close it if you have to for all I care," I mumbled, throwing clothes in a duffle bag.

She was an organizing whirlwind, thinking out loud—*Gas? Money? Snacks? Water jug?* From our bathroom, she grabbed my razor, shaving cream, and deodorant before adding it to my bag. From our closet, she retrieved my dark blue suit—the one I'd worn to Katherine's funeral. She held it in my direction, her face questioning.

We both stopped. "Yeah, I suppose," I conceded with a twinge of melancholy.

She added a white shirt and a complementing tie.

We hustled downstairs, where I grabbed my faded Levi's jean jacket from the closet. "I'll call you when I get there. I think it's an eleven- or twelve-hour drive."

She stood on her tiptoes to kiss me with an accompanying hug, further communicating her sympathy and love. "You drive careful, Jimmy Marino. And don't you worry about a thing here."

There was a nip in the morning air. "I know you can take care of things here," I assured her, looking over my shoulder as I breezed across the wet lawn to my truck. "I love you ... "

Sarah stood inside the porch, holding the door open. "Jimmy come back here a sec."

I threw the bag on the front seat and half jogged back to the top of the steps.

Her eyes drilled into me. "If this is it, you know . . . " She grabbed both my hands in hers, looking away, looking back. "Don't leave anything unsaid." She continued to hold eye contact, her face tight with determination. "Trust me, I wish I had a chance to tell Katherine a few more things."

I bent to kiss her. "Thanks. I won't." I dashed down the steps and across the yard.

"Love you, Jimmy!" she said behind me.

I clamored into the truck, the lingering scent of Connie's perfume still present. I threw the truck into reverse, tires ripping out of the gravel driveway onto the road. Waving to Sarah, I punched it, and the tires squealed goodbye on the asphalt.

Keeping the speedometer right at five above the speed limit on the two-lane highway, my pace was often slowed by the small towns east of Painted Rock. They all had Victorian homes surrounded by overgrown foliage and dusty pickups at crowded diners. In between towns, the highway was straight and empty, except for the occasional dead animal or shredded pieces of tire littering the road. On either side of the highway, the landscape featured skim ice in the little swales situated between subdued, rolling hills. In the distance, combines combed fertile acres for the harvest. The radio played Jim Croce and Bill Withers as the odometer spun out the miles.

In concert with the hum of the road, I began to journey back to my happiest memories with Grandpa. There were a bunch. I remembered my first largemouth bass out of Lone Star Lake, him showing me how to throw a spiral, teaching me how to drive. The happiest was when we found the Thomas Jefferson Peace Medal, which resulted in hugs, tears, and an admiration that forged our grandfather-grandson relationship at a deep, emotional level. As if reliving the experience, I exhaled through my nose with an audible *humph*. Finding it had been half the adventure. The second half of the adventure wasn't happy but taught us both about the will to survive, culminating in the confrontation with the Staties. Back when the Staties saga happened, Grandpa and I had found it hard to believe nothing ever became public about their disappearance.

Passing excavated mountains of sand and gravel, which were long ago buried, reminded me of how Grandpa taught me that all of it had been left behind by a receding glacier. The steep rolling hills north of Sioux Falls made the horizon appear much closer, practically touchable. The character of the landscape changed to thicker tree lines; burr oaks clinging to their leaves were intermingled with yellowing green ash trees, clustered enough to be called woods. Off in the distance, white, black, and chestnut horses grazed in the trampled pasture. Above me, a soft blue sky was filled with swatches of clouds linen-cloth thin. In the distance, a skein of snow geese resolved to follow a centuries-old flyway to the southern United States. Fall was my favorite time of the year.

My legs started to cramp up with no comfortable position to alleviate the tightness. I stopped for gas, a salted nut roll, and a Styrofoam cup of bitter coffee. The worry about Grandpa's condition was building. I used the pay phone to call his house, hoping Joan was there. No answer. Returning to my truck, I kept my head down to fight off a cold bluster from the north, and I shifted my mind's eye to Grandpa lying on white sheets in a hospital bed attached to machines. My nose smelled the sterility of the room. My mind's eye scanned to find the vinyl chair in the corner. Monitors beeped softly in the background. My gut wrenched as if I'd been transported back to my mom's room again.

Sarah's voice reentered my head. What were the things I wanted to talk to Grandpa about? Any regrets about tossing the medal? I wanted to ask him if he wished he would have kept it. Of course, I'd tell him about Sarah being pregnant. Would he recommend I get married? What would be the things he wanted to ask me? Tell me? I begged God to make sure I got there in time.

Crossing into Iowa with its outdated motels, slaughterhouses, and truck stops packed with eighteen-wheelers, I passed Sioux City. By this point, the truck cab had begun to smell stale. I rolled down my window for air as I picked up the Missouri River on my right. Here it was mud-brown and shallow cut, a marked contrast to the water's width at Painted Rock. I tried to imagine how Lewis and Clark had navigated this stretch of mostly unused waterway. Grandpa would have fit in on their expedition, I knew it. He was never afraid of anything. They would have learned a thing or two from him, too. Yep, he had been born a hundred and seventy years too late.

My eyes were getting heavy. My lower back and legs screamed with stiffness as my tires headed west at Kansas City, Kansas. The strong ammonia smell of urine and manure from the livestock yard seeped through my truck vents, wrinkling my nose. I found a station with a deep-voiced DJ playing a "commercial free rock block" from six to seven. That would be long enough to keep me awake until Lawrence.

16

The highway crossed the Kansas River before I took the off ramp and a couple of left turns on side streets to the Lawrence Memorial Hospital. I was surprised to see a brand-new hospital had been built right next to the original building built in the 1920s. The smell of antiseptic surrounded me as I zigzagged through doctors and medical staff hopping from room to room. Stopping at the nurse's station, I asked about Grandpa. The nurse told me his doctor was talking to him but to wait in the hallway outside room 909.

The shimmer of the polished floor mocked my dark situation as I approached his room. Peeking through the open door, I saw the doctor positioned at the foot of Grandpa's bed. The white-jacketed doctor was murmuring, which made me nervous. Joan stood on the other side of the bed, her eyes fixed on the doctor. She wore a pale face full of anguish. Her hands, drained of color, clutched the upturned bedrail.

After I paced back and forth a couple minutes with my heart knocking, the doctor emerged. We passed by each other without recognition.

"Hey, Grandpa," I started in a soft tone. "How ya doing?" I tried to conceal my shock at how salty-white his skin had become. His perpetual tan from years in the field was gone. His eyes had dark circles around them, the centers hollow.

Joan acknowledged me with disconsolate eyes, subsequently shifting her attention to the opposite side of the bed.

"Dad!" I blurted, stepping toward him but unsure of how we would greet one another. Hug or handshake?

My dad stood with an outstretched arm to shake my hand like we were meeting for the first time. Although we talked on occasion, I hadn't seen him in three or four years. His stature had shrunk, with stooped shoulders and a thinner face, still tan. His gnarled hand with sausage fingers still had a good grip. The other hand held his ball cap, revealing his untanned dome sprouting less hair. "How was your drive?" was all he offered before sitting back down, resetting his ball cap on his knee.

His greeting caused a flare of upset within me. "Good to see you, Dad," I responded with a hint of sarcasm. "The drive was fine."

I turned away and leaned over the bedrail, extending my hand. Grandpa's eyes recognized me but lacked his usual animation. His mouth started to open, as if wanting to say something. Instead, he settled on raising his hand with great effort.

I met it, held it. "You need to get well, Grandpa," I softly encouraged him.

He swung his head over to Joan. They both made eye contact with me. "I don't think that's going to happen, Jimmy." He strained to get the words out. "Doc says he doesn't know how long I have."

We talked about what the doctor had said about pancreatic

cancer and Grandpa's condition. Joan went on to say the doctor had drawn a crude picture and described how the tumor was on the tail of the pancreas, wrapped around a big artery. Surgery, therefore, would be too dangerous. It might kill him.

"Well, it's getting late. I should be getting home," Dad said, standing to straighten the leg of his Dickies overalls. He stepped toward the foot of the bed. "Take care, Colby. I'll check in with you tomorrow. Make sure they're feeding you." Dad forced a smile under a wink, and Grandpa weakly smiled back. Dad motioned to me. "I'll wait outside."

Silence filled the room after Dad left. The pause was interrupted by a soft double chime. A woman's voice filled the room and said, "Visiting hours conclude in fifteen minutes."

"You've got to be kidding me," I groused. "I'm not leaving. Not after I drove eleven hours or whatever. They're going to have to kick me out."

Joan took Grandpa's hand. "We should let you rest." With motherly eyes, she nodded to me. "We can all catch up tomorrow."

Grandpa said, in a loud whisper, "Joan's right. I'm struggling to keep my eyes open."

Another flare of upset surged through me before I capitulated. "Yeah, I guess." A couple beats of silence. "Mind if I stay at your house, Grandpa?"

He nodded. "You know where the key is."

"Thanks, Grandpa. I appreciate it." Over the bedrail, I managed a hug. "See you tomorrow. Love you."

I stepped into the hallway, almost running into Dad. Neither of us spoke as we leaned our backs against the wall waiting for Joan to say her goodnight. The three of us took the elevator down to the lobby, silently self-absorbed. Stopping in front of the revolving door, Joan said she planned to be back midmorning.

Dad said he wasn't sure because of his work schedule, and I said I'd come over when I woke up.

After Joan split, I followed my dad to his car. The parking lot had inadequate lighting, making it difficult to see. I broke the silence. "You want to get a beer or somethin' to eat?" I wanted to tell him about the baby, that I might be getting married, and about life in general. Try to have a grown-man conversation.

"I have to drive a car for the Chevy dealership to Topeka early tomorrow." His answer was quick, without regret. He kept his eyes focused on using his key to unlock his Caprice Classic. "How about later in the week if you're still here?" He swiveled his head, opening the door. "Shouldn't you be getting back to work, though?" He stood with the door open, one leg in the car, hurried.

Stunned by the question, I tried looking into his eyes, wanting to make a connection. He offered a fleeting glance. "No. Sarah's got it handled." My heart ached for his attention, but his standoffish body language made it clear to me he was uninterested in rekindling our relationship. "Hey, I was going to tell you there was a mountain lion spotted north of town."

"No kidding," he replied with a blank stare. His taut face contained torment. Below the surface, he was waging a war with demons. They'd gotten ahold of him after Mom died.

"Didn't you scare one up with the tractor during planting season one time?"

"Might have. Can't say for sure." His interest switched to observing the people walking from the hospital to their cars.

I was getting nowhere. Shifting my tone to a wish, I said, "Call me at Grandpa's when you get home, okay?"

"If I get time, I will." He closed the door with a thump.

I stood as he pulled away, the slam of the door echoing in my head. I drove to Grandpa's and fell asleep in the spare bedroom under the brown and orange plaid quilt that Grandma Phillips had made.

I rested against the wrought iron column bracing the entrance canopy of Grandpa's house, taking in the morning. I held a coffee cup in my right hand, the rich aromatic vapors trying to offer comfort. His neighborhood was dotted with towering hardwood trees surrounding a mixture of clapboard ranches, as well as Victorian and Tudor style houses. Muted golden-yellow honey locust leaves covered the front yard, dislodged from above by fall winds and leaving a skeleton of branches reaching for the rising tangerine sun. The early morning sun blanketed me, the air fresh and light, but my heart was heavy with heartbreak. The beauty of the day offered hope that the doctors were wrong and Grandpa would make a miraculous recovery. If anyone was going to beat this cancer, it was him. I prayed Grandpa had the will to get better. Somewhere above, squirrels chattered their agreement.

Grandpa's neighbor, Mrs. Fouts, still in her threadbare housecoat, poked her head out of her front door to grab the morning paper from the front steps. She smiled and waved, so I smiled and waved back. A burgundy Caprice drove by, throwing me into remembering Dad hadn't called. Another wave of disappointment crashed into me but receded quickly.

I refocused, watching clusters of students, laden with books and backpacks, disappearing into cream-colored brick buildings. Seeing the college kids going to class made me think of Grandpa. To everyone else, he was Professor Colby Phillips of the University of Kansas, winner of multiple awards in his fields of anthropology and archeology, revered by his students and peers alike, recognized at one time as being the best in the world. To me, he was simply Grandpa. I pictured him lying in his hospital bed, weak and unable to care for himself. I dismissed my disturbing vision, returning to memories of the Patton-esque man of bravado from my youth. If this was it, I told myself, that was how I would remember him.

Anxious to get the day moving, I dumped the last of my coffee into the bushes and went back inside to call Sarah. I filled her in on Grandpa's condition. She filled me in on how things were at The Caboose. No one had said if they'd found the other D.I.P. agent. I told her I wanted to get up to the hospital, so our conversation proved short.

The nurse leaving Grandpa's room stopped me in the hall. In a hushed tone, she informed me he hadn't had a good night. Grandpa, she said, had used his call button incessantly throughout. He'd wanted his pain meds increased because the pain was becoming unbearable. She had upped his dosage of pain medicine—morphine, she called it—twice during the night. Thinking of Grandpa in pain made my skin itch with anxiety.

"Morning, Grandpa," I said in my cheeriest voice. "Is your pain going away yet?" Happy to have gotten this one-on-one time, I affectionately squeezed his shoulder.

"I'm not in any pain." He smiled, but his words carried a tinge of a thick tongue. His eyelids carried the weight of the medication.

Sarah's admonishment had played on a loop inside my head since I left Painted Rock. It needed my voice. "So, Grandpa," I waded in, "I've always wanted to ask you, do you have any regrets about throwing the medal in the river?"

A shadow of seriousness crossed his face. He squeezed his eyes shut.

Puzzled at his behavior, I recoiled. "What's the matter?"

He mustered a defiant tone. "I'm fine, Jimmy." His eyes searched the room before finding mine. In a loud whisper, he volunteered, "I didn't throw the medal in the river."

Muscles flexed in my neck and shoulders. The medications had clearly affected his memory. The downhill slide had begun. I spoke in a voice mixed with distress and pity. "Yes, you did. I was there for the showdown on the bridge with the Staties, remember?"

"I remember," he mumbled. "Sit me up." Using the hand control, I raised the head of the bed. "Put a couple pillows behind my head." Grandpa cleared his throat as his eyes shifted from side to side. It was hard to tell if he was going to relive the Staties' confrontation or if he didn't know where to start with explaining our contradictory memories. He stammered, flattening out the creases in his white cotton blanket. "I've done a dumb thing, and I'm really sorry."

I sat down on the vinyl chair located under the TV. "I have no clue what you're talking about."

He waved his left hand through the air dismissively. "I'm doped up, but not so much I don't know what I'm saying." He wriggled under the covers. "The Thomas Jefferson Peace Medal I threw off the bridge was a fake."

My jaw dropped; my eyes got big. "*What?*" I exclaimed. Was it the drugs or Grandpa talking? I studied his eyes and the lines on his face, looking for a hint of his frame of mind.

There appeared to be an aura of resignation, disappointment. "This may take a while, so get comfortable," he started, licking his lips. He began with the day we'd found the Thomas Jefferson Peace Medal and had it stolen by two hillbillies from Tennessee before being tied up and left to die on the prairie.

I helped him with the part where we had freed ourselves using our machete and rushed to town to see Jay and Robert carrying the hillbillies' beaten-up bodies out of The Caboose. In the aftermath of the bar fight, Jay had grabbed the medal one of the guys had left on the bar.

Grandpa nodded in agreement. "I was too physically wounded, not thinking clearly . . . to ask about it right when we got to The Caboose. Big mistake on my part." He grabbed the Styrofoam cup of water and sipped through a straw. "So, I have recently come to find out that Jay . . . took the medal to ask his father what he would like done with it. Standing Bear said he would have to . . . you know . . . consult with the Tribal Council, because of their belief it contained bad medicine or a curse."

I acknowledged his accuracy. "Yep, go on."

"What you and I didn't know is Barking Coyote was there when Jay showed up at his parents' house . . . on the reservation. Barking Coyote offered to put the medal in his safe at the jewelry store until the Tribal Council decided its fate the next morning."

I leaned forward, my elbows on my knees. With fragmented sentences and pauses, Grandpa continued to tell me about the visit he and Joan had had with Barking Coyote. Grandpa said Barking Coyote had seemingly wanted to unburden himself of a guilty conscience because he was in poor health from a heart infection. I recognized the irony in Grandpa's statement.

Barking Coyote had figured out that, with the real medal, he had an opportunity to make some money. As a jeweler, he easily made a duplicate, dirtied it up a bit, and gave the counterfeit to Standing Bear at the Tribal Council Meeting. Grandpa narrowed his eyes. "Barking Coyote . . . deceived the Tribal Council, his father Chief . . . Standing Bear, and the tribal Medicine Man . . . Eagle . . . Elk about the authentic medal's whereabouts."

I stared at Grandpa, my brain in overdrive, trying to process what I had just heard. My stomach churned from its acid. "So, what did he do with the original?"

"I'm getting there." Grandpa, in between catching his breath, filled in the picture for me with a couple of missing pieces. Without his knowledge, Standing Bear had passed the fake medal to Grandpa, and Barking Coyote had sold the real medal to an antiques dealer in Montana. Since we'd presumed we had the real one, which Grandpa wanted to purge himself of, he threw it off the bridge right in front of the greedy D.I.P. Staties.

"Lots to connect here, Grandpa," I said, prepared to blitz him with more questions. "At least I know the real reason you didn't want me to go looking in Lake Oahe for the medal."

"Knock, knock," the nurse said, walking into the room. With an effortless rhythm, she made her assessment visually, asked questions, checked his vitals, made some notes on his chart hanging at the foot of his bed, and administered the pain medication with a couple of clicks. She smiled at Grandpa as if to say, "Have a nice flight." Reaching from her tiptoes, she pulled back the white curtain, generating a sharp clanking sound along its track. Withdrawing it revealed an empty bed, lanced by bright sunbeams piercing through the window. Head down, she rushed out.

Joan joined us in typical cheery fashion, carrying donuts, coffee, and the morning newspaper. Her cheeks were flushed. The expression on her face dimmed as it dawned on her that she had come during the middle of an intense conversation. Her typical greeting banter abbreviated, and she sat in the other chair and focused on her donut and coffee. "Please finish your conversation. Don't mind me."

Grandpa picked up where he had left off, telling me the antique dealer in Montana had died three or four years earlier, and an Arizona collector out of Winslow bought the contents of the entire store from his estate. The collector had sold off most of what he'd bought but kept the finest pieces, including the peace medal.

Joan's cup stopped midway to her lips. We exchanged a glance. "Do you know how crazy this sounds, Grandpa?" His expression remained a face of stone, his eyes searching mine. "There's more?"

"Three or four years ago, I was approached at a conference in Tempe. I was told this guy from Winslow would sell it to the right buyer. I told his intermediary I wasn't interested and, well . . . figured we were done." His face tightened, and he took another pause to catch his breath. "Last year, I fell back into old habits, like an alcoholic falls off the wagon." His eyes dropped. His face reddened.

The walls of the room closed in on me. My chest tightened. I shook my head, jumping ahead of him. "*Oh no.* You bought the medal, didn't you?" I bowed my head, covering my eyes, gutted with disbelief. After all we had been through to find the medal, lose it, get it back, and free ourselves of it—we were right back to square one. We had faced death in the process. I shook my head, speechless.

Grandpa ran his trembling finger under his nose, sniffling. His lower lip quivered as he answered my nervous fear. "Oh, Jimmy . . . I-I was up against an irresistible force. I had to have it . . . all over again." He swiveled his eyes to the ceiling and came back to me. "I-I had to know . . . I still had it. I still had . . . game." His lower lip quivered; Grandpa's forehead creased. "Look at me," he said in a whisper, disgusted with himself. "I-I believe the damn medal . . . cursed me with cancer."

My body had tightened. I pushed off the arms of the chair to stand. "No!" I shouted. "The medal has nothing to do with it. It's ridiculous to believe you got cancer from the medal," I said. I glanced at Joan, who sat with arms and legs crossed, her face taut. With open palms, I pleaded, "You didn't need the medal to

prove your worth. We talked about this. You said so yourself."
I shrugged, disappointed. "You were lying to yourself, I guess."
I walked to the window, hands on my hips, feeling dejected, cheated, and alone. For the first time in my life, I was filled with genuine frustration toward my grandpa. Turning back, my face kinked in restrained outrage. In a terse tone, I spat, "I hate to ask, but where is the medal now?"

Grandpa cleared his throat before taking a hearty drink of water. "Jimmy," he regained his composure, talking calmly. "Let me explain. I-I . . . like I said earlier, I talked with Barking Coyote when we were at Standing Bear's . . . After he was done with his story, I told him how I came to have it. I said I wanted it gone so no more harm would come from it. He said . . . he wanted nothing to do with the medal ever again before directing Joan . . . and me to talk with his dad."

Joan explained that they had spoken with Standing Bear and Eagle Elk, the medicine man. "In order to break the spell of bad medicine," she said, "the medal must be taken for sacrifice to the sacred waters at Tower Buttes." She described in vivid detail passing near the small town of Crook, the entrance road, and the named buttes. Animatedly, she told me how they had walked "a long way on a deer trail," through pine trees and towering bluffs of light-colored sandstone, to a large meadow of rock intermingled with scrub brush. A big smile accompanied her excited voice. She beamed with pride, reliving their "adventure" as she called it.

I glanced over at Grandpa, his face an unhappy mask. He took another sip of water and swallowed hard. In a gruff voice aimed at Joan, he exclaimed, "That's enough, don't you think?"

"Don't be silly, Colby," she poo-pooed. Undeterred, she recounted the fine mist that hung over the meadow. With enthusiasm, she added that they were astonished at the faint smell of rotten eggs coming from the area of the springs. They had found a spring with a number of ceremonial items placed around it. Joan described items such as a necklace of elk teeth and beads, a turquoise cross, a child's small clay pot, and a cluster of bald eagle feathers. She said they had both experienced a spiritual presence, so Colby tossed the medal into the shallow puddle surrounding the burbling water.

Leaning forward off the pillows, he pointed his index finger at me, his voice growing hoarse. "We fixed everything. We left the medal on the reservation." The stern look on his face softened into appealing. "I beg you, Jimmy. Damn it, leave . . . it . . . be!" Grandpa sank back into the pillows. He briefly stared at the ceiling, coughed twice to bring up some phlegm, and spat into a tissue. With his tank empty, Grandpa closed his eyes.

His chest rose, followed by a soft whistle of an exhale. My posture frozen, I hesitated before slowly approaching and kissing him on the forehead. Pangs of sorrow shot through me, yet I still loved him with my whole heart. I'd been hoping he had no regrets about throwing the medal off the bridge. At least, that would have reinforced that he'd done the right thing. I never expected to get such a messy answer to such a straightforward question. I leaned over the bedrail, heart heavy but still full of affection.

"Get some rest, Grandpa." I stood back from the bed, unsettled about my hero. The arcing static inside my head from our conversation was deafening.

What else had he not told me?

17

I went back to the house to decompress. The midday sun's warmth loosened the coolness of the hospital's air conditioning from my body. While I dug in my jeans pocket for the house key, my nose picked up on the smell of a city's worth of car exhaust drifting up from the road. It reminded me of my visits here as a kid. An agitating squeak of brakes from a city bus pierced the hum of local traffic behind me, and I wished for the solitude of the prairie. I retreated inside to make a peanut butter and jelly sandwich, struggling to make sense of Grandpa's confession. The silence of the kitchen wrapped itself around me.

Seated at the maple dining room table, I replayed the entire conversation with Grandpa. I wasn't okay with him buying the medal, but I could see why the temptation had been too strong to overcome. He had been under the spell of fame and glory for his entire career. To change his values one hundred and eighty degrees in a relatively brief period of time was asking a lot. Despite the ask, I told myself that people overcome temptation all the time. My hero had let me down.

I adjourned to the couch, pondering what my life would be like without Grandpa in it. It didn't feel good. I curled up with a red, white, and blue afghan, wanting to take a nap. Restless, my mind was tumbling—Sarah, Dad, The Caboose, Paul, Grandpa, death, travel, baby, marriage, and back to Grandpa. A pall fell over me at the prospect that Grandpa might not meet our baby. In the next instant, a tightness formed in my throat as I began to reminisce again about some of our times together. How would I fill the void he would leave?

The doctors had to make him better. It was 1977—modern medicine should have been able to cure anything. Surgery? Pills? Something. I wanted one more fishing trip, one more trip to the drive-in, one more Saturday afternoon of playing catch, one more...

> *I am in the middle of a crowded hotel conference room dominated by the din of conversation. Faceless bidders mill around, scrutinizing the items for auction. The auctioneer takes the podium, microphone in one hand, a bouquet of dogwood flowers in the other. The voice from the outline of a woman is my mom's. "Mom!" I shout. "Mom!" I wade through the people to get to the front of the masses. "Know what you're buying," she opens. "And buy with confidence." She starts an intoxicating, rapid first chant. "All to go ... lookie here ... Well, who's got two thousand?" The theater of my mind is illuminated, and Mom's face has gray tombstones for eyes. Back to the auction patter. "Let's go ... all clean ... " And emerging from behind a curtain is Jenny, my girlfriend from high school. She has the medal around*

her neck. I reach out toward her, but the tombstone eyes return as Jenny dissolves into pixie dust. The medal drops and spins like a quarter on the floor. I reach for it as the spinning stops, halted by the weight of a granite tombstone crushing my arm.

I woke up, keeping my eyes closed in the hope of seeing the image of my mom return without the tombstones. The dream had felt so real—exciting, yet haunting. I sat up, thinking of death and the questions surrounding it. Different questions than the ones my teenage self had asked when Mom died. What do we know about death? It comes to us all, mostly not at a time of our choosing. But it comes to everything: animals, plants, even the stars. Humans try to control longevity. Everything else in the universe accepts it, and time moves on. What does the rest of the universe know that we don't? Can death be beautiful? Can the sting of losing a loved one ever heal? Can death be overcome? The simplest answer I came up with was that it depended upon your perspective—how you look at the world, how your life experiences have molded you, what you believe this world is all about.

Driving through town back to the hospital, I kicked myself for not telling Grandpa sooner about the baby. My becoming a father should have been the first thing I'd told him. When I returned to the hospital, I would tell him first thing, even if I had to wait until he woke up. This was too important to wait another day. Things needed to be said.

Joan was sitting on the edge of the bed holding Grandpa's hand when I arrived. When I walked into the room with a knock, she forced a smile. His eyelids opened fully, closed halfway, and opened fully again. I hated to see him struggle so. The pallor of his skin had lightened further, and his lips were dried and cracking like they used to after a day of artifacting on the prairie. His few tufts of hair were disheveled. He was fighting the good fight, but his body was losing—and fast.

I approached the bed and a used tender tone. "Hey, Grandpa."

Eyes flickering, he slowly lifted his hand for me to hold it.

I took it, noting the thinness of his wrist and the brownish-purple blotches on his arms. "Can you hear me, Grandpa?"

He slowly rotated his head toward me, eyes barely open. Once he found focus, he nodded. Joan faced me from across the bed, rivulets of tears ruining her impeccable makeup.

"Guess what?"

Grandpa held my gaze, waiting.

"Sarah and I are having a baby. You are going to be a great-grandpa!" I smiled, squeezing his hand and hoping it registered. "If it's a girl, I'd like to name her Mary, after Mom. If it's a boy, I'd like to name him Colby, after you."

Grandpa's eyes found Joan. Returning to me with a weak smile, he reciprocated my hand squeeze.

"Oh, what wonderful news, Jimmy! Isn't it wonderful, Colby? Congratulations." She swiveled her head. "I bet Colby on our way home from Painted Rock that Sarah was pregnant. Sarah had a special glow about her."

The smile never left his face as he nodded. I imagined how proud he would feel if he wasn't so drugged. A satisfied smile creased my face.

"And we're talking about getting married . . . but we'll have to see what happens." There was hesitation in my voice. Joan's face expressed a puzzled look, and I wanted to explain myself. "Well, I mean, I don't know if I'm ready." I smiled, comfortable in sharing.

Grandpa's face came alert with a throaty growl. "Come . . . closer . . . Jimmy," he ordered in a thick-tongued whisper.

I took a tentative step closer.

Slowly and seriously, he said, "I . . . n-never devoted my full self to my wife . . . your Grandma Phillips." His voice contained pain and longing. He took a deep breath. "It was the . . . biggest mistake." He paused to cough up phlegm. "Of my life." Another deep breath. "I was so full of myself, the accolades . . . chasing the ghosts of success." He pinched his eyes tightly together, wincing. I wasn't sure if the origin of his wincing was physical or mental. "I know it hurt her deeply. I feel . . . " Grandpa's voice trailed off. His shoulders shuddered as his eyes reopened. He squeezed my hand tighter for emphasis. "Don't make . . . the same mistake with Sarah."

His body relaxed into the bed, but my body stiffened from a visceral pushback. I'd always appreciated his advice and willingness to share, but in this case, I wasn't ready to hear it.

He slept during most of the rest of the day, waking for brief periods to sip water, acknowledge our presence, and comply with the nurse's orders. Joan and I stayed until the visiting hours were over. A low ceiling of heavy clouds launched sheets of rain on us as we parted for the evening. Once I got home, I dialed my dad's number. Ten rings later, I hung up.

Rain continued off and on for the next two days as Grandpa's condition worsened. He slept for longer periods of time. His skin began taking on a mottled appearance, and he had lost his appetite. Shortly before noon, the physician in charge of Grandpa's care, Doctor Waterfield, took Joan and me to a small sitting area at the end of the hall for an update.

"You both should know the end is approaching for Doctor Phillips," he said with a sympathetic tone. He explained further, "Our bodies are programmed to shut down in a methodical way. There has been a shift in his vitals, indicating he is actively dying."

His eyes shifted from me to Joan and back, letting the enormity of his statement sink in.

Joan and I turned to each other in the way people do when they want to share their misery. Her face was pale, and mine undoubtedly was, too. Grandpa's death was inevitable, but I was completely unprepared for the reality. My body went limp.

The doctor continued, "I'm sorry. The cancer has progressed too far. Other than keeping him comfortable, there's nothing more we can do." He clutched Grandpa's chart tight to his body. "The hospital offers grief counseling, clergy, and our chapel is open twenty-four hours a day." He laid his hand on my shoulder. "Doctor Phillips has done a lot for our university and community. He's a great man."

We both sat in stunned silence as sleet beat against the window behind us. A full-body shiver forced me to stand. "I need to be with Grandpa," I said.

Joan lifted her head, eyes glistening with tears.

18

A crushing pressure from the stress made my head feel like it was in a slow-closing vise. Joan and I returned to Grandpa's bedside, watching the nurse place an oxygen mask on him. "This will help keep him comfortable," she said. With particular attention, she wiped his shoulder with an alcohol-soaked cotton ball before injecting Loraz-something and then Morphine. She filled out his chart at the foot of the bed in a businesslike manner before leaving the room.

Unable to shake the fog from my brain, I bent close to his face. With quivering lips, I murmured, "I know you can hear me. I want you to know how much you have shaped me into the man I am today and ... I'll be forever grateful I had you as a role model ... and mentor." I swallowed hard; my throat was tightening. "I'll carry the lessons you taught and ... the memories of our good times forever. I love you, Grandpa. Love you so much." I grabbed his hand and squeezed it tight, desperately wanting the transmission of life to heal him.

Deep within me, a surge of tears overcame me. I needed to get some fresh air and talk to Sarah. When Mom died, the grief had been overwhelming, but Grandpa was right there for support. Now, the person I needed most in this world to share my grief with was miles away. Grandpa's admonition to give my whole self popped into my head. I had to call her right now.

On the way out, I stopped at the nurse's station. "I'm Colby Phillips' grandson. He's in 909. Do you think it'd be okay if I ran out for a bit—not more than forty-five minutes to an hour?"

The nurse continued charting without looking up. "Yeah, should be fine."

I held it together until I got back to Grandpa's house to call Sarah. I filled her in on Doctor Waterfield's talk with Joan and me. Each of us had a bout of trying to talk between the gasping and sobbing. I let her know Grandpa's reaction when he'd learned she was having a baby. Sarah told me she was glad I'd told him. I told her how grateful I was that I could share these matters of the heart with her.

"How are things with you and The Caboose?"

"Jay and Robert are using their vacation time to cover your hours," Sarah reassured me. "Paul has kept his same hours, and I've been feeling better, so I'm doing my old hours."

A weird sensation ran up my back as I realized that I might have to plan a funeral. In an even more morose moment, it occurred to me I might have to pick out a casket. "I'm sorry. I zoned out. What did you say?"

"I said things are under control here and not to worry," she said confidently. "Range Detective Ross stopped in to talk to Paul about something and said if I needed anything while you were gone to give him a call. He's so nice."

I was relieved to hear the strength in Sarah's voice. "Yeah, okay. I don't know when I'll be home. Kinda depends on what transpires in the next few days. I'll keep you posted." After we said our goodbyes, I stood in the kitchen feeling powerless, unhappy. I was leaned against the counter and rubbing the tension from my forehead when the stark ring of the phone caused me to flinch. It was Joan tearfully telling me to come quick if I wanted a final goodbye with Grandpa.

Lawrence traffic was oblivious to my gut-wrenching sorrow as I hastily wove through the streets to the hospital. I screeched to a stop as the automatic gate of the railroad crossing closed inches from my front end. Peering down the tracks, trying to see the end of the slow-moving train, I thought I was going to crawl out of my skin. I tapped my fingers on the steering wheel. I chewed my fingernails. I counted cars. Would it never end? When I thought I couldn't take it anymore, the train finally passed. It wasn't long before I thumped into the parking lot. Running into the hospital, I ignored the command from a greeter at the welcome desk to walk. I should have never left. My pace quickened down a narrow hallway. I dodged the people waiting for the elevator before throwing open the stairwell door. I needed Grandpa to know I was there for him. My fleet steps scurried up the stairs two at a time, the stairwell echoing to the ninth floor. I slowed to a fast walk, trying to catch my breath before entering his room.

Too late. Two empty beds with sheetless mattresses in a darkened room filled only with the hum of the HVAC confronted me. A guttural sound of anguish erupted from deep inside me. I wheeled around to make sure I hadn't walked into the wrong room—the gold numbers on the door were 909. A nurse flew in the room and asked, "Are you okay?"

My voice gushed with rage, "No! Where is my grandpa?"

She put her hands up defensively, taking a step back. With a practiced voice, she said, "The doctor was summoned, and he called the time of death. Once the call is made, hospital protocol is for the orderlies to transport the body downstairs and wait for the funeral home to arrive."

"Why didn't you wait 'til I got here?" I asked.

"I'm sorry for your loss," was all she volunteered before she left.

Shuffling out of the room, I stood aimlessly in the hallway. What could I do? Where could I go? A voice called my name. Joan was at the sitting area, head in hands. I went to her, full of sorrow, my world rocked. She stood, wobbled a bit, and sat back down. "He's gone, Jimmy, he's gone." She took a well-used tissue from her cuff to wipe her nose. "It was awful. Not long after you left, he took a deep breath, let it out, and that was it." She nuzzled into my shoulder before pulling back. "It was as if he waited 'til you were gone. I don't think he wanted to die in front of you."

The space around me started spinning. I sat down. I sensed no colors, no movement, no sound. Head bowed, I stared at the blank tile, my mind straddling the void between the present and the alternative reality I sought. The cushioned chair consumed me for an indeterminant amount of time, my brain zipping between memories like a pinball bouncing off bumpers. A gentle sensation on my back registered, but the garbled words directed toward me did not.

I lifted my head, trying to focus on Joan's fuzzy outline, her heels clip-clopping down the hallway and stopping at the nurse's station. Leaning back, my eyes drifted shut as I rose out of myself and hovered above, the camera lens seeing me below. For a moment, I was detached from a world I wanted no part of. The lens zoomed in on me as I returned to myself, a nurse shattering my peace by offering me a glass of water, a package of Ritz crackers, and her condolences.

The service took place at the funeral home two days later. Sarah's doctor had advised her against traveling. I was talking with one of the other mourners when, to my surprise, I spotted Jay on the other side of the room. His entrance at the wake, confident in a bolo tie on a snap button western shirt and wranglers, sparked a few cautionary glances accompanied by less than discreet whispers. Grateful for his presence, I left the reception line to vigorously shake his hand and thank him for making the long trip. I introduced him to my dad, who greeted him with marginal acknowledgement.

Dad had offered no help in planning the funeral, which angered me, given it was his wife's dad. But, given his life of emotional indifference, his lack of participation in the service made perfect sense. Joan, ever stoic throughout, asked him if he had gotten back to the hospital to see Grandpa. "I wanted to but didn't get there. Got tied up at work," he'd answered with a blank face. Throughout the viewing, he hung by the back of the room, seated in a wing chair, fidgeting like he had somewhere to be. On occasion, women in "church dresses" stopped and offered a hug of bereavement, along with a tilted head in sympathy. Men looking uncomfortable in ill-fitting sport coats—plaid, deep brown, or powder blue—offered him obligatory handshakes. None of it elicited an emotional reaction from my dad. How could anyone be so devoid of humanness? Especially at the funeral of a family member. The day of my grandpa's funeral, I discovered there were others besides myself Dad was emotionally detached from. Anger rose inside me, dissolving into pity.

The procession of university and government types came and went, each with a story to tell and offering their condolences. Former students who had gone on digs or had him for a class came and offered fond memories. A few colleagues from other universities within driving distance came, too. Even the CEO of the nursing home where Grandpa had volunteered showed up to pay his respects. Greg and Louie, two of my high school football teammates, came to express their condolences. It was good to catch up on what some of the guys and girls were doing since we'd graduated. The throng of attendees caused the wake to run long. After an extra thirty minutes, the funeral director cut the line off, asking people to take their seats. All the wonderful things people had to say about Grandpa strengthened me during the service and burial.

Joan and I didn't plan any formal gathering after the internment. I tracked down Dad on the way to his car to ask him again if he wanted to get a beer or food. There was so much I needed to tell him about my life. Importantly, I wanted to share with him that Sarah and I were going to be parents, making him a grandpa. I would tell him how the work ethic he'd taught me on the farm translated to the success of the bar. I'd tell him what my life was like these days in Painted Rock, how I'd found a church like the one we used to attend when I was growing up, how I would love to have him come visit and hang out. Somewhere in the conversation, hopefully, he'd tell me he was proud of me. Even show some affection. Unfortunately, none of this came to be.

With an expression of consternation over my invitation, he shuffled his feet. Lifting his head, he stared past me, apparently searching for someone or something more worthwhile. He didn't seem to know how to respond. Was he getting dementia? I remembered the times we'd talked when we were close—he would teach me how to fix things, ask how my day was, what was I going to do on the weekend. At those times, he was a regular chatterbox, but he'd changed. I believe something inside him died when Mom died.

"I'd love to, son, but I have a few things at home I've gotta get to. How about tomorrow?" He forced a smile, showing no teeth.

My cheeks blushed warmly. He knew I was heading home tomorrow. "No." I paused a few seconds to hold his eyes. "By the way, Sarah's pregnant."

"Hey... I guess congrats are in order," he grunted, padding his pockets for his keys. He moved on. "I'm sorry it didn't work out to get together this trip. Let's plan on next time, okay?" he offered meekly, opening his door. As if a transaction were consummated, he offered his oversized right hand, which I shook. He patted my shoulder as he withdrew. "Drive safe, ya hear?" The car door slamming echoed in my head as he drove off.

I stood there, flanked by Jay, feeling embarrassed, hurt. Consumed with rage, I wanted to shout after him that he wasn't half the man Grandpa was. I wanted to tell him I still carried the scars from Mom's death. Mostly, I wished he were capable of seeing my scars, because it wasn't hard to see his. With my hands trembling, I told myself to breathe. *Next time?* Screw him. I didn't know if I'd ever be back. Maybe his funeral. Maybe not.

19

Sunrise winked as it escorted me onto the freeway. Traffic was light, mostly local delivery trucks or commuters heading into Kansas City. To my right and my left, a layer of fog hovered above the cornfields that shouldered the road. In my rearview mirror, Lawrence had diminished to the tops of downtown buildings. I slumped against the back of my seat, giving flex to my legs, happened upon "Free Bird" on the radio, and settled in. The limited stops I was going to make would be for food, fuel, and pee. Ahead of me lay a long drive, with plenty of time to think of the last few days. Grandpa, Sarah, the baby, marriage. Marriage. Dad.

Jitters of agitation ran through me. Why? Dad had brought out feelings of no connection—or was it no commitment?—I didn't know I had within me. I was struggling with his emotional distance. Maybe that was what had been holding me back with

Sarah. Did my insecurity or confusion around commitment stem from my relationship with my dad? The questions I was asking myself made me feel uncomfortable. The Doobie Brothers were rockin' the radio, so I cranked it.

My stream of consciousness was interrupted when a girl driving a flatbed Ford pulled up alongside me. As I caught her eye, she pushed back her shoulder-length auburn hair, smiled, and waved like we'd met before. I raised my hand to reciprocate the wave, but she accelerated. She was vaguely familiar—high school? Jenny? Sarah was all I ever wanted, but I'd never been able to completely discard Jenny's memory. God, what a painful time. Our hearts had been young, open, and vulnerable. Jenny had considered it "puppy love," but for me it was more. She was my first love and she'd dumped me, crushed me.

At the wake, my buddy, Louie, had shared that she'd been back to our hometown from out east for her sister's graduation. I wondered if she ever dreamed about me or became a writer like she wanted to be. I pictured her at a desk, writing about us. I wanted to believe she would have come to the funeral if she was in the area. Who was I kidding? She'd likely married some rich lawyer who graduated from Harvard. Wouldn't doubt if they had one home in Chestnut Hill and another on Martha's Vineyard, Lawrence—and me, a mere blip in her past.

In need of gas and coffee, I stopped in St. Joseph. Slowing as I entered the town limits, a freshly painted wooden sign to my right boasted that St. Joseph was *"Where the Pony Express started and Jesse James ended."*

I gassed up and went inside for my free cup of coffee with fill-up, and to call Sarah. Using the spare change from the ashtray, I dialed the pay phone. She picked up on the first ring. My emotions flooded as I recapped that past couple of days—having to watch Grandpa deteriorate and eventually die, the stress of the funeral, and I confessed Dad had pissed me off. I described myself as shell-shocked since his passing. I needed to change the subject. "I need a distraction. Tell me, what's new with you?"

Hesitating, she said, "Well . . . there was a gentleman—Staubach was his name—here from the Department of Indian Properties in Pierre. He said he needed to talk to Paul." She continued to tell me what the agent had been wearing—black tie, white shirt, black sport coat—and about his creepy demeanor.

"Is Paul in trouble?"

"I asked, but he didn't answer. He rudely repeated that he needed to talk to Paul. I told the guy it was Paul's day off and I had no idea where he was." Sarah's exasperated inflection reflected the mysteriousness of the encounter. "This guy was super persistent, but I honestly didn't know where he was."

"Hmm. Possibly it was something to do with his dad or the dredged car." I was as much in the dark as she was. A sense of dread came over me. "Wait . . . do you think the two are connected?"

"I have no idea," Sarah said. "Before he left, the agent said he would be back but didn't say when."

I stood with my hand on my hip, watching traffic go by through a plate glass window the size of a car. "Huh." I paused briefly, pondering how the D.I.P. agent, Paul's dad, and the car in the river might somehow be linked. "Anything else I should know about?"

"The Range Detective, Ross, shot the mountain lion north of town. Apparently though, not before it had killed another calf. Ross told me the poor calf had been shredded. Like it had been attacked with a knife. He said the mountain lion's teeth and claws are razor sharp." I imagined Sarah's face racked with disgust.

I knew how vicious big cats could be, especially with vulnerable livestock. We'd lost a calf or two on Dad's farm, too.

"Before you go . . . he said our lawn needed mowing and he'd get a guy to take care of it."

I paused. Huh, he'd never offered before. And why was he driving by our house? "Tell him thanks for the kind offer, but I'll take care of it."

We said goodbye, and I took an armful of snacks to the checkout. The cherub-faced checkout lady asked if all the snacks were for me. I replied with a smile and a nod. I hit the road, buckled in with a large black coffee, a Snickers bar, a small bag of Planter's peanuts, an oversized bright yellow bag of Lay's potato chips, and a handful of Bazooka bubble gum to keep me occupied on the asphalt carpet home.

Pointing the nose of the truck north through Iowa with the hum of the engine serving as a copilot, I continued to have a melancholy feeling about Grandpa's death. I soon became aware that the transition to late fall was complete, thanks to the absence of leaves, a lack of greenery, and the increased waterfowl heading south. Even the farm animals were bunched tighter together, hanging close to barns and feed pens. Blue sky formed the ceiling above, improving my dour mood. I changed the radio station from "Bohemian Rhapsody" to settle on Willie Nelson's "Whiskey River."

About the time the sun passed its zenith, the shroud of Grandpa's death began to lift. The vinyl seat squeaked as I shifted, trading my right hand for my left on the steering wheel. Trolling the AM dial, the novelty of a baritone voice caught my attention. The NPR host was sharing his review of a book entitled, "Seasons of Your Life." The reviewer talked about seasons of relationships inside and outside the family, jobs, family dynamics changing with births, the progression of age, and deaths. He said that seasons in our lives intertwine or compound each other. I tried to find examples in my own life and recognized my "seasons" were about to change big time.

Once back in South Dakota, crossroads came and went. The road worked as my partner again, widening on hills to allow me to pass farm implements, offering vistas to shake my boredom, and posting encouraging signs telling me the miles needed to reach home. I tapped my fingers on the steering wheel while singing to "Brown Sugar" by the Rolling Stones.

As I crested the hill overlooking Painted Rock—nestled between the wide expanse of pale blue sky above and the dammed up Missouri River beyond—pangs of loneliness ricocheted inside my stomach. Not because of the view of the town's gridworks, the shimmering steel gray water, the fingers of emerald draws on the horizon, or the tan-yellow grasslands capping the midnight black shale bluffs. The loneliness had to be from elements contained in the panorama, the space where Grandpa and I had made deep connections on so many levels. My life felt untethered with Grandpa gone. The curtain of sadness for his death reappeared before cascading down with a boom.

I began withdrawing, hoping resurrected memories would back-fill the unwelcome void, when my ears suddenly picked up a recognizable melody. Dean Martin crooned "Everybody Loves Somebody" —one of Grandpa's favorite songs. Hearing the song helped some of the sorrow to flit away, but before doing so, it left a remnant for me to consider.

Grandpa wasn't coming back, and my life had to go on without him... but how? I should have grabbed a toy I had played with as a kid or reminder keepsake from the house. It would help soothe the darkness when the inevitable loneliness visited again. During my stay in Lawrence, I had never gotten a break from overwhelming circumstances constantly swirling in my head. It never occurred to me to look around for a remembrance. The house had offered a haven, but the turmoil kept me from feeling settled in it. What would keep me connected? I needed Grandpa's help...

I halted at the red light by the closed A&W, mentally paging through the photo album of our lives together. God, I loved him. Family photos at holidays, trips to KU football games, my high school graduation. Many pages in my mind were filled with pictures from our trip to find the medal. I recalled our conversations about the medal's power, which I figured was dictated by the belief system of whoever possessed it. I had never truly bought into the mystique surrounding it. True, there had been a fair number of coincidences with unfavorable outcomes. Coincidences. There were plausible explanations also available. It might have had some kind of grip on those who were truly convinced it had spiritual, albeit bad, powers. But I had never believed in those types of voodoo curses. I would have the power over the circular piece of metal, not the other way around.

As the sun slid below the clouds to rest on the dim horizon, slivers of golden beams fanned down toward me. One beam brought a special intensity, rendering my sunglasses ineffective. An *aha* moment hit me, and clarity followed. My mom had passed, my dad might as well have, and I had no siblings. Grandpa, and by extension the medal, represented my last connection to family. My hand slammed on the steering wheel—I had to have the medal as a keepsake of the most remarkable man I would *ever* meet. The medal was not going to jinx me! The connection to him would remain in vivid memories but also in the tangible essence of grit, history, and notoriety.

All I had to do was find it.

20

Like an old friend, the farmhouse welcomed me as I turned into the driveway. A pale afterglow of twilight melded into evening as the cold rose from the darkness. After being chased into the house by the sweep of a northern wind, I felt the penetrating warmth of the kitchen melting the crispness of the evening. My travel fatigue vanished the minute I saw Sarah's cheerful smile upon my arrival. Her swollen breasts pressed against me as I hugged her. Her tummy had popped more, too.

We used a dinner of green bean casserole with French fried onions to fill in the details of my trip. I told her of my desire to find the medal, despite Grandpa's warning. "This is something I have to do. You get it, don't you?" I asked, seeking her approval.

She took another bite. "I get why, but I'm not sure it's a good idea. Sounds like Colby was pretty clear you should avoid it."

"I figured you wouldn't understand, but it will truly give me a connection to Grandpa. It's a *need* of mine, Sarah," I explained, rising off my chair to get a second helping. "I have to have it."

She took a big gulp. "You know there are many reasons why you shouldn't. The number one reason being your grandpa said not to. Numbers two through ten are the curse." She set her fork down and folded her arms across her chest.

"I know he did, but he bought into all the hocus pocus about the medal," I countered, my eyes unwilling to meet hers. "I don't."

"Okay, *fine*, Jimmy." She pushed her chair back with an irritating screech. "Go get it for Pete's sake. I wish you were this committed to getting married and being a father." Her voice had a sharp edge. She rinsed her plate under the faucet.

Anger rose inside me from her conflating the two subjects. She had to have known the importance of Grandpa and the medal. I bristled at her pushback. "Jeez, I get home and you start on me right away," I shot back. "I am committed to being a good dad, and I'm committed to you. I need time to process the whole marriage thing," I replied with Grandpa's admonishment ringing in my ears.

She spun around, daggers for eyes. "Well, I'm not waiting around forever for you to," she raised her hands to make quotations, "'*process*'. I have to say, I think your priorities are screwed up." She narrowed her eyes, index finger extended. "You should work through whatever your hang-up is with marriage. Talk to Pastor, read a book, ask Jay, whatever."

The idea of losing Sarah curdled my stomach. My temples throbbed. She had to see my point of view. Pleading, I said, "I . . . I will, I swear. I'll do whatever I need to do for you to know I'm committed. But first I have to talk to Barking Coyote and Standing Bear to see what they told Grandpa about Tower Buttes," I said with excitement. "And given the last few days I've been through, saying my," I mocked her use of the air quotations, "'*priorities* are screwed up' . . . is a bit harsh." A stare down accompanied an uncomfortable silence.

She rolled her eyes and withdrew to the living room with a huff. She didn't *really* get why I needed the medal. In order to break the tension, I suggested we curl up and watch some television. In the past, vegging out in front of the TV—particularly at stressful times like we were experiencing now—had allowed us both to calm down. She reluctantly agreed. I stretched out against the back of the couch with her in front of me, pulling her tight before throwing the afghan over us both. The peppy tune brought a smile to my face. We watched kids having fun in a simpler time. Jukeboxes, Hula-Hoops, drive-ins, sandlot baseball—the good ol' days.

We had settled into an evening of "Happy Days" followed by "Laverne and Shirley," but she wouldn't let it go. "You know how you were telling me how distant your dad was the entire time you were in Kansas?"

"Yeah." The red warmth of embarrassment returned to my face. Tired from the drive and emotionally spent, I wanted to relax and watch the Fonz.

"Don't take this wrong but . . . " She stopped, putting her finger on her chin. "I mean, was he kinda distant with your mom?"

I cringed. "Never occurred to me. Grandpa kept me busy when he was around, or I was busy helping my dad with chores. I guess I was occupied with being a kid and didn't pay much attention to how my parents interacted." I hated it when she cornered me for answers requiring feelings. I punched back. "How about we talk about your mom and dad's nonexistent relationship?"

"I'd be happy to another time, but their relationship has nothing to do with what I'm getting at," she said. There was an uneasy air between us. She continued. "I'm not the one pushing back against getting married." She continued to look at the TV. "Don't get mad, okay? But it seems to me you're having trouble with a marriage commitment because of the way your dad and mom were. Like they never acted married?" She quartered to look at me for a reaction, and after not getting the one she must have wanted, she returned to the TV.

A cauldron of anger, impatience, and fatigue boiled up inside of me. "Can I get back to you? Let it go. Seriously, I'm too tired to talk."

"I'm going to hold you to that, Jimmy."

The television blurred as I retreated back to when I was a kid, possibly nine or ten. My parents had been at an ice cream social, hosted by the Layne family, right before school started. It was the first time I'd ever swum in an aboveground pool. The yard was well manicured and surrounded on two sides by deep green stalks of sweet corn so tall they touched the sky. Dad and the other farmer dads were sequestered out beyond the clothesline drinking beer, while the moms huddled around the picnic table keeping an eye on the kids. Looking back, I thought life was pretty normal for me. Mom had the domestic responsibilities and Dad had the farm responsibilities. There was rarely a deviation from their roles, regardless of the month or day. I don't remember them ever arguing. When they were together watching television, going out to dinner, or traveling in the car—which didn't happen much—they acted happy to be with each other. So, had my dad been distant from my mom? I didn't believe so, unless the work of the farm demanded it. The next time Sarah wanted to psychoanalyze my childhood,

I'd open up more. As for the aversion to getting married? Yeah, I needed some help.

About the time Lenny and Squiggy were going to pick up Laverne and Shirley for a hot date, I fell asleep. Sometime later, Sarah woke me with light kisses. Softly she breathed, "You've had a rough few days, Jimmy. Let's go to bed."

Grateful that she'd let our argument drop, I nuzzled her neck and whispered how much I'd missed her. She cast her seductive eyes upon me, licked her soft lips with the tip of her tongue, and bared an irresistible smile. Her eyes met mine, which led to shared whispers of apologies, which led to whispers of passion.

Into the night, we were entwined in perfect cadence.

21

The overnight temps forced a noticeable drafty current in the house as I lumbered through the living room to make coffee. I parted the kitchen window curtain to read the thermometer. Thirty-five degrees. I started the coffee and raised the thermostat to sixty-eight. A hint of mustiness clung to the warm air rumbling up through the painted iron heat vents as the gurgle of coffee brewed. I leaned against the counter, staring at the floor, thinking. Sarah's directness about my parents' relationship still resonated within me. Her probing had caught me off guard.

My mind jumped... The whole D.I.P. visit with Sarah added another layer of questions I needed to resolve.

Pouring myself a cup of coffee, I theorized that Paul had prompted Staubach to come and investigate what had happened to Gritzmacher and Calhoun. The agent wanted to know why Paul was poking around D.I.P. headquarters. Or ... maybe the agent was, in fact, after me and had hypothesized that Paul was aware of my involvement in Gritzmacher and Calhoun's disappearance. A queasy feeling hit the bottom of my stomach. Too much to think about this early in the morning. Hearing Sarah plod down the steps, I poured her a cup.

"You should look at something," she said, withdrawing a crisp white business card from her purse as she shuffled from the living room. "I have to fill you in on the guy from Pierre who came looking for Paul." She waved the card in front of me.

I read it out loud. "*Dean J. Staubach. Department of Indian Properties. Special Agent in Charge.* Huh." I rubbed my finger over the shiny, raised black lettering. "Looks pretty official. I'll have to ask Paul when I see him if they talked."

"This guy was bizzarro, Jimmy. He had a black suit on with a black tie and these creepy eyes. One eye was straight at me, and one eye was looking over my shoulder." She pointed divergent fingers to illustrate. "He talked in a super deep voice and stood stiff as a board." She took the card from me, placing it back in her purse.

"Sounds like he should be featured in the *Close Encounters* movie they're advertising on TV."

"And I haven't seen Paul since the agent stopped in." Her eyes got big, her face full of suspicion. "Doesn't it seem odd to you Paul wouldn't at least stop by? He stops in every day whether he's working or not."

"Who knows?" I paused for a couple of seconds as anxiety crept up my back. A D.I.P agent questioning Paul about the car in Lake Oahe, his dad, and other potential trouble could add up to nothing good. "Paul's in his own little world."

Sarah and I enjoyed each other's company over a cup of coffee before I had to get to The Caboose.

I eased out of the driveway. The familiar comfort of my truck was like I'd never left it. My route took me past Pastor Dawson's church, where I caught a glimpse of a group of bundled up ladies carrying their brightly-colored knitting bags through the side door. I steered south at the corner and saw smoke spiraling above chimney after chimney, coiling high enough to parade as one to the southeast. Yards fresh off their final fall cut were still white from the overnight lick of a ghost. I drove past the apartment building Range Detective Ross had recently moved into. The solitary dulled light behind the window shade made his second-floor corner room look lonely. It looked out over the darkened plaza across the street from the flat-roofed Waltson Inn. The town was waking with a yawn.

I stood on the stoop behind The Caboose, startled by the approaching beat of *flump, flump, flump.* I fixed my eyes to the sky. A dragonfly-like speck increased in volume as it approached from the south, transforming in a matter of seconds into a big helicopter. Probably a charter of high rollers from Denver coming to hunt or fish. A black belly with white call letters cruised overhead before disappearing beyond the treetops in the direction of the grass landing strip.

Shaking off the aviation curiosity, I tugged on the screen door. It offered more resistance than usual. The old closer had been replaced. After removing my jacket, I paused to survey the tidy kitchen under the humming fluorescent bulbs. The residual smell of stale cigarette smoke received me. I unlocked the drawer below the cash register, where we kept the financials. I reviewed the day slips, deposits, and the pile of bills from when I was gone. After confirming the numbers, I began to kitchen prep for the day.

Midmorning, Paul showed up. "Hey, Paul." I smiled. "The prodigal son returns."

Paul's face showed confusion. "What are you trying to say?"

A recoil of disbelief shot through me. I opened my mouth to explain but let it pass. "Never mind. So, *whassup*?"

"I've got some stuff to show you." He opened up a one-gallon opaque plastic ice cream bucket. "Oh, and I had Rick from the hardware store help me fix your screen door."

"Thanks," my voice filled with appreciation. "What ya got to show me?" I was less interested in his time walking the river since I'd found out where the real medal was.

Paul put an unlit cigarette in his mouth before reaching into the bucket. He held up a rolled piece of metal with a green tint to it. "Is this copper?" he asked.

"Heck, yeah," I said in an enthusiastic voice. "Well, technically it's a brass bead." Total beginner's luck, but I didn't call him out. "It's got copper in it, which gives the metal the green tint. Don't find these very often or in this good of condition. You been walkin' the river?"

"Yeah, off and on the last couple of days. I'd say four or five hours a day." No wonder his face looked dry and red. The South Dakota sun and wind would do that. "I had to go see the dentist in Keogh two days ago. Doc said I got an infected tooth. Said they'd call me when they had an opening to get 'er yanked." Paul began to shake his head. "Hope he doesn't nick me too bad with the cost."

No wonder he hadn't been around. We went through his ice cream bucket, tossing the small, broken remnants of Indian artifacts but saving an unnotched arrowhead, a nice notched arrowhead made of Montana moss agate, a couple of thumb scrapers made from knife river flint, and a broken pressure tool made from a deer bone. He didn't have a lot to show for his time, but I wasn't going to dampen his mood.

I asked, "Hey, did a guy from the Department of Indian Properties talk to you recently?"

He closed the lid on his ice cream bucket, his face pulled tight. "No. Why?"

"While I was in Kansas, Sarah said a guy showed up looking for you."

He tilted his head. "What did she tell him?" He took a deep pull from his cigarette and blew smoke out of his nose.

"She told him she had no idea where you were. It sounded to me like he wanted to know where you lived, which she never told him," I replied.

He went to the sink to get a glass of water. I spotted a slight tremor in his hand as he lifted his glass. "I guess if he wants to find me bad enough, he'll be back." He shrugged. I was surprised he'd blow it off like it was no big deal. He put his bucket away and joined in helping me get ready for the lunch bunch.

A while later, there was a knock at the back door. Figuring it to be another beggar from the rail yard, I tried to ignore it and finished cutting up the tomatoes. Another knock. I wiped my hands on my apron before opening the door. No one. I stepped onto the stoop looking left and right. A man in a black sport coat marched across the rutted alley toward his black Ford LTD with the State of South Dakota Department of Indian Properties seal on the driver's side door. In bright red, trimmed in gold, were the letters D.I.P.

"Can I help you?" I used my outside voice as I stepped off the stoop onto the gravel parking area. His partner occupying the front seat swung his head to make eye contact with me.

The man's clothing fit the description Sarah had given me of Agent Staubach. He snapped his whole body around. "Yeah, I'm looking for a guy by the name of Paul Van Brocklin." He stood ramrod straight with a voice flat and deep.

"I'm him," Paul said from the stoop. He cupped his hand around the cigarette to block the wind. His voice sounded like he was ready for confrontation.

"I'm Special Agent Staubach from the Department of Indian Properties." His tone carried a cold confidence as he flashed his badge. He was joined by a man whose chest, biceps, and quadriceps had been stuffed into his undersized black suit. His thick neck lapped over his collar. "This is Agent Michael Kelly." Kelly appeared to be eager, younger, and wore a gold wedding ring. "Who are you?" Agent Staubach asked, pointing at me, baring his upper and lower jumbled teeth. There was an authoritarian swagger in their gait as they approached.

"Name is Jimmy Marino. I'm his boss," I said with my hands in my pockets, tilting my head in Paul's direction.

His stare hardened. "Uh-huh. You're Sarah's boyfriend." Agent Staubach moved on from me. "Paul, I'd like to follow up with you regarding your visit to our offices in Pierre. Is this a good time?" He used a helpful tone.

Paul came down beside me, standing with his feet shoulder-width apart, arms crossed. The wind whipped his hair and hid his face. "I suppose." His tone was snarky. He tucked his hair behind his ears. "Like you have information on my dad?" He took a deep drag from his cigarette, making his lips smack.

Agent Staubach pulled a small notepad out of the inside pocket of his suit coat. Flipping through the pages, he began to recite his notes. Staubach said his superior had filled him in on the conversation he'd had with Paul, Paul's desire to find his dad, and where the Bureau suspected Paul was headed next. Paul confirmed it was all true. Agent Staubach warmly said he was new to the agency, in the area on another matter, and willing to help if needed. Serve and protect.

"So, what you're telling me is you have no clue where my dad is." Paul made no attempt to hide the impatience in his voice. He used his cigarette as a pointer. "I bet you're here because you're hoping I would have found him. Tell you where he is. Or perhaps you're here trying to find him as well but for different reasons?"

Agent Staubach ignored Paul's attitude. "Have you located your father or talked to anyone who might know his whereabouts?" His tone had gotten snippy. A wave of nervousness followed. I dreaded the possibility of Paul or Staubach bringing up how the D.I.P. car had ended up in the water. Or who the occupants were. Despite the late fall temperature, a bead of sweat ran down the middle of my back.

"You Pierre guys are all the same. You know where my dad is or at least what happened to him." Paul spoke with clenched fists.

The big diesel motor of the dredger fired up in the distance, shifting my focus to Lake Oahe. In the distance, Range Detective Ross was watching us from his green Bronco parked a block down on Railroad Street. Was Ross backup for the D.I.P.? My body tightened involuntarily. The confrontation was reaching a crescendo. I feared Paul might say or do something to piss off the agents and get arrested.

"There's something you're not telling me." Spit flew out of Paul's mouth as a furious dark storm cloud engulfed him. "Who was in the D.I.P. car they got out of the water?" He took a step beyond me, pointing in the direction of the dredger. I lunged, grabbed his arm, and held him back before things got physical.

A sweep of wind carrying dust off of the alley interrupted the confrontation. A scuff of gravel from Agent Staubach's direction, followed by a dry chuckle, caught my attention. Staubach reassumed his rigid posture. "I'm not sure what you're implying," he countered with a sly smile. "We are still working on identification. But I think we're done trying to help. Good day, gentlemen." The D.I.P. agents pivoted in unison back to their car. Staubach stopped abruptly and pointed an accusing index finger at him. "Oh, one more thing. On the scanner a couple of days ago, there was a report of a .22 long rifle being stolen from a pickup here in town." Staubach let the inference dangle in the air between us. Then, he said, "Paul, you want to tell us anything?" Dust swirled at our feet. "Last chance."

"Nope." Paul threw open the screen door and flicked the butt of his cigarette toward the agents. "You can shove it!"

As he stomped inside, I was taken aback by the entire exchange—in particular, Paul's boldness. Looking out past the railyards toward the placid gunmetal water, I figured there had to be more to the story from the D.I.P. side. The way Agent Kelly had stared at me the whole time made my body shiver. Did the Department guys have an ulterior motive to find Paul's dad? Did they know I knew what had happened? Was their real motive for being there to scope me out? I wondered if Paul had played the hard guy because he truly believed the agency *did* know what happened to his dad.

My scalp tingled from overthinking the possibilities. My ears, hands, and the tip of my nose began to sting from the brisk temperature, so I hustled up the steps to the warmth of the kitchen. Running the scene back in my head, I felt like I'd been a spectator at a tennis match. Behind me, the Ford's big engine growled as its tires sprayed gravel. With all my heart and mind, I hoped never to see them again.

Sarah came by to help me with the bar after Paul left at eight. The bar was slow, so we closed around ten. I told Sarah to head home; I'd grab a couple of turtle sundaes at Chubby's Drive-In on my way home to treat ourselves while we watched *The Tonight Show*.

Coming down our road, I noticed the plume of exhaust drifting from a dark-colored sedan pulling away from the front of our house. The driver didn't turn on his lights until he reached the end of the block. I sped up, but with tires screeching, it pulled away before I could get close enough to read the license plate.

As I bumped down the driveway, I looked over my shoulder at a trail of exhaust vapors that hung above red taillights. Sarah had left her truck parked next to the back steps. Weird. I chalked it up to her pregnancy. After parking, I ambled around her vehicle and up the back steps, balancing the sundaes as I opened the screen door. The inside door was locked.

"Sarah!"

"Jimmy, is that you?" came a muffled voice.

"Yes, of course. Who else would it be? Open up!"

The door flung open. "I got followed home by a black Ford car. I didn't get a good look, but it might have been those two guys from D.I.P." Sarah was talking fast without taking a breath. "I was so scared they were going to kidnap me or something."

"It might have been them." I filled her in about our encounter with the D.I.P. agents. "There's something going on here I don't know about." I tried to calm myself, but jitters of fear had me unnerved. "Something doesn't add up."

"I'm wondering what's going on, too," she replied without offering a hypothesis.

My eyes found the shotgun on the kitchen table. "You got my twelve-gauge out of the gun cabinet?"

Sarah nodded. "I didn't know what to do."

"Whoever it was, they were parked out front with their lights off. They spooked when I got closer. I set the sundaes on the table next to the open box of double ought buck shot. "Did you load it?" I asked.

"No, but I was going to," she said, putting the sundaes in the freezer. "I'm saving these for later. There's no way I can eat this right now." She had eyes full of annoyance, then alarm. "Why were they following me?"

"I have no idea. Like I said earlier, these guys are serious. Get upstairs, pull the window shades, and I'll make sure the doors are locked."

She hustled up the stairs. I grabbed a kitchen chair and wedged it under the doorknob of the locked back door. She had already started to push the sofa toward the front door. The legs squealed on the wood floor as I rammed it into the door with a bang. My pulse quickened, and the back of my neck bristled with anger. By scaring Sarah, they had pushed me over the edge. The conflict with the D.I.P. had become personal; a surge of paternal protectiveness of Sarah and the baby fortified me.

Retreating to the kitchen, I picked up the shotgun. I liked the way the gun fit in my hands. I plucked three shells out of the green and black box. The pump clattered, the first shell in the loading portal followed by two more in the magazine loading port. My mind amalgamated all the loose pieces from Paul's comments since he'd arrived in Painted Rock and what the D.I.P. agents had said earlier in the day. Only one conclusion remained: the agents were out to get me over the death of their colleagues. How they figured out that I had anything to do with it, I had no idea. Chastising Paul had been a ruse to get to me. I knew what had happened with the combine, and it wasn't Grandpa's or my fault. No one in their department cared about the truth. Whipped into a fury, I was ready for a fight.

I bounded up the stairs two at a time, carrying the shotgun in one hand and the box of clanking buck shot shells in the other. Sarah was sitting on the edge of the bed chewing her nails. The harsh ceiling light emphasized the veil of worry on her face. I put the shotgun at the foot of the bed before pushing our dresser in front of the door.

"What happens if I have to pee in the night?" she asked.

"You're going to have to wake me up." I hit the light switch.

Sarah nestled on her side against me, draping her arm on my chest, my arm under her to bring her closer. We lay there in silence, staring at the ceiling, listening to every creak and groan from old floorboards. "I'm going to Brave Eagle early tomorrow, and I want you to come with me." For no apparent reason, I spoke in a whisper. "It's not safe for us to be here. I think they're trying to kill me . . . or us, for revenge."

"Yeah, okay." She spoke in a barely audible voice. She pulled up the duvet close to her chin, wriggling closer like she wanted to crawl inside me.

"I think I can use the medal to bargain with the agents if Standing Bear will help me find it."

Sarah lifted her eyes up. "Bargain for what?"

I lowered my eyes to meet hers. "Our lives."

22

We were moving about the darkened house quietly as the sun began pulling back the curtain on a new day. Sarah made us coffee for the thermos and ham sandwiches for the drive. I checked the streets and surrounding properties by peeling back a corner of window shades on all four sides of the house. My stealthy behavior revealed a predawn sky of faintly lit stars and a beautiful blue ribbon along the horizon to the east. All clear.

I found Sarah in the kitchen. "You ready to roll?"

I was first out the door, carrying the shotgun and the sandwiches. With my head down and my front pockets bulging with clinking buck shot shells, I ran to my truck. I threw the sandwiches on the front seat and shouldered the shotgun, waving Sarah on. Clutching the thermos against her chest, she cupped her other hand on her midsection and tottered to the truck.

Hustling over to her side, I helped her into the front seat. The truck started right up. I pulled the lights on, hammered it into reverse, and we were headed west with the heater on full blast.

There wasn't time to try calling Standing Bear to let him know we were coming. I was hoping he would give me directions to Tower Buttes and specifics as to the sacred spot where Grandpa had left the medal. Barking Coyote might have some information that would help us, too. I figured he owed me one.

Sarah faced me with panic in her eyes and haste in her voice. "You have to remember to call Jay and tell him to put a sign up saying we are closed."

I banged my hand on the steering wheel. "Damn it. For sure, when we get to Standing Bear's."

"Does Paul have a key? I don't want him in our books or freeloading our food and booze."

"Nope. No worries there."

We thumped onto the mile-long bridge over Lake Oahe, its silver-colored superstructure stifled in the predawn light. Off the bridge, the potholed road made a sweeping curve with a view toward the south, where the hardpan prairie was desolate and foreboding, interrupted only by sharp ravines. There were lifeless undulations, washed out draws, pockets of sagebrush, and a rough two-lane road through it all. As the road climbed over worn hills and bottomed out through dried creek beds, I kept an eye on my rearview mirror. We hadn't seen a car approaching, nor one behind us. The farther we got from Painted Rock, I was sure I'd see a black Ford LTD racing up behind me.

My mind flashed back to Grandpa's Scout getting rammed multiple times by the Staties on this same road. My palms started to sweat all over again. Sarah's head was rotating like a turret, eyes wide open. In a conversation filled with anxiety, we exchanged ideas and scenarios for how the next couple of days might play out. We agreed that lying low in Brave Eagle where we would be protected was the best idea—at least for a day or two. I caught a glimpse of myself in the rearview mirror. The lines on my face made me look old, my eyes pinched into a grimace of fear. The instinct for survival took over, causing me to push the pedal deeper to the floor.

In the distance, the sun's dawning light brightened the outline of a single pedestal-style water tower against a blue-gray sky. Three years earlier, we'd come to the community center in Brave Eagle to celebrate Jay's twenty-fifth birthday. I remembered the Lakota words *Wanbli Ohitika*, meaning *Brave Eagle*, were painted on the water tower. A bright half-moon sat above it, finishing its nightly arc. The tension I carried in my neck and shoulders relaxed a bit because we were getting close to safety.

Rusted old cars without engines, trucks, and farm machinery peeked through overgrown fireweeds next to an empty corn crib at the town's edge. The familiar clusters of tired willows, graceful poplars, and dense osiers were taller but emaciated with no leaves. Within the town limits, we passed a gray cinder block building on our left with its roof collapsed. To our right sat a two-story, weathered brown post and beam log building containing the "Last Chance General Store" on the first floor and Barking Coyote's jewelry shop above it. Hot, dry summers and long, harsh winters had caused the off-white chinking to become pitted or crumble away, leaving visible gaps. Behind the store, small houses dotted the sunlit hillside. Many of the homes had broken windows, missing shingles, or additions made from repurposed materials. I mentioned to Sarah how depressing it was to me that nothing much had changed for the better since we'd been there last. She hesitated a beat and agreed.

We took the winding gravel road between homes, around scattered clumps of box elder and buckthorn, to Standing Bear's home near the top of the hill. The engine whirred as we climbed the last tenth of a mile before parking in his driveway. We stood by the truck, pausing to look east as the curtain of dawn finished lifting to reveal a majestic sunrise. Light blues, faded yellows, orange reds, and bright pinks sprayed the horizon between folded clouds. Sarah waited near the front door of Standing Bear's modest house, watching me eject the shotgun shells before I put the twelve gauge back in the truck.

We were about to knock when the door opened, startling us both. Standing Bear, dressed in a white T-shirt and a black pair of pilled sweatpants, reached for Sarah without saying a word. He pulled her inside to share an embrace. I followed, closing the door behind me. The smell of oak burning in the potbellied stove filled the house.

"To what do I owe this honor?" he asked, pulling out a chair for Sarah. A shade under six-foot-four with broad shoulders, he glared down at me intently. He carried a calmness about him with a presence few challenged. His once jet-black crew cut contained prominent dapples of silver. His round face wore a few more creases of aged wisdom, too. Sarah and I exchanged uneasy glances. Standing Bear smiled at me. "You finally ask for Sarah's hand in marriage?"

Sarah got right to it in a voice of contempt. "Yeah, right. I'm starting to think it will never happen, Howard." *Never* came out as *NAH-vah*. She turned to me with a quick, damning eye roll for emphasis.

I diverted my attention out the window. "C'mon Sarah. Give it a rest, will ya?" An awkward pause followed. Addressing Standing Bear, I said, "We're here because we need your help."

The shrill sound of water boiling in the tea kettle let us know it was time for instant coffee. "Excuse me." His bare feet chafed on the plastic runner as he made his way to the kitchen.

Sarah was curious about Standing Bear's wife. "Is Doris Walking Thunder still teaching third grade?" Sarah asked.

Standing Bear raised his voice. "They moved her to fourth grade this year." Cabinet doors banged, and his voice projected differently. "I'm sorry I don't have much for breakfast food." He returned with the tea kettle and his massive fingers intertwining three coffee cups, motioning for us to sit.

I used the phone in the hallway to dial Jay's number and asked him to put a *closed* sign on the front door. When I returned, Sarah opened her jacket to reveal her baby bump, which brought a warm smile from Standing Bear to go with gushing congratulations. He recounted Grandpa and Joan's visit with gratefulness and offered his condolences. With pride, he showed us the latest pictures of Iris, "the prettiest granddaughter in the world."

Our empty coffee cups and completed pleasantries transitioned to empty glances. Standing Bear opened. "Okay, so how can I help?"

Sarah motioned for me to take the lead. "After Grandpa died, on the drive home I concluded that the quintessential way of remembering our relationship, as well as paying homage to the man he was, would be to have the medal."

Standing Bear's chair skidded on the wood floor as he pushed back from the table to cross his left ankle over his right knee. He crossed his arms. "And how do you propose to get it?"

Sarah joined in, "That's where you come in, Howard. You told Colby where to take it. Tower Buttes, right?"

Standing Bear clasped his hands in front of himself and uncrossed his legs. "Yes. Tower Buttes has been used for hundreds years by our ancestors as a sacred place, a holy place. Specifically, the springs there contain spiritual powers of cleansing." His dark eyes focused on me. "Your grandfather spoke with Eagle Elk to gain permission to enter the area within Tower Buttes, where no white man is allowed. Our people call it the Springs of the Great Spirit. It is not for me to help you. You must gain favor and permission from our spiritual leader, Eagle Elk."

From down the hall came the click of a door opening, followed by the scraping sound of shuffling feet. Barking Coyote's pale, thin figure emerged out of the dim hallway. His eyes, once bright and engaging, were set in joyless sockets. He braced himself against the dingy white wall as he inched toward the dining room table. Stopping short of the dining room, Barking Coyote faced us, but with hesitant posture he peered over his shoulder—three times. Was it embarrassment? Was he looking at something?

Sarah got up to give him a gentle hug before helping him sit in her chair. Seeing him in this condition, especially after what I'd gone through with Grandpa's cancer, made me feel sorry for him. It was tempting to want to rip his head off after what Grandpa had told me about his deceptive handling of the medal. He'd deceived his dad and all the members of the tribal council, which was no small thing to do within the Indian culture. The shame alone, I figured, would be enough to kill someone. Primarily since he was Jay's brother, I chose to forgive the past and demonstrate grace in the present.

Barking Coyote spoke. "It is necessary for me to tell you I am sorry for the pain my transgression has caused you." His small voice contained remorse, eyes directed toward the pine table. "I told Colby how to break the medal's spell of bad medicine once he gained permission from Eagle Elk to go to the springs. I came clean with your grandfather to release myself from the bondage my lies had put me in." He glanced with sheepish eyes toward Standing Bear, next Sarah, and lastly me. "My father," his voice cracked, "and our people have forgiven me, but I cannot forgive myself. I am dying. and my one wish for you both is to leave the medal be. No good can come from you retrieving it."

Sarah grabbed a tissue from the center of the table and excused herself. We all paused. Could Barking Coyote be right? Had I overinflated the medal's importance? *No*, I decided! This was all about me and Grandpa. I wasn't going to let it go; I was on a mission. "Standing Bear, Barking Coyote, I respect you both. Thank you for hearing me out, particularly at this early hour. I hear what you are saying. I'd like to visit with Eagle Elk and gain his perspective."

Standing Bear paused to read my eyes before pushing off of the table. "I'll set up your meeting with Eagle Elk for tomorrow at sundown." His penetrating eyes met mine. "Only you and him, Jimmy."

I extended my hand to Standing Bear. "Thank you. I'll be forever in your debt."

Standing Bear pulled back. "Don't thank me. It's up to Eagle Elk. I don't want to have anything to do with the medal or the bad medicine associated with it."

Sarah returned to the dining room to hug Barking Coyote one more time. I offered words of encouragement, for which he thanked me. Sarah and I exchanged glances as Standing Bear passed behind us, headed for the door. He started to reach for the doorknob when Sarah said she needed a favor. Standing Bear immediately said yes, smiled, and asked what it was. She filled him in on each of our encounters with the D.I.P. agents.

"Would it be possible for us to stay in Brave Eagle tonight?" She continued, saying we didn't feel safe in Painted Rock. The next day I had to go to work at The Caboose but would return to meet with Eagle Elk at sunset.

Standing Bear was unable to conceal his concern. His forehead furrowed. "Yes, of course. As long as you must." He picked up the phone and began to dial. "I'm going to have a couple of my men swing through town." Sarah and I listened as he delivered the crisp order for a couple of trusted tribal members to go to Painted Rock and see if the D.I.P. agents were still there. "Okay, they'll get back to me later today or sooner if they find anything out." He motioned to the tawny-colored living room with a rose-colored couch and an avocado-colored easy chair facing an RCA console television. Standing Bear and Walking Thunder's wedding picture adorned the wall above the television. "I'm sure you didn't sleep well last night. Please, make yourself at home," he said, pulling the shades. "A nap will do you good."

Relieved we were able to stay, a tired calmness came over me. I opened the easy chair to stretch out. Sarah wasn't shy about curling up on the couch.

For today, we were safe. Tomorrow would bring its own dangers.

23

The next day, I prepared to return to Painted Rock. "I'll call you right away if I hear anything," Standing Bear said. His men had not seen the D.I.P. guys around town, nor had anyone they'd talked to.

Even so, I'd had a restless day and a terrible night of sleep. "I'm going to close after lunch, clean up, and I'll be outta there."

"Hurry back," Sarah said, closing the front door.

In the truck, I turned up the radio. The weatherman on KOLW forecasted wind gusts out of the north at forty to fifty miles an hour. Howling gusts bucked the truck as I left town. In the fields to my left, the prairie grasses bent severely, noticeably flattened into swirls by powerful downdrafts. The morning had started with bright sunshine, but as the wind picked up, the conditions became damp and gloomy. Under threatening clouds, horses grouped up around water troughs and converted old tractor tires filled with feed at a couple of places along the serpentine road. The wildlife had to be sensing the drop in pressure. "Weather is coming," I mumbled.

The morning light made visible the solitary double- and single-wide trailers in the middle distance tethered to the highway by two dirt track driveways. Dust blew off a trafficked space below empty clothesline poles. Small children in sweatshirts played around in a yard marked with a collection of abandoned vehicles, scattered bikes, and a fifty-five-gallon drum for burning garbage. I had forgotten how difficult life on the reservation was for these good people.

As I got closer to Painted Rock, trepidation began to roam in my brain. Drawing parallel to Lake Oahe as white caps rolled in the distance, I pondered the possibility that the D.I.P. might have my house staked out. Would they arrest me? No, they'd wait and make a scene at The Caboose in front of customers. Sarah had some extra clothes she wanted me to pick up in case things spiraled in a bad way. Following that, there were some things at The Caboose that needed my attention. Pushing away my paranoia, I resolved to deal with whatever the agents tried to throw at me when the inevitable time came.

Our house reflected my somber mood as I pulled into the driveway. I gathered the items on Sarah's list before going to The Caboose to serve the lunch rush. As the crowd was thinning out, Range Detective Ross showed up. I must have been wound tight, because when he hoisted himself off his good leg and onto his bar stool, a certain tension left my body. He would vouch for me if the D.I.P. showed up.

"What can I get ya, Ross?" I asked, sliding a cardboard coaster in front of him.

"Scotch and a burger." No please. No thanks. Then he warmed up, just a bit. "Sorry to hear of your grandpa's passing. A man's man from what people tell me."

"Yes, he was. Thanks." I got him his scotch and burger while he used the mirror behind the back bar to keep an eye on the other customers. Once the lunch crowd had cleared out, I took the opportunity. "Hey, Ross," I said, coming to refresh his scotch, "you work with the Department of Indian Properties sometimes, don't you?"

He swiped a napkin across his mouth and thick mustache, then casually tossed it onto his empty plate. "Yeah, on occasion. Why?" He glanced at me then looked away.

I told him about the D.I.P. agents questioning Paul about his dad and how we suspected they'd followed Sarah home. I confided in him that we were holed up in Brave Eagle out of fear. Ross didn't act the least bit surprised.

"First thing I should tell you . . . and this stays between the two of us, because this is all confidential. It'd be my job, all right?" he said, leaning forward. "I was backup, *ah*, surveillance, *er*, watching—your vantage point was better than mine—when the D.I.P. guys were talking with Paul. Okay? It's not you or Sarah they're after. Nobody around here should be worried. Nobody. Second, the D.I.P. guys left yesterday morning for west river country because they were alerted about a potential situation over in Whitehorse. They might be back, but you have nothing to worry about."

For as long as I'd known him, my friend had proven to be trustworthy and blunt. "How do you know all this?" I opened my palms. "You get why I'm going to have to reassure Sarah."

He picked at something in his teeth.

"She's going to want to know why they followed her home."

Ross put on a sloppy smile, placing a five-dollar bill on the bar. "As to why, I don't know. I don't. Honest." He held his right hand aloft like he was swearing an oath. "Look, Jimmy." He spoke with kindness. "I'm involved in a multi-department investigation. Sorry, but no more questions." He raised his glass to drain the last drop of scotch, "*Ah*, good stuff."

I pushed the five back. "On me." Our eyes met. "Thanks."

He stood with a half-smile and a nod, meticulously refiling the five-spot into his wallet on the way to the door. "Is Paul around? Haven't seen him around town."

"My guess is he's walkin' the river." I circled from behind the bar to follow him. "You think they were interested in helping Paul find his dad?"

Ross put his hand on my shoulder. "Oh yeah, I'm sure of it. You can tell Paul, too." He took another couple of steps toward the door. "Those D.I.P. guys take care of their own."

"Good to know," I said.

Out the door he hobbled. I wasted no time locking it. A wave of doubt coursed through me as I flipped off the *open* light in the window. He had been emphatic with his answers. As I carried the dirty dishes tub into the kitchen, my mind wouldn't let go of the idea there was a boogie man out there that law enforcement was after. Was there a drug dealer staying at the campground peddling dope to the Indians on the reservation or at the high school? Tittle's responsibility. Poachers on the reservation? Sheriff Owl's department. Did Paul have a long rifle? I should have felt relieved with his answers to the agents, but something about their exchange still nagged at my insides.

The ringing of the phone boomed through the silent bar. I put the tub next to the sink and wiped my hands on a towel.

Clearing my throat, I picked up the receiver. "The Caboose, Jimmy speaking."

"Hi, Jimmy. This is Jenny. Remember me?" Her voice was as delicate as it had always been. "Jimmy, hello?"

My mouth got dry. I swallowed hard, too shocked for words. "Yeah, I'm here. How are you?" I wasn't sure what to say.

"I'm good. You're doing okay?" There was a nervous edge in her voice.

I pictured her as I'd last seen her. We had been at the pavilion at the park back home. She was wearing cutoff jean shorts, topped by a polyester halter top in a mod pattern of bright colors tied up behind her neck. Her skin was smooth and summer-tanned. We had roller skated a few blocks from her house and stopped at the Mobil station to grab a Sun-Drop out of the vending machine. The air was oppressively hot, so we'd sought refuge in the shade of the park to drink them. She was about to head off to school in Boston, and I was leaving for KU. We had been inseparable the summer of '69—family camping at River's Edge Campground, the county fair (of course, I'd won her a stuffed animal), ice cream at The Ice Cream Store, and hanging out with friends late into the evening. Some days, we'd lie by her pool and talk for hours. But she was emphatic that our relationship wouldn't work. She said our conversations had gone flat—whatever that means. I could still remember my eyesight being blurred with tears when she walked away. She never looked back. It was last time we were together. Ever since, I'd tried to convince myself I was okay with it. I questioned if I would recognize her—was her hair still red?

"Yeah, everything's cool by me." I had twisted the phone cord around my hand, perplexed as to why I was talking to someone who had hurt me so badly. I was happy with my life with Sarah. "Where are you?"

"Um, I'm in Jacksonville . . . Florida." She made it sound like I didn't know where Jacksonville was. "The reason I'm calling is because Louie got my number from my parents and called to tell me your grandpa passed away. I wanted you to know I was sorry."

I paused. "Thank you," I said, still wondering if this call was really happening. On occasion, and most recently around the time of Grandpa's funeral, she'd crept back into my memory. I guess I'd never had the closure to the relationship I wanted because it had ended on her terms. The conversation had a surreal dimension to it. I didn't hate her, but I was caught between respecting what was an unforgettable summer with this person and where I was in my life. Curiosity got the best of me. "How did you end up in Jacksonville?"

"Long story, but my ex-husband was a naval officer at the base here. It's nice; you should come visit." Her voice gushed with excitement. I began to doubt this was a condolence call.

"Yeah, I don't know," I said. This conversation had gone in a direction that forced me back to reality. It was time to clear the air. "Jenny, I gotta ask. Why are you calling me?" Dead silence on the line. "It's been since high school that we've even talked."

The silence on the line was broken by a sniffle. "Louie mentioned you were in South Dakota, but I didn't know you were seeing someone." Her voice was nasally. "I'm sorry. My life hasn't been the greatest since high school, and when I got the call from Louie, I don't know . . . It made me miserable." The sniffles became more pronounced between chopped words. "I was sad for you, sad for me, sad for the good times."

Her timing was horrible. Sarah would be wondering where I was. Jenny continued to ramble on about her degree in English from Springfield State, her heavy drug use and eventual rehab.

She talked about how cool it had been to travel the country protesting the Vietnam War in the summer during her early college years. Everyone hated President Nixon and the war, wherever they went, she had been certain of it. It was a party every day, with pot and pills passed out like Halloween candy, she said.

She rambled on. I began pacing and chewing my nails. I sat down. I stood up. I sat again. My heart beat faster, and I wanted to scream, "I have to go home!" I coiled up, ready to pounce on an opening to cut her off.

She paused before continuing on about being at the University of Wisconsin campus in August 1970 protesting a few days before a bomb blew up a research lab, killing a researcher. After she heard someone had died, Jenny became disillusioned and quit protesting. She graduated in 1972 and went to work in Washington D.C. for an environmental advocacy group writing grant requests. She met her husband, the naval officer, and fell in love. Their marriage lasted a couple of years.

My mind began to wander through the maze of Sarah, the baby, Grandpa, the D.I.P., and Paul. Finally, I had to interrupt. "Hey, Jenny, it's good to talk to you, but I have to go meet Sarah."

"Okay, sure. Um, if you're not too busy, we should talk more soon. I'd like to hear what you're up to." There was resignation in her voice.

"This phone call is going to cost you a fortune." I had enough on my plate, so I was not encouraging. "Let's catch up with everybody at our high school reunion in a couple of years." The last thing she said to me was that hopefully we'd meet again someday, and she hung up.

As I finished cleaning up, memories washed over me—but not the fond ones I'd clung to before. In my mind, I'd created better times with Jenny than they actually were. Leaning against the back bar, I surveyed The Caboose, and a feeling of melancholy washed over me. My heart let go of both the joy Jenny used to make me feel and the abrupt pain of her breaking up with me.

I flicked the light switch off in the kitchen. It was time to leave the remnants of this past relationship in the past. The present with Sarah was what mattered to me.

24

Despite Bradshaw's assurances, I checked my mirrors frequently on the way back to Brave Eagle. My tires buzzed as I traveled along the high ground, both sides of the road darkened by the recently finished rain. The sun, low on the horizon, laid acres to shadow from bare buttes and mesas to the west. Similarly, shadows at obtuse angles fanned out from fenceposts, creating a complicated matrix on a simple palate. To the east, three deep Ranger fishing boats sliced south, surely headed to the boat launch at LeBeau Creek Campground, weaving around crescent-shaped sandbars and driftwood hazards due to the low water level. Lake Oahe would have to be patient until spring to be made whole again. The lead boat was driven by the best walleye guide in these parts, old man Bub in his signature red jacket.

The last hour of sunlight caused an instinctive change in prairie dwellers. I caught a glimpse up ahead of three pheasants scooting along the fence line, suddenly flushing out of the attempted reach of a stalking tan-gray coyote who disappeared into the sagebrush. The pheasants caught the breeze and became specks, alive for a bit longer. An adult mule deer and her yearling crossed ahead before they cleared the barbwire fence on their way to the water. Above, two turkey vultures rode thermals, patiently waiting to scavenge roadkill. It was a busy time as nightfall held its residents in check until the sun yielded the day.

I knocked twice as I let myself into Standing Bear's house. Sarah and Standing Bear's voices drew me to the kitchen. Passing by Barking Coyote's closed bedroom door, I shook my head. Life could be so unfair. Without hesitation, I went straight to Sarah with a big hug and kiss. Her face flushed from my forwardness in Standing Bear's presence, but she mustered she was glad to see me, too.

As they put away groceries, I told them about my conversation with Ross, the pang of doubt concerning the agents' reason for being in Painted Rock, and my worry with Paul's handling of the confrontation.

"What concerns you about each of those?" Standing Bear had a way of using his wisdom to ask discerning questions. He lit a burner on the stove.

"Well, Ross was working way too hard to sell me on the fact we were all in the clear," I said, folding the paper grocery bag. "Plus, it seems like Ross has been hanging around the bar a lot more than usual. He's keeping an eye on Paul from what I can tell . . . kinda weird."

Sarah nodded her head in agreement.

"And how is it we hardly ever see D.I.P. agents, but they are fixated on talking to Paul about his dad? And randomly ask if he has a long rifle? And say nothing about the D.I.P. car?" I was out of breath.

Sarah swiveled her head. "You never told me they asked him about a long rifle." The smell from frying the hamburgers combined with the sizzle and pop of grease had begun to fill the kitchen.

I continued with my hands in front of me, palms up. "Paul's belligerence with the agents . . . he told them to shove it . . . also seems weird. Especially if he seriously wants to find his dad. He was either frustrated he had traveled so far with nothing to show for it, or he's hiding something from them."

Standing Bear tilted his head, contemplating for a few seconds. "No longer concern yourself with the D.I.P. car or agents. I had a *nice* talk with them this morning at tribal community center north of Whitehorse, reiterating the facts of what happened with the car and making it clear that if they wished to ever receive cooperation from our people again, they should let it go." His face wore a mask of indifference as he continued, "They were not pleased with my approach, but they were smart enough not to cross me. As they were leaving, I expressed my condolences without remorse. It's over." Standing Bear settled his attention on me. "But I have a feeling all is not as it seems in Painted Rock. Your time with Eagle Elk will be good for you." He indicated he had spoken to Eagle Elk. He would see me at six o'clock sharp. "Eagle Elk will have the Inipi prepared."

My head jerked. Sarah's eyes went to Standing Bear. "What's an Inipi?"

Standing Bear's face showed seriousness. "I will take you after we eat."

"Did Grandpa have to do the Inipi?"

"No, he did not. Eagle Elk told me when he met with Colby, he saw the spirit of death hovering over your grandfather." Standing Bear's face was apologetic. It wouldn't have been hard for him to read the pain on my face. "Colby would have been too weak for the ritual. Eagle Elk thought it best for Colby and Joan to travel to Tower Buttes right away. He granted permission but did not reveal his vision."

I stared at the linoleum floor until it blurred. I mumbled softly, "I wonder if Grandpa had a premonition or something. You know, he had to get rid of the medal on his last trip to see us because time was short."

Sarah tilted her head to the side, eyes filled with pained sympathy.

We left Sarah and Barking Coyote at the dining room table chatting about the good times they'd had as kids. Clattering down the hill and barreling to the right at the general store, Standing Bear drove his dusty '67 Cadillac Coupe DeVille. The soft gold-colored behemoth was topped with a black vinyl roof, clearly recognizable, as we received waves from a cluster of men smoking cigarettes in front of the abandoned brick gas station on our way out of town. The last gasp of sunlight lay on the horizon ahead on top of the dark belt of highway.

Standing Bear must have sensed my anxiousness, perhaps by my fidgeting. "Eagle Elk is close to eighty but still holds a remarkable connection to *Wakan-Tanka*, our God. He'll be wearing a headdress of four eagle feathers representing the four directions: east, west, north, south." My heart began to beat faster as the ritual was becoming more real with every word. "When he was a teenager, his spiritual leader taught him the sacred lore of our ancestors. Through constant prayer and days of fasting, he received visions that blessed him with unique powers he has used for the good of our tribe." Standing Bear finished by explaining Eagle Elk had served the tribe in many roles. He had been called upon to act as medicine man, prophet, and spiritual leader.

With no warning, the spacious Cadillac slowed, approaching a two-track access road on our left. Standing Bear crossed the double yellow lines and clunked off the pavement to the prairie. The car began to vibrate as we continued down through a dip, winding through a grove of cottonwoods to descend farther into a hollow where two men waited for us.

Our car doors bellowed in the three-sided amphitheater nature had created. The prairie grass, brittle underfoot, smelled sweet in the crisp night air. The night's coldness ran under my jean jacket and down my neck. Standing Bear left the car running with its headlights on as he introduced me to Eagle Elk and his helper, Black Deer, both dressed in traditional Lakota ceremonial clothes. Their posture was solemn and stark, and neither offered a greeting. Black Deer submissively stood a pace behind Eagle Elk, his eyes dark like a crow's. His face had a strong chin set below razor-sharp cheekbones. Eagle Elk had a deeply fissured face and peaceable eyes. Twenty yards behind them, beyond our shadows, was a circular dome-shaped structure.

"The sweat lodge, or *onikare*, Jimmy," Standing Bear said, pointing to it. "We use sixteen young willows for the frame, and it gets covered with hides from fox, deer, wolf, coyote . . . There are some beaver pelts mixed in, too."

It was a surreal setting down in the hollow. Casing the area, I felt like we were the last people on earth. It was a cloudless night with stars above, calm and cold. A glowing moon, three-quarters full, bathed us with its white light. There was no sound, save for the timing belt's muted hum from the Cadillac. Eagle Elk remained focused on me with a blank face, which caused an uneasiness within me.

"Eagle Elk will take you through Inipi, the rite of purification, which involves using the sweat lodge," Standing Bear said, standing tall. "He knows your motivations and your desire to travel to Tower Buttes, specifically the Springs of the Great Spirit."

I immediately felt like I had fallen under the spell of Standing Bear, this powerful leader of the Indian people. His instruction left me appreciative and moved by the radiant glow of good from him. He had always been a relentless advocate for his people. Over the years, he had lobbied in Washington and Pierre for better education, better medical care, and better housing. Standing Bear was constantly pushing forward, trying to give his people a better life. At the same time, he passionately believed in the customs of his ancestors and trusted in his people's spiritual leader, Eagle Elk. He had treated me as one of his own, so I wanted to honor him by doing what Eagle Elk told me to do.

"Once completed," Standing Bear assured me, "you will have gained the necessary strength, humility, and purity necessary to find your grandfather's medal safely." Within a second, Standing Bear spun out of the headlight beams and into the darkness, heading to his car.

It took a few seconds for my eyes to adjust once he pulled out of the treeless hollow. Black Deer approached and nodded toward the sweat lodge, gesturing for me to follow him. Eagle Elk followed me. The entire layout was before me: the sweat lodge with an opening to the east, and a path from the opening that led to a mound of dirt. On the other side of the mound was an unlit stack of small willow branches by a firepit. From the lodge's opening to the firepit, I'd guess it was about thirty feet. The wind *whooshed* overhead, but I felt nothing. It was a spiritual reminder that we had withdrawn from the elements of the outside world.

Rotating in place a full 360 degrees, the space around me felt like a cathedral, which, of course, it was.

We moved to the firepit end, where Black Deer lit the sticks. Its construction had four sticks facing north-south, and on top of them were four sticks facing east-west. It was finished with sticks placed over them to form a tipi. A circle of baseball-sized granite rocks, Black Deer explained, represented Grandmother Earth and bordered the arrangement of sticks. Eagle Elk took off his top, revealing a wiry physique and an upper body ornately painted with spiritual symbols. He began a husky chant to the Great Spirit *Wakan-Tanka* over the firepit, joined by a chorus of pops and snaps from the dried willow. Under faces intermittently illuminated by splashes of firelight, an ember shot from the circle, followed by another.

Once his prayer had finished, he removed a pipe from his otter pelt pouch, trimmed with buckskin fringe and multicolored trade beads sewn on in an indistinct pattern. Looking unsteady on his feet, Eagle Elk carefully navigated the uneven ground before he lifted the hide flap to enter the sweat lodge. Using a wishbone-shaped deer antler, Black Deer passed a hot rock into the lodge. Having participated in the sweat lodge ritual himself, Black Deer told me what was happening inside. "Eagle Elk will travel clockwise to the west side and light the sanctified sweet grasses situated in a hole in the middle of the lodge. He'll rub the smoke over his entire body, making everything sacred, including the pipe. Should there be anything bad in the lodge, the power of the smoke will drive it out." Black Deer leaned into my ear and added, "Remember to concentrate on your breathing."

I nodded.

After some minutes, Eagle Elk emerged and walked the sacred path to place the pipe on the small earth mound with the pipe bowl full of tobacco herbs, *kinnikinnik* he called the mixture, to the west and green ash stem to the east. Eagle Elk motioned for me to strip down and follow him. I flicked a glance at Black Deer, immediately returning to Eagle Elk. Within my chest, a repeating thump of doubt pushed back against emotion. Stripping down in front of strangers, in the cold, out in the middle of God knows where ... This wasn't what I had signed up for. Their stone faces confirmed for me there would be no debate. During a few seconds of uncomfortable silence, I searched the heavens. A shooting star arced, vanishing into the void. It ignited a shapeless vision of Grandpa, which flared through me and served as a reminder of why I was here.

Naked, I felt coldness assault every pore of my body. I feverishly rubbed my arms, legs, and torso for warmth. Bowing as we entered the lodge, a thick, dull, smoky smell enveloped me. Eagle Elk prayed in a quiet voice as he took his place in the penumbra near the east-facing entrance. I took my place on the north side, sitting on the hard ground with my legs crossed. Both of us sat on the sacred sage strewn across the lodge floor. Eagle Elk placed his index finger to his lips for silence as he pointed to his left, before demonstrably circling both arms vertically and horizontally. I took his demonstration to mean I should remember the maker of all things around us.

Black Deer passed in the pipe, which Eagle Elk placed on the west side. After a few beats, he passed another hot rock from the sacred fire using the deer antler, which Eagle Elk placed in the center. Four other rocks were passed in for each of the four directions. The rocks passed in were oval-shaped and smooth like river rock. The rest of the hot rocks were passed in to fill the hole. To complete the preparation, a black pottery bowl full of water, the size of a cake mixing bowl, was set inside the entrance. Eagle Elk dipped his hand and spread the holy water on himself. I began to feel a current inside me when I put my hand in the bowl. It was an unnatural flutter in a way I'd never felt before. With the door flap closed, a serenity of black filled the lodge.

Eagle Elk spoke in a clear voice, with a bit more capacity than before, "The darkness represents our ignorance, our dark soul from which you must purify yourself, so you may have the light." Eagle Elk sprinkled water from a sprig of sage over the rocks, giving the air a fragrant aroma.

The lodge became hot in a hurry. It felt good to sweat, the combination of fire and water purifying. The door opened and closed after the pipe, stem first, entered into Eagle Elk's hands. I was directed to take a deep breath and blow into the hollowed-out stem. Smoke rose from the pipe bowl. Pushing down a rise of nausea, I chased the smoke with a cupped hand, rubbing it all over me. With a faint voice, Eagle Elk prayed in his native tongue, circling the helix of smoke around him.

A comfortable silence followed before Eagle Elk spoke, "We are to be reborn when we revisit the light. All impurities and ignorance will be left here." He put four splashes of water on the rocks, raising the humidity, and my chest involuntarily expanded for maximum oxygen intake to avoid suffocating. The door opened for a second time. We puffed again; the door closed. Beads of sweat began popping up on my chest and arms. I closed my eyes and focused on the solitary bead traveling down the curve of my spine. My hands—and my feet—were tingling. Eagle Elk began to sing a prayer to *Wakan-Tanka*. I caught myself spellbound by the fire, allowing the beautiful melody to bathe me.

Water splattered to white steam, condensation clinging to the interior of the lodge. After the third opening of the door and a welcome rush of cool air, Eagle Elk insisted I partake once again. I was happy to oblige. This time, the thick air stung my nose and throat. My entire body was slicked with sweat. Darkness, again, became my friend. I entered the blackness, floating through a soupy haze and crossing into another plane of consciousness, like a confluence of rivers—memory, dream, and prayer. One flowed into and through the other; three as one combined to enhance my sensory awareness. The smoke, colored as if a rainbow, swirled around me to cross over the circle, encasing Eagle Elk. The dark eyes of the aging medicine man bore into me as words traveled to me but did not register. Lakota spiritual symbols danced above his torso—red, black, yellow, and white in color—a thunderbird, bear, and geometric shapes among them. My hand reached in an attempt to touch them, but they returned to his midsection. A certain euphoria came over me, leading me to chant in a loud, boisterous crescendo in unison with Eagle Elk. He nodded approval at my heightened spiritual awareness. I felt as if we were one—souls bonded.

In a blink, Ma's Sauce filled my nostrils, and Katherine's face appeared and melted away on the tanned hide of the lodge opposite me. Mom floated in front of me, clutching the fragrant pink roses I had cut for her from our garden when I was in first grade. She mouthed, "I love you, Jimmy." My eyes blinked repeatedly, trying for a lucid vision. Instead, Grandpa appeared next to a green Coleman camp stove, looking like he was reading out of a journal, twirling the medal in his hand. Eagle Elk placed a handful of sweet prairie grass on the fire, causing sparks to fly and me to flinch. Behind me, there were the sounds of a baby crying and a mother's comforting voice. I turned, but Sarah was not there. Shimmering sequins on an empty white wedding dress burned bright like a Fourth of July sparkler. A familiar voice I could not place descended from above the lodge to affirm the circle of life would begin again.

Water was splashed again on the fire, causing a steam geyser, which was chased by coiled smoke. Eagle Elk took water from the bowl and patted my head four times, returning me to reality. Speaking with a normal voice, he said, "In a moment, the door will be opened for the last time. Light will enter as it is sunrise. The darkness you have experienced will stay here. You will enter the light seeing with both your eyes again. The one eye of your heart will also now see. It is with that one eye you will see all which is good and pure."

The door opened, and I raised my hand to shield my eyes, stooping to follow Eagle Elk out. Though I had no rational explanation, I felt stronger, empowered.

The sky to the east had lightened, golden and diffuse. Surveying, I found that the soft morning light brought the grasses and wildflowers a different-looking texture from when I'd arrived. Dew sparkled throughout the entire hallowed depression. From elsewhere in the hollow, a meadowlark sang greetings. Standing Bear was leaning against the grille of the Cadillac, arms folded on his chest, waiting like a patient parent ready to pick up their child after school. Black Deer had positioned himself at the tip of the sacred path, squatting to poke the embers of the smoldering fire.

Eagle Elk and I traveled the path, purifying our hands and feet with the smoke. Together, we lifted our eyes, offering thanks to *Wakan-Tanka*. Overhead, a hawk paused before resuming its ride of the thermals with elegance. Although naked, I was not cold.

Eagle Elk took a step toward me with his eyes warm and his voice hoarse. "You have completed Inipi. Cantecikiya. You may enter the Springs of the Great Spirit."

I felt my face loosen, nodding with respectful gratitude to Eagle Elk.

25

Dawn sharpened into morning as we bounced out of the hollow and back onto the calm of the highway. Dressed, I slumped in the front seat, equal measures tired and thirsty. Standing Bear offered me a plastic jug filled with water. I drank all of it, still feeling the grips of thirst as I placed it on the floor at my feet. The gracious leader started. "Eagle Elk called out, 'Cantecikiya.' Are you aware of its meaning?"

Still coming out of the fog of my dream-state, I tried to guess. "Congratulations?"

Standing Bear creased a smile. "No, it's more significant, much deeper. In Lakota, it means, 'My heart is inspired by you.' He is honoring you."

"Why would Eagle Elk be inspired by *me*?"

"Because you completed the Inipi. Not everyone does," Standing Bear said.

"All I know is I feel different." I sat up, altering my lap belt. "I went in one person and came out another, ya know? I need to pay attention to what's going on in my heart." The car became quiet as I reflected on this revelation, watching the prairie whizz by me.

After a couple of miles, I began to think about what was going through Standing Bear's mind. Right on cue, he asked, "Would paying *attention* have anything to do with Sarah?" He gave me a good-natured wink and a smile.

He told me he and Sarah had talked a lot while I was in the sweat lodge. He reminded me she was like the daughter they never had. Sarah had recapped her displeasure with my lack of willingness to make a lifelong commitment, dealing with my dad in Lawrence, and how she believed the two might be related. Standing Bear also said she had talked about her pregnancy, parenting, and my lack of enthusiasm at first but coming around to being supportive.

"Pretty much sums it up," I said, a bit embarrassed by her reveal.

I slumped back down in the seat as he spoke with a manner-of-fact tone.

"If you haven't already, you will realize the Inipi was more than a purification for the Springs. If you believe the prayers Eagle Elk offered on your behalf, then the self-doubt, the disappointment, and the fear of connection have all been left behind."

We drove in comfortable silence, allowing this wisdom to sink in. In many ways, he was the father figure I wished to have, wished to be. Standing Bear used the appropriate tone to share his wisdom, and I always felt he was "present" when we were together, even though I'm sure he had a lot on his mind. "Why are you slowing down?" I asked, surveying the road ahead.

"See the wolf? A good sign." He pointed as he slowed the Cadillac for the gray wolf standing broadside in the middle of the road.

"Oh, wow. Why is the wolf a good sign?" The wolf walked off, but not before stopping on the shoulder and turning back to look me right in the eyes as we passed.

"The wolf is a spiritual symbol for us. It represents strength, intelligence, and leadership. Valued traits of our people for centuries. Also connotates good hunting."

"As in hunting for the medal," I said with confidence.

When we pulled into the driveway, he parked the car next to my truck, making no movement to get out. For a reason I can't explain, I wasn't ready to get out either. It was as if he wanted to keep me separated from the outside world even longer to contemplate. After a few pulses, I asked bravely, "Can Sarah stay with you for a few days? I need to take care of some stuff. I don't want her sitting at home with the D.I.P. possibly coming back, or feeling work pressure, you know?"

He nodded once. "Yes, of course. I think you are beginning to see with more than two eyes."

We went inside, and I told Sarah some of what had transpired over the last twelve hours. I wanted to tell her more details, but anxiety was building, pushing me to move on. She hesitated but agreed to stay, understanding the D.I.P. concern. Although, she did want to know what the "stuff" was.

"Please trust me," I said. Once completed, I would be back for her. We would get back to normal.

Her face expressed reservation. "I hope you know what you're doing," was all she managed to say.

After a shower and big breakfast, I drove the lonesome highway back to Painted Rock. The prairie spread big and empty, and the afternoon azure sky was cloudless. I slipped into second-guessing myself. Had I made the right choice to leave Sarah in

Brave Eagle? She'd be protected, less anxious, and both of those elements made my life easier, too. She would worry about me, but Walking Thunder would use her calming demeanor to relax her. I told myself I'd made the right choice.

The silver shine from the bridge jolted me from a deep spiritual review of the Inipi. I took a shortcut down Railroad Street to get to The Caboose. I waved to Pastor Dawson as we passed each other. The wind was whipping off the water, causing the cottonwood trees to bend and sway. A cloud of dust from the alley caught up to me as I parked behind the bar. Fishing my keys out of my pocket for the back door, I saw movement through the sheer curtain of my peripheral vision on my right. I stepped off the stoop, squinting toward two boxcars coupled on the side rail. Nothing moved except the tall grasses in the wind. Suddenly, a lumped dark shadow passed from my right to my left, crawling underneath a lonely boxcar and dragging an indistinguishable shape. A person?

Pinching my jean jacket closed to block the cold gust of wind, I hustled across the street to the railyard. It was a man wearing a green Army jacket with dark stains on the front dragging a dirty yellow blanket. The blanket was lumpy like Santa's bag. He drew it close to him as I approached. The guy wore no cap, so his strands of thinning dark hair were windblown. His eyes were full of fear, right arm cocked, fist balled up for defense. He clutched a Bible in his left hand.

"Hey, buddy, you get to town recently?" I stopped five yards short of the rails and squatted down. The strong smell of creosote from the railroad ties filled my sinuses.

He shimmied on his butt using his arms for levers over the ties and coarse red granite track ballast. He retreated against the train axle like a cornered animal, shaking his head no.

I lost his face in the shadows, so I stepped closer, which drew an outstretched arm from him, palm up. Stop. "You all right?" I asked, backing up and modifying my angle to see him.

He froze. His jaw muscles clenched. His darkly circled eyes darted in different directions, assessing the quickest escape.

"It's okay. I'm not going to bother you." I waited a few seconds. "Where are ya from?" The wind made a rushing sound under the box car.

No answer. He sat up in a squat, ready to bolt, and I saw the ripped front pocket. Confirmation clicked. "Wait . . . I need to tell you something," I pleaded. The wind became more pronounced, so I found myself talking louder. "I hoped I would see you again." I mustered a gentle smile. "I've felt bad ever since, you know, when things didn't go so well in the bar." I thumbed in the direction of The Caboose.

He released the tension in his body, allowing his shoulders to fall from his ears.

I didn't know what to say next. In a quick moment, I flashed the peace sign. He leaned forward into the sunlight with his upper lip curled in a snarl to spit in my direction. A thick scar traversed from above his left ear to his widow's peak. A remnant of war or a mugging?

"You a vet?" I asked.

He pushed the bag off himself. "*Yeah*, 'Nam." His delicate voice carried a hint of disgust.

I extended my hand. "Hi, I'm Jimmy." I had Eagle Elk's voice in my ear, his fresh teachings in my heart.

"*Larry*," he strained, shaking my hand.

We made casual conversation, and Larry began to warm up to me. I asked him if he was hungry. He paused, leering to gauge my intentions. There was despair in his eyes.

"What do you say I get you a couple cheeseburgers, some fries—ketchup, mustard, whatever you need." The corners of his mouth rose, and he nodded. I invited him into the bar, but he mumbled something about wanting to eat where he was. Nodding in agreement, I scampered back to The Caboose to fire up the grill. While the burgers cooked, I got curious about Larry's background, his life's journey, and his head wound. The cost of war. How had he picked Painted Rock? Where would he go from here?

Balancing the burgers and fries on a paper plate, I crossed back over Railroad Street to the stunted sage mixed with switch grass next to the train car.

Larry was right where I'd left him, staring toward the water's edge. *"Thank you."*

Opening a bottle of Pepsi, I set it down by his side. His bites were ferocious and focused. "Let me know if you need anything else, okay?" I offered, backing away.

Without lifting his head, he waved me off. The air following me smelled of diesel as I left the rail yard for The Caboose. I felt bothered by Larry's depressing truth: a man—no, a *disabled veteran*—cast aside, homeless, an afterthought of war. West of town, the dull, thunderous churning of an approaching freight train filled the air. Puffs of black smoke intermittently rose, each one closing the gap to Painted Rock.

I stood on the back steps, watching Larry emerge into the unkind wind from under the box car, dragging his yellow sack. He chucked the Bible into the fireweeds as he headed in the direction of the approaching train. He would do what others had done. When the train slowed to come through town, he would run alongside the chugging monster and either get a hand from a faceless cohort or grab the ladder to swing himself in. I'd seen it done dozens of times over the years. A succession of short warning blasts from the train's horn satisfied my heart, causing a smile to arc. Within minutes, Larry would be gone.

The blustering wind grabbed his discarded, ketchup-stained white paper plate, tossing it in the air. The plate dipped, fluttered, and skittered to the road. Far beyond, the sky was lit up with a yellow-orange burst of fire, extinguishing itself to dusk.

One day closer to finding our medal.

26

"It was your first sweat?" Jay asked out the side of his mouth, chewing on a corned beef Reuben.

The midday crowd was fairly quiet; the clanking of silverware on dishes surrounded subdued conversations. The season's first snowfall—or the cold dead air of late fall—had people depressed, I reasoned. People coming in for lunch reported that it was a fine snow, fine like sugar. Ross sat to Jay's left, sipping scotch. Robert sat to his right, working on a Hamm's. Ruby and Lee sat a couple of stools down, filling their ashtray with butts and listening to Andy Williams—but not to each other. Lee had cleanly peeled two labels off his empties by noon.

"You talking to me or," Range Detective Ross nodded in my direction, "him?"

"I was asking Jimmy. *You've* done a sweat before?" Jay's head swiveled in Ross's direction.

"I have. Years ago, we needed to get on the Springs to gather evidence for a poaching case." His chest swelled as he continued. "Did the sweat, caught the poacher." With a sharp cadence, he blurted, "Bada-bing, bada-boom!" An enormous guffaw followed, his prideful smile washed away by a healthy gulp of scotch.

Bringing the trio up to speed regarding Grandpa's cancer, funeral, and subsequent need for the medal was a longer story than it should have been because it was complicated. It didn't help that I was interrupted by customers looking for food or drinks. I got into the whole D.I.P. fiasco, which renewed Ross's attention—particularly my reference to Paul's attitude. Ross interjected he hadn't seen or heard anything about the agents being back in the area since. Telling them about the agents following Sarah to our house made Jay and Robert's eyes get big. Plus, it resurfaced the anger I should have left in the lodge. Continuing after a phone call from a food distributor, I picked up the story with our trip to Brave Eagle. I described to Jay his father's insistence that Eagle Elk okay my travels into the Springs of the Great Spirit. We got into a discussion of the Inipi, Lakota traditions surrounding it, and ultimately Eagle Elk's blessing. I didn't feel it was necessary to interject my phone call with Jenny into the timeline.

"Everyone's experience in the sweat lodge is different," Jay explained before taking a pull from his bottle of Blatz. "Most people, if they are willing to allow themselves to open up, feel lighter. Free."

Robert nodded in agreement.

I leaned toward them, arms braced on the edge of the bar. "I definitely felt different. I'm ready to go find the medal. And I *will* find it." Jay and I slapped some skin.

"Find what?" Paul brought out the tray of clean glasses, setting it heavy on the counter behind me with a clang. He put his lit cigarette in the ashtray on the bar. The smoke coiled upwards like unraveling strands of braided rope.

I backed off the bar so as to include Paul in the conversation. "Well," I said, full of confidence, "you'd hear about it sooner or later."

Jay and Robert almost indiscernibly moved their heads from side to side as if to say, "Don't say any more." Ross narrowed his eyes at Paul, like he was appraising his reaction.

Feeling empowered by the Inipi, I continued. "I'm going to a place west of here called Tower Buttes. At the buttes are the sacred Lakota Springs of the Great Spirit."

Paul faced me with parted lips, pinpoint pupils, and head tilted inquisitively like he wanted—no, *needed*—to know more. I caught him sneaking a glance in Ross's direction. "For real?"

"I hope to find something my grandpa left there. A personal thing to remember him by." I wanted Paul to understand this was an important item.

"Well, what is it?" Paul asked, throwing his hands in the air.

"A Thomas Jefferson Peace Medal." My tone was smug. I let my words hang in the air.

"So, I was right!" Paul puffed. "Your grandpa did find it and hid it there!"

An uncomfortable pause followed, all eyes on me to see my reaction. "Not even close."

Paul grinned. "Whatever. That's cool he found it. How are you going to know where to look?"

Ross hadn't taken his eyes off Paul this whole time for an unshared reason. The thought occurred to me that he wanted to rip his throat out, or Ross was trying to figure out what made Paul tick.

I swung a glance over to Jay and Robert, who were sitting passively, listening. "Anyway, I'm still working out the details. Grandpa's friend, Joan, outlined the general area with a few landmarks to help me find it." I grabbed Jay's empty bottle and popped the top on a new Blatz. "With some luck, I think I can."

Paul took a drag from his cigarette and returned to putting the clean glasses under the bar. "Yeah, good luck. I'd be careful if I was you. It's not worth dying over."

Jay and Robert reacted with surprised glances. I snorted in Paul's direction. "Nope, definitely not."

Later in the afternoon, I was prepping for dinner. It had continued to snow, the wind getting angrier by the hour, with nothing on the prairie to slow its wrath. The glass of the kitchen window rattled with each muscled rush of air. I turned up the heat to combat the draft.

Paul pushed through the saloon doors. "We're all stocked for tonight in case anybody shows up, you know." He ran his fingers through his uncombed hair and tucked it behind his ears.

"Yeah, people braving the weather to come here for dinner might be an issue." I hadn't finished cutting the cherry tomatoes for the house salads. "You can start setting up the salad plates with the iceberg lettuce. Grab the dinner rolls off the bread shelf, and I'll get them ready to warm." I followed Paul as he took the salad plates from the cupboard. "And I moved the bacon bits to the middle shelf by the parmesan cheese."

We both sank into our routines, moving around the kitchen, completing the tasks necessary for dinner prep. Taking a break from the tomatoes to clean the grease layer off the grill, I recalled my previous conversation with Ross to Paul. "Oh, I meant to tell you I was talking to Ross the other day." I leaned against the grill. "He believes those D.I.P. guys did want to help you find your dad."

"Oh, yeah? That'd surprise the hell out of me." He kept his head down, handwashing utensils at the sink. "I'm pretty sure he's not alive—or at least he's not around here."

The way he spoke caused me to feel a twinge of feeling bad for the guy. I tried to be supportive. "The D.I.P. must think he's still alive, otherwise they wouldn't be wasting their time, right?"

Paul had no reply for a few minutes. He had begun to set up the stainless-steel counter in assembly-line fashion to get the house salads made. He stopped halfway down the line. "You know, I was thinking, I'd like to go with you to look for the medal. After we find it, I'm going to thumb it west. I got no reason to stay here anymore."

I tensed up. I hadn't seen that coming. "Honestly? You giving up?"

Barely audible, he replied, "Yeah. I've had no leads on my dad. I mean, if I haven't found him by now . . . "

I felt a bit of empathy for him. "Okay, I can get you west, but I'm not sure you can go with me to look for the medal. You have to have special permission from the Lakota to go on the land by the springs."

"How about this," he offered. "We find a place to camp, hangout or whatever, drink some beers . . . you know, climb the bluffs . . . "

I squared myself to Paul, considering his plan. This part of his personality was pleasant.

"Look, I won't even go to the Sacred Springs," he suggested. "I'll hang out at the campsite near Tower Buttes while you do your thing. Once you find it, I'll head out." He threw his arms in the air and cocked his head as if to say, "What d'ya think?"

"I like the way you're talking." I finished garnishing his salad plates of iceberg lettuce with cherry tomatoes and a sprinkle of bacon bits. "I've got to see a guy tomorrow, so I would think we'd head out in a couple of days," I said, hoping Jay and Robert would work The Caboose while I was gone. Sarah would want to, I was certain, but it would be best for her to stay in Brave Eagle.

Paul glanced up at the clock. "Hey, I have to run to the clinic in Keogh to pick up a prescription for Valium for my appointment tomorrow. I gotta get a hind tooth out." He stuck his finger in his mouth wanting to show me. "On my way back, I'm going to stop at the hardware store to get a new sharpening stone," he said, grabbing his jacket. "I can't find the first one I got at Richard's. I should be back in an hour." As he fumbled to put his arm in his blue parka, his KA-BAR USMC knife tumbled out of the inside pocket of his jacket, falling to the floor with a dull clunk. Fortunately for Paul, it was still in the sheath. "Holy shit, that was close," he said, nonchalantly picking up his prized possession.

"What do you carry it around for, anyway?" I asked.

"Never know when I might need it," he snarled with ice in his voice. He held a stare as he wheeled out the door.

I shook my head, questioning whether bringing Paul with me was a good idea.

27

Paul returned from his excursion to Keogh, excited to tell me there was a semi and a Bonneville in the ditch east of town. Glittering flakes of snow imitated dandruff on the shoulders of his parka. Once he closed the door behind him, he stomped the shiver out, sending flakes flying. The snow-ice combo had made the roads super slick. "Slicker than a greased hog," he said with an accentuated southern drawl. I made the decision to close at seven and go home to call Sarah.

There was a hollow quiet in the lifeless air as I headed to my truck. The windshield got a strong scraping to clear the film of ice. Streetlights illuminated a gray canopy of low clouds. Painted Rock was eerily empty as I passed through the intersection by Gus's, the yellow streetlight flashing caution. I put the defroster on high and followed a solitary set of tire tracks toward our house. It occurred to me the tracks might be from the D.I.P. agents. My anxiety ramped up a notch with every block until the last turn, where the tracks went right. I went left.

The back porch light of our house reflected its white beams off the hushed snow, brightening the back steps. I flicked on the kitchen light to find the house cold, stuffy, and quiet except for the metallic clicking of the grandfather clock. It felt good to be home. I dropped my stuff on the kitchen table before picking up the phone to call Sarah.

Standing Bear picked up, and we exchanged greetings before he handed the phone to Sarah. We talked about the weather (snow and ice there too), The Caboose (slow night because of the weather), Paul (pleasant—other than his weird defensiveness about his knife—and he was heading west after Tower Buttes). She was surprised he was leaving (I was too) and asked if he was going to miss work after getting his tooth out (I didn't think so). She was appalled he was carrying the KA-BAR around in his jacket (me too).

"I miss you, Jimmy."

"I've been thinking of your safety all day," I told her.

We sat in silence, listening to each other breathe through the line.

"You know, Jimmy . . . Howard, Doris, and I have been catching up. It's been nice." Her tone was sweet and relaxed. She was with her adopted family, in effect, her second home. "Yeah, you know, um, I happened to be talking to Pastor Dawson on the phone about doing a bake sale again to raise money for the youth group workcamp." Her story felt true, but it lacked confidence.

"What are you trying to say?" I prodded. "Cut to the chase."

"Well, you and I already talked about you talking to Pastor about our lives with a baby, marriage, you know, working out some stuff . . . right?" I pictured her standing with one hand on her hip. "So, I didn't feel like I was tattling on you," she said it as if she were apologizing to me. "I told him we had talked about you giving him a call."

"As a matter of fact, I was planning on calling him in the morning," I said proudly with the hope she would take my proactiveness as a positive sign.

"No kidding?" Her voice rose an octave. "Howard kinda talked to me, too. He said I might want to think about backing off, you know. He said you would figure out I'm worth it and our child would need a committed father and husband." She stopped to catch her breath.

"Uh-huh," was all I got out. I stretched the cord as I took a seat at the kitchen table.

She went on. "If you decide it's not the right time, I'll wait." Her tone indicated she meant it. "I can't believe what I just said, but I also believe in you and us."

"Me too."

"Like Walking Thunder, er, Doris said, if I push you into something you don't want, you're going to resent me anyway, right?"

"Yeah, I guess," I said, although I hadn't ever considered the possibility of resenting her. "I mean, we'll figure it out. I respect Howard's . . . er, Standing Bear's opinion. And Doris Walking Thunder's, too, of course. It sounds like you guys had a good talk."

"We did," she bubbled. "It gave me peace." Since Howard and Doris were spoiling her, Sarah said she was in no hurry to come back. "So, when are you going to Tower Buttes?"

I told her Paul had to throw his camping stuff together after his dental appointment. Also, Jay and Robert had committed to cover for Paul and me. Sarah was concerned about Paul quitting. She wanted to know why I was bringing him with me. I told her he'd run out of leads with finding his dad. I gently reminded her that, as much of a pain in the butt as Paul was at times, he'd helped us out more than I'd expected. Given the circumstances, it wasn't a big deal. She reluctantly agreed. If everything fell into place, we'd leave the day after next. With winter beginning to ramp up and the forecast not great for the next few days, I had a day or two to find it, or I'd have to wait till spring.

"Oh man, Jimmy, you're talking about a pretty narrow window." Her tone was tainted with anxiety. "And our baby's due April sixth . . . " Her voice trailed off.

"Yeah, tell me about it. I hope Joan's clues will get me close," I responded with equal anxiety in my voice. "I have to find it. I have to."

Immediately after we said our goodbyes, fatigue hit me. Adrenaline had been keeping me awake the last couple of days, but my tank was empty. My head hit the familiar pillow; sleep came to me.

I overslept because my alarm didn't gone off. As I get closer, the organ music propels me to the base of the steep steps. My dad and Louie are dressed in gray tuxes with gray bowties. They open the arched wooden doors of the church. I take the steps two at a time, wearing my green puffer jacket and Sorel boots. In the narthex of the church, I find myself in the middle of an Indian village. From a shroud of Indian men and women appears one man in a circle of light holding the hand of a pregnant woman, wearing a deerskin covering, her face unrecognizable. He is broad-shouldered, muscular, in full ceremonial finery—buffalo horn headdress, elk tooth necklace, brass tinklers, beaded loin cloth, rawhide moccasins, and leggings adorned with multicolored trade beads. I ask if he is the Arikara Chief Kakawita. Has he met Lewis and Clark? He pulls back the shiny jewelry covering his chest to reveal the Thomas Jefferson Peace Medal underneath. May I touch the medal? He smiles with pride as the woman's face comes into focus. It is Sarah. He offers me the medal with his right hand and Sarah with his left. I look down at my Sorels as I try to keep my balance, walking a tightrope high above water.

28

A blast of wind buffeted the windowpane, snapping me into the dawn. I rolled on my side to look out the frosted windowpane at the glow of an oblong orangish-yellow sun sitting fat and soft on the horizon. Last night's dream had me thinking again about the weight of my circumstances—baby, marriage, medal, work, Grandpa's death, my dad's distant behavior, and D.I.P. agents—battling with my will to untangle the web I was caught in. The Inipi had helped strengthen me, but I still had to confront a lot of uncomfortable issues ahead. Were my panic and occasional rapid heartbeat the harbinger of drowning in circumstances? Was I struggling to rise up to catch my breath, merely to be pulled under by unexplained forces? Would it be a painful death, or would I simply fall asleep?

The stench of beer, smoke, and grease rose from my bell-bottomed flares and T-shirt piled on the floor by my feet. I stepped over them to put on a clean T-shirt and my blue polyester warm-up suit with white pinstriping. With a slow walk down the stairs, I tried to rehearse what I'd say to Pastor Dawson. "I want to honor my grandfather by giving all of myself to Sarah, but don't know how." Or I could start with, "Sarah is pregnant, and she wants to get married." How about, "So many questions for you. I came here for you to give me the answers." By the time I got to the kitchen, I had given up on where to start or why I was even going. Click went the brew button, leaving me to wait for the familiar aroma of coffee brewing to comfort me.

I sat in my truck parked next to the church with the engine running for a minute, tapping my foot and mulling over the pros and cons of going in. I was hoping to find an answer to my issues. Deep down, I knew this talk would complement my soulful sweat experience. On the other hand, I was going to hear something I didn't want to hear—like I was a bad person for living in sin. I didn't know Pastor Dawson well, and talking with him kinda scared me. He'd probably want to pray, and I wasn't even sure how to. The pros outweighed the cons, so I took a deep breath and got out of the truck.

The white paint on the side door of the church showed cracking and peeling from the prairie sun as I pulled it open. To my left, up a couple of stairs and down a lonesome hallway, a light came from Pastor Dawson's office. Stiffness racked my body, legs heavy like sloshing in quicksand. A lonely typewriter clacked away as I approached. As I entered, he came out from behind his desk, extending his hand with a warm smile and kind blue eyes. He still had on his flannel shirt, bird vest, and brown brush pants. There was duck smell coming from him, so I didn't ask if he'd shot any.

"Tell me what's on your heart, Jimmy," he asked, pulling up a fan-shaped office chair with muted gold vinyl. I straightened up when I connected the familiar voice in the sweat lodge, affirming the circle of life would begin again, to Pastor Dawson. He gestured for me to sit down while he closed the door and pivoted back to his desk chair. The double hung window behind him had cream curtains pulled together with heavy water stains along their lower edge. A peaceful violet plant on a small plate at the corner of his desk contrasted with the clutter of books and papers surrounding it.

"Sarah said she had talked to you but . . . I'm not sure where to start," I stammered.

He wore a pensive expression. "Start anywhere. We can fill in the blanks as we go."

My ears burned, and my face got warm. "Okay." I wiped my hands on my pants. "Sarah has been talking about us getting married for a year or so. It's not like I don't love her, but for some reason, I haven't asked her to get married." His face showed no emotion as he listened. "And . . . she recently told me she got pregnant. I should be happy, but . . . " My voice trailed off. I shifted in my seat and crossed my legs.

"Sarah got pregnant, or she told you she was pregnant by you?" His head tilted to the side as he attempted to clarify.

"She told me she was pregnant. I mean, I'm going to be a dad," I fumbled.

"Glad we got *that* established." He half chuckled. The other half communicated seriousness about my situation. "Congratulations."

I reciprocated his half chuckle. My other half contained a large dose of discomfort. "Thank you. Yeah, that's what I meant." I squirmed, diverting my eyes to the floor.

"Let's back up a few steps." Our discussion retreated into my family history—I was an only child, had a distant farmer father, closeness to my grandpa, Mom dying when I was in my mid-teens, how close my mom and I had been. Our talk turned to how Sarah and I had met, how long ago, her family dynamics, and Katherine's passing.

He went right for the piece of my past I feared the most. "How much of your mom's passing do you think still affects you today?"

My sinuses began to get stuffy, and building tears made my eyes get heavy. Pastor read my face and handed me the box of tissues from his desk. "Well, with the baby coming I especially miss her. She'd have been a wonderful grandma." My eyes were focused on the floor in front of me. *Damn it!*

"Is it possible, Jimmy, you're afraid of commitment . . . getting too close . . . " His hands opened in an asking-the-question fashion. "Maybe you don't want to lose Sarah like you did your mom?"

"I guess. I mean it's possible."

"It's not uncommon after the loss of a loved one, especially a parent, to build a fortress around your heart as a means of protection." My ears picked up on his sermon voice. "The walls serve two functions. Protection from others hurting you emotionally. And, in some cases, protecting yourself from loving another and having your heart broken again." He paused; our eyes met. "As you reflect on our talk here today, consider if you have built a wall of protection over the years."

Emotions and intellect were colliding at a rapid speed inside my head. I got what he was saying but needed time to fully process.

He shifted gears to my relationship with Sarah. "What do you see in Sarah?"

A measure of calm returned. Even though I had never been asked what I saw in Sarah, the answer came easily. "She is an amazing woman. Strong, independent, attractive, dependable, a bit untamed. She makes me a better person." I paused. "Oh, and I always liked the fact she has a mind of her own."

"Jimmy, do you *really* love Sarah?"

The way he asked it rattled me. I flinched, thinking it was a dumb question. "Yeah, of course."

"Okay, you say love her." He squinted at the same time his index finger rose. "But do you *value* her? It's what she is asking you, ultimately, when she's talking about marriage."

"I never thought in those terms," I confessed and took my jacket off. The room had become noticeably warmer since I'd arrived.

Leaning forward with his elbows on the desk, he continued. His tone moved from inquisitive with a relaxed posture to stern. "If you'll allow me to be frank," he said with a direct voice, "Jimmy, you've been gettin' the goods—and I don't mean just the sex. I'm talking support, companionship, the fun times, all the components of a committed relationship. But what has she been getting in return?"

The castigation intimidated me. My body sank into the padding of the chair. The cumulative effect of this discussion had left me raw and humiliated, with my insides tumbling. I wished myself right out the window.

"Let me explain it to you this way. Love in its truest sense is an action, not a feeling. There has to be actionable *sacrifice* for it to be love. More action than feeling. The actionable sacrifice by you creates value for you in her."

His emphasis on the word *sacrifice* bore through me.

"See, love isn't the thing we call love until it costs you something." He tilted his head before opening his palms. "What has your love for Sarah cost you?"

"Not much, I guess." I grasped at thin air to find a lifeline. "I mean, I didn't go back to school, moved from Kansas away from my friends and family."

"If love doesn't, or hasn't, cost you something significant . . . it has been merely convenient. You left your friends and family and moved to a different state. An enormous sacrifice. You *have* paid a cost. If I'm her, I'm thinking, your sacrifices eight years ago were because she was lovable. She was worth it, right? With your unwillingness to commit, she might be thinking there is something wrong with her." Pastor stopped to let his last statement sink in. "I'm not here to tell you what the answer is. You have to figure it out."

The room got quiet except for the ticking of the clock on the bookcase. As the walls were closing in around me, I stared at him, forming the courage. "It's not her; it's me. When my grandpa was dying, he said to give my whole self to Sarah. I don't think I have been. If I'm being honest with you, I'm not sure if I know how to."

He leaned back. "I don't mean to be hard on you, Jimmy, but you have some serious decisions to make. Life altering decisions. There's no way to sugarcoat this. I'm sure you wouldn't want me to." His voice contained a tenderness contradicting his facial expression.

"True. I came to you for answers." I was the small child in the overstuffed chair, so naïve, engulfed by this gigantic, nebulous vapor of Pastor love-talk.

He interlaced his fingers on his desk. "Seems to me you have three choices. One, you can leave the relationship. Two, you can continue on the road you're on. Or three, you can commit to Sarah and your child by marrying her. If you're willing to make a commitment, I can help you. Seems to me you know the man you want to be but . . . you're not sure how to get there and what it means to give your whole self to her." There were a few beats of silence. "In the emotional gear shift of life, you are stuck in neutral. Paralyzed, unable to move, as it were. As a pastor, I want to help you move forward to become the man you want to be."

The conversation went dead. I thought about the weight of what he was proposing. The quiet made me ache, making me even more uncomfortable. I picked at my fingernails, feeling his gaze as he continued.

"The first two choices will leave you empty, searching, unfulfilled. I have found with the others I have counseled that the last choice will complete you."

I shifted in my chair silently, allowing his words to sink in. My neck cracked when I pinched my shoulders together, chasing the tension from my upper body. I had a hunch his eyes were on me until he abruptly stood up.

"Think about what we have talked about, okay?" His voice soothed me. "Come back when you want to dig deeper or have questions." We shook hands across his desk. "Share with Sarah what we've talked about." With a glint in his eye, he spoke with reassurance. "Think of it as an opportunity to deepen your relationship with her." He smiled. "Open your heart completely, without condition, and you'll be richly rewarded. God bless you, Jimmy."

"Thank you, Pastor." I'd never gotten a blessing in close proximity. I was consumed by a deep feeling of comfort. As I walked out of the church, it clicked. He had echoed what Grandpa had said. Pastor was right. Marrying Sarah would give me the deep joy I wanted for my life. My chest swelled with happiness.

29

Quiet houses along the empty streets of Painted Rock became a blur as I drove back through town. I was reeling from all Pastor had said. Competing legions of humility, confusion, and encouragement fought for my attention on a field dotted with potential relationship landmines. Echoes of the conversation I'd had with Grandpa, Sarah, and Chief Standing Bear about the Peace Medal eight years ago reverberated in my head. The discussion had proven to be a seminal point in our understanding of Indian perspectives and our reacquisition of what we'd assumed was the original medal. Today's talk might have been equally impactful on my life.

Pastor had ripped off the Band-Aid on some of my issues and, in the process, helped me begin to understand what may have contributed toward avoiding commitment. The Pastor talk generated a feeling of liberation in me like the sweat lodge had.

I'd discovered with both experiences that I had a lot of personal growing to do. My willingness to self-examine was helping me gain the confidence to get there, to make things right with Sarah, to be the man she deserved. Stopped at the red light by Gus's, I smiled for the first time at the thought of being married to Sarah.

As I passed the police station, I noticed Range Detective Ross's green Bronco angle-parked next to the building. Two unmarked black Crown Victorias with whip antennae sat next to a gray Ford LTD with short antennae on the trunk and roof. Their municipal-style plates weren't familiar to me, but there was no doubt they were all law enforcement. At first, I didn't think anything of it, but by the time I pulled into the alley behind The Caboose, the voice in my head said something was up. The presence of lots of cops in our little town of nine hundred was worrisome. Things in Painted Rock were about to get crazy. I circled back and parked down the street from the police station.

"Hi, Karen," I started, approaching the counter. Karen drove twelve miles one way from their black angus ranch outside Benteen for her job as Tittle's secretary. She was stout, short-haired, and always wore a smile on her round face, eager to help. Her oversized square frames of her glasses matched her brown hair and eyes.

"Officer Tittle, please. He's expecting me," I lied.

"I'm sorry, Jimmy," she answered. She leaned forward to whisper; her perfume smelled like baby powder. "He's in there with Range Detective Bradshaw and some other bigwigs." She straightened with authority. "Don said under no circumstances should he be disturbed." A wink, and then she lowered her voice. "Must be important."

"Must be," I groused. There had to be a way in to find out what was going on. Did it have to do with the D.I.P.? Paul's dad?

Was this related to what Range Detective Ross had mentioned to me? Grandpa used to tell me the simplest solutions to a problem were always the best ones. "May I use your bathroom?"

She pointed. "End of the hall, take a right."

I pushed through the batwing door, tiptoeing to position myself out of Karen's sight by Officer Tittle's closed door.

The men in the room were loud talkers, so it wasn't hard to hear most of the conversation. Ross was telling the others about our conversation regarding my required experience in the sweat lodge. Feeling anxious, I glanced up and down the hallway. He had started talking about the medal when Tittle piped up and said the backstory was old news to him. Ross continued to talk about the medal, Grandpa, and Tower Buttes. A voice I did not recognize bellowed, "Lock him up!" A collegial laugh followed.

The frosted glass in the door went dark except for brief flashes of color accompanied by short bursts of a muted voice. Was it a slideshow or overhead projector? Someone said "Paul," "Department of Indian Properties," "the dredged car," and "the medal." Another said, "Four states and eight years ago." Were they talking about Paul Gritzmacher or Paul Van Brocklin? An inaudible buzz followed before a deeper voice said something about a warrant, questioning "him" and "armed." The rest was unrecognizable. My jaw tightened, while my brain tried to make sense of it all. After about five minutes or so, the lights came back on, and the patter of voices picked up. At one point, the banter got heated until Ross let everyone know in a voice of authority, he was in charge. The room grew silent before he asked if there were any more questions. I began to panic, knowing the meeting was ending. Sounds of paper shuffling, books or binders closing, and chairs dragging along the marble floor made my face warm. I backpedaled away from the door, my heart beating faster than a jackrabbit.

I turned on my heels and ran right into Officer Keith Jurgensen. "Oh, jeez," I said with big eyes, stepping back. "I'm sorry, Keith."

"Hey, Jimmy. Can I help you with something?" His tightly wound face featured narrowed eyes. "Why are you so jumpy?"

"In a hurry. I wanted to talk with Don about an issue I'm having with the transients sneaking into The Caboose."

He stood with one hand on his hip, the other checking his wristwatch. "Don should be wrapping up soon." He had a serious look on his face.

"No biggie. I'll try to come back tomorrow. I gotta get home. Sarah's pregnant, you know," I said, walking to the door.

"Congrats!" he yelled as I exhaled.

Karen interrupted shuffling papers long enough to roll her eyes at me as the batwing door slammed against the wall. I pushed through the double doors and out into the cold, bending at the waist to exhale my panic. Whatever was going on inside had me stumped. Why would they want the medal? Money? Who brought up Paul? Did they want to hold me responsible for Gritzmacher and Calhoun? Had Tittle and Bradshaw been lying to me the whole time? My gut instinct was telling me I'd better find the medal before they did or before the weather derailed my quest. The medal belonged in our family. Once I found it, they'd have to pry it from my dead fingers.

Whoever "they" were.

30

I was restless, concerned with what had been said in Officer Tittle's office. Lying awake with my eyes open at three in the morning, I contemplated various explanations. The outcome I drew from the scenarios I had concocted was that the assembled law enforcement were after the medal. Pangs of ignorance hit me hard when it dawned on me. Ross had been at the bar when I explained that the medal was at the Springs of the Great Spirit. He'd passed on the information during the law enforcement meeting in Tittle's office. It was all my fault. *Ugh!* My stomach curdled.

A wave of guilt rolled through me as I revisited the meeting, and headlights swept through the room. Pipes rattled in the walls startling me. A knocking sound in the wall mimicked a door closing. Somewhere below me, the house creaked. The *thump, thump, thump* of my heart played in my ears. The darkness had made me paranoid. After tossing and turning to release the worry, I finally went to sleep thinking of Sarah and how much I missed her.

Jumping out of bed, I'm cussing at my alarm clock for not waking me up. My Econ 101 final starts in fifteen minutes in the Ag building on the other end of campus. My first final exam of freshman year, and I oversleep. Ugh. I throw on the clothes left next to my bed, slide on my backpack, and head out of my dorm. Snow has dusted the sidewalks, lighting a dark morning. I hustle up the railroad embankment to take a shortcut along the railroad tracks. The backpack with my heavy economics textbook bounces against my back. I'm mindful of landing my Adidas on the railroad ties as I jog. It feels like I am running in place until the Ag building's façade of columns and brick appears. Next scene, and I'm in the lecture hall filled with a sea of students, their heads down, furiously writing. The professor, in a suit and tie, peers over his black reading glasses with a look of contempt. He has my blue answer book and test booklet in his hand, waving me to an open seat in the front row. My sweaty hand sticks to the blue book as I write. I see myself pounding my hand on the desktop, trying to unstick the paper. I look up to see my failing test score is posted on the chalkboard.

I woke with wide eyes, reassured by my surroundings that it had been a dream. Through the window, the morning had broken crisp and still, the cover above formed by shades of blue, mixed with small saucers of dark gray clouds below racing to the east. From the distance, the *flump, flump, flump* of a helicopter transitioned to softly vibrating the windowpane. Throwing back the covers, I hustled down the steps to the front porch to see the black and white underside of the chopper heading west toward Tower Buttes before turning southeast over Lake Oahe into a weak morning sun. Another charter coming and going? Business must be good. I returned inside to get dressed and to scrounge up coffee and toast prior to heading down to The Caboose to pick up Paul. Despite my lack of sleep, I was positively wired, ready to win the race for my medal.

I bounced down the alley, waving to Range Detective Ross as we passed. Finally, I pulled in behind the dumpster, gravel popping under the tires. Paul was sitting on the back stoop of the bar, smoking a cigarette, his oversized backpack next to him. Taking my duffle bag from the front seat, I was greeted by the ripe smell of yesterday's garbage.

I asked, "Where's the tent?" My breath curled white in front of me before dissipating.

Paul stood, approached the back of the truck and patting his backpack. "Everything we need is here." He threw the backpack into the truck bed with a heavy thud. Paul showed no lingering signs that he'd had a tooth pulled. He insisted on showing me the extraction site, which I vehemently declined.

"Where are you going?" I asked. My eyes followed him as he went behind the dumpster and produced a gun case. A jolt went through me. "What the hell are you doing?"

He wore a wicked smile. "My .22 long rifle might come in handy for prairie dogs, or whatever."

I nodded. "Holy shit. So you *do* have a long rifle—you stole it!" I shook my head, disgusted. "Why did you lie to the agents? They were trying to help you." My face must have expressed my disbelief.

He laid the gun in the back of the truck. He growled at me like a pit bull with daggers for eyes. "Damn right I lied. C'mon,

Jimmy. You think I was going to tell them I had a gun? They'd confiscate it from me." His face was clouded with anger.

"Why would they take it from you?"

"Because where I'm from and everywhere, it's what cops do." His irritation and mistrust of authority were once again front and center.

"You bring it from Georgia?" My jaws had tightened.

He scrunched his nose and mouth together, baring his yellow teeth. "Yeah right," he scoffed. "Like I'm going to hitchhike with a rifle." He took his anger up a notch. "I got it from the hardware store about three or four weeks ago. Ask Rick if you don't believe me." His breath billowed forward as he flicked his cigarette butt to the alley.

I made eye contact, and he averted his eyes. He had to have seen the anger in my face. This trip was not starting off on the right foot. Moving toward the back of the truck, I rested my forearms on the truck box while I scuffed at the gravel. Raising my head, I refocused. "Look," I said, trying to reason with him, "I don't know what's going on with you, your dad—if you even have one—the Department agents, the questions . . . all of it." I stopped and pointed at him. "But a second ago you told me you can't hitchhike with a gun, so leave it here. You can pick it up on your way back."

"I was going to hunt with it around Tower Buttes."

"Nope. It stays here, or you don't go."

Paul grabbed the gun case and put it inside the back door of The Caboose. He mumbled something about me being a pussy or wuss.

"What'd you say?" I stepped toward him.

"Nothing, man. Sorry, okay?" He snapped, heading back to the truck.

"All right." My voice was tentative; a sharp cramp from acid irritated my stomach. "We gotta stop at the Red Owl for some groceries."

We climbed into the truck, slamming our doors simultaneously against the nippy elements and each other. The cab was filled with an uncomfortable quiet on the way to the grocery store. We picked up more food than we'd need, but where we were going, there wouldn't be a grocery store within twenty miles.

Once we crossed through the superstructure of the bridge, things changed. An hour into our journey, the sky transitioned to darkened clouds that looked like clumps of steel wool. Some were angrier than others, but there was no doubt we were driving into some weather. I started to tell him western South Dakota was mostly reservation and one of the least inhabited areas of the United States. "Underneath our drive is the Williston Basin. It holds the world's largest lignite coal deposit. You know, the black stuff in those open boxcars you see passing through town. The center of the coal mining in South Dakota used to be in Firesteel, which is about fifty miles ahead. It's pretty much abandoned." I glanced over to see if he was listening to my tour guide speech.

"Whoa! What the hell are those?" He quickly quartered to his right, pointing at a wave of movement on a field of harvested corn.

I glanced to my right. Antelope. I had difficulty trying to count how many antelope there were because of the camouflaged white and tan against the light yellow and tan-brown terrain. "Oh, yeah. Those are antelope. They can accelerate to sixty miles an hour in the blink of an eye." I let him ponder for a second. As if on command, bobbing white butts exploded up and over the rise, single file.

His face went from amazement to delight. "Wow . . . so cool."

Something wasn't right. Their skittishness had to mean a bad storm was coming. Dark purple-gray clouds had quickly appeared on the horizon, and we were heading right for them. Rain freckled the windshield at first, but in an instant, it required the wipers to be on high. The pitter of ice slivers followed. Miles later, it became an ice and snow mixture, driven by a wind that was gaining force. I threw the defroster on high, knowing that, in time, the battle for a clear windshield would be lost.

Paul intermittently placed his hand on the dash, rubbing his forehead, rubbing his hands on his pants, and squirming.

Finally, he came clean. "Mind if I have a smoke?" His large eyes were filled with panic.

"Crack your window."

We traveled on, visibility getting tougher as the wind out of the northwest blew sheets of snow across the highway. I reduced my speed in an attempt to mitigate the worsening conditions. A Mack truck crested the rise ahead, barreling toward us and splaying a wall of snow. My knuckles became white as I held the wheel tight, praying the behemoth would stay in its lane. Pain shot up the back of my neck from shoulders bunched by wracked nerves. The passing snow slush combination pelted my truck, leaving me unable to see ahead until the wipers swept away the deposits. The Doors' "Riders on the Storm" drifted out of the radio as if we needed a haunting reminder.

In the middle of Paul's third cigarette, he started, "Did I ever tell you about the time I fell in a well when I was like, seven or eight years old?"

"No. C'mon," I snorted. "How big was the well? I mean, how did you fit?" This was an odd time to bring this up.

He took a strong drag, the tip of his cigarette bright red. "Big enough, I guess. It's not like a well around here." He took another drag, putting pursed lips to the opening and channeling the smoke out the open window. "Me and my mom lived in the country in a side-by-side with an old well in back. It was one of them early morning, beautiful summer days, you know? Mom's clothes flapping in the breeze on the clothesline. So, anyway, me and Herschel were playing catch with a baseball out back. He threw me a deep fly ball. So, I go chasing it and down I went," he said matter-of-factly. He popped another cigarette out of his pack. "The well didn't have a fence or brick around it."

"You get hurt?" I kept my eyes focused forward. The port of visibility, which I needed to keep us on the road, was closing. The passenger side of the windshield had become virtually useless.

"Nope. You know what I remember thinking when I was in the well?" He rolled up his window. He had rotated his upper body to me. His face was electrified with excitement, and his speech got faster.

This story had better be going somewhere. "No idea."

"The sirens started out barely noticeable at first. My mom was frantic, telling me help was on the way. And I'm thinking, you know, if I had a dad, he'd get me out of here like those other kids' dads would have." His voice was rising, and he softly punched the dashboard. He stared straight ahead for a few seconds before gradually turning to look at me with these primeval eyes, void of sensation. "But I didn't have a dad. He left me. And I still don't."

His story gave me the creeps. Although, in a way, I related to what Paul was saying. My dad had left me, at least emotionally, and Grandpa had stepped in. I told myself I was going to be there for my child.

"You know," he sneered, "I got this gut feeling before I started my trip out here that someone had taken him away from me for good."

Paul flexed his jaw muscles, gritting his teeth. He twisted to look out his window, fists clenched, and exhaled. He mumbled, "They should have left me in the damn well."

31

We were hemmed in with retreat impossible. Ice had formed along the edge of the wiper blades, limiting their effectiveness. The buildup of snow on the road from nature's relentless attack had me guessing where the shoulders were. Going up a small hill, the truck fishtailed toward the ditch, forcing me to ease off the accelerator. Mini cyclones of driven snow, *snow devils*, dashed through the field to my right, warning me there was more to come. A group of Red Angus cattle with backs covered in snow huddled near the fence line, unable to escape the first major storm of winter. We had been silent for a while, listening to weather updates on the radio when the signal was strong enough. The snow was predicted to continue through the day, but the weatherman said, in a voice tinged with doubt, the temps could well reach the forties the next day. The melt could allow me to start my search. "Midnight Train to Georgia" came on the radio. Paul cranked it up.

The fury of the white veil surrounding us was interrupted by a line of faint red dots ahead. Glowing flares had been stretched out over a quarter mile, ending at two squad cars topped with rectangles of flashing red lights. A feeling of dread came over me. I slowed to a crawl, seeing the sheriff's squad cars blocking the road beyond the pasty white, hexagonal stop sign. My headlights reflected off their cars, and the two officers' bright, red-tipped flashlights waved at us like they were helping a North Central Airlines plane taxi to the terminal. The snow made a squishing sound under the tires as I stopped and cracked the window.

One of the officers leaned into the wind as he trudged through the snow toward us with his gloved hand on top of his hat. He sidled up to the truck, yelling above the gusts, "Officer Blanda!" He nodded man to man. "Can't go any farther. Semi jackknifed, blocked the road. Can't clear it 'til morning." His words were choppy. "Storm is . . . expected to get . . . much worse. Predicting sixty . . . mile an hour winds." The wind howled through the opening.

"Sixty?" I asked in disbelief. Turning, I glanced at Paul, whose mouth hung open below eyes the size of teacup saucers. "Guess we're not camping," I snickered.

"Yeah, you have . . . to go left here and Crook is . . . less than a mile south of here." The cop pointed. He braced his hat with his free hand, his yellow slicker snapping against itself. "There's a motel for ya . . . to spend the night."

Officer Blanda and I exchanged a look. I was reluctant but said, "Okay."

He barked, "Get going." He peeled away, and as I cranked up the window, he turned his head for a muffled, "And good luck!"

We crept forward, turning left and catching a bit of a tailwind crossing over the hill. Lit by blurred amber lights, Crook appeared—through the weather—to be ahead and below. The main drag had a few houses on either side, tapering off down the valley. I headed down the hill, struggling to stay on the road. The motel's bright pink and aqua neon sign cast a fuzzy image through the snow.

"Gotta love their sign." I pointed to the blinking *Vacancy* sign below the obscured *Crook Motel* sign. It had a retro appearance of functional simplicity, a leftover from the bygone era of post-World War II mom-and-pop motels, which had sprung up along highways across America.

"Jeez. Good to know the rooms are air conditioned," Paul added in a sarcastic tone.

Finding a haven of refuge from the storm did little to improve my mood. We pulled in, and to my amazement, there were two other vehicles. One truck had a horse trailer attached to it, and the other one was similar to the gray Ford LTD I'd seen parked by Tittle's office.

The white enamel paint on the trim around the office door reflected the muted pink from the bright *Vacancy* sign in the adjacent window. I swept back the aluminum screen door with a metal *C* monogram on its front. The hollow wooden door behind it was stuck and screeched against the door jamb as I pushed it open.

The lobby had a homey feel—magazine rack, green-toned paisley upholstered furniture, thick wooden end table and lamp. A heavy pine air freshener was working hard to tamp down the residual cigarette smell. A thinned, tan carpet led me to the counter.

"Howdy, fellas. Name's Chet. Quite a storm out there we're having," said the man with the rosy-red cheeks set below his matching beady bloodshot eyes. He had a half-moon shaped scar on his chin and a shiny, sloped forehead. "Radio says warmer tomorrow. One of those early winter freak snowstorms." Short and egg-shaped, he had on a maroon cardigan sweater over a mustard gold turtleneck. Chet reached out to shake my hand. His small hand was soft, his grip limp.

A woman about the same age as he was poked her head out of the single door behind the welcome desk like a turtle. She checked us out, then quickly retreated behind the closed door.

He read the look of confusion on our faces before nodding over his shoulder. "My wife, Sue."

"Oh." What else could I say?

"May I assume one night for you gentlemen?" He had the sympathetic voice of a funeral director, the presence of an owner. "We have ten rooms, of which numbers nine and ten are taken. All the rooms have two full-size beds. I have room eight all ready for you." He curled his lips into a smile, full of pride, first to me and then at Paul.

"One room, one night," I said. "What do I owe you?"

He slid a pad of paper closer, taking a pencil and mumbling, "Carry the one . . ." His movements were twitchy.

Impatience crawled through me. Paul met my eyes with a look of disbelief. He shook his head.

"Eleven dollars and fifty-six cents," Chet announced as if we were the lucky winners. "Includes taxes." He winked.

I handed him a ten and a five. He handed me two keys for room eight and proceeded to count back my change with more care than necessary. "Right out the front door and down the sidewalk," he said in a helpful tone, pointing.

We grabbed our snow-covered gear and got settled in room eight. It smelled old and stale, the smell of disuse. One wall had mahogany paneling, and the other three were painted in a light yellow. I flopped down on my bed to give it a test run. Cement was softer. As I lay on my back, I noticed the ceiling had a couple of tan-brown water spots above the television. The frosted glass bowl covering the light was speckled with dead flies and a couple of miller moths. Not long thereafter, nature called, so I got up to pee. The tub faucet had a drip, which, over time, had left a teardrop-shaped orange-brown stain above the drain. The mirror above the sink showed its age, along with reflecting my consternation, as I washed my hands.

Back in the living area, I pulled back the stiff beige curtain. The storm showed no signs of letting up. The white rage was increasing in intensity. The platinum snow blew sideways, creating chalk white drifts—a blanket covering everything. I strained to see beyond the road before scanning to my right, recoiling. The LTD was gone. Where?

My heart sank. We were going nowhere anytime soon. The room filled with the sound of a furious wind howling, causing our window to chatter. "I won't know 'til morning when I can go look for the medal. Gonna depend on the weather," I said, annoyed. The room's light flickered once, once again, and out. I tilted my head to the ceiling. It came back on, but a few seconds later, it went out again.

My eyes met Paul's blank expression, eye sockets devoid of feeling. What *was* he thinking? An eerie sensation filled me as I waited to hear a generator kick on. Something wasn't right. It felt like there was someone else in the room. Were we being spied on? We sat in uncomfortable silence for a few minutes until a knock on the door jolted me. A blast of wind entered as I cracked the metal door.

Chet had on his army green parka zipped up to his nose, looking like a cartoon character. With his head tilted back, his bloodshot eyes peered up through his snorkeled jacket. He muffled, "The wife went to the neighbors to get a new battery for the generator." Only his upper torso rotated as he extended his arm to point. "Won't be long 'til we get power back." He stared at me like he wanted me to respond. "Okay, thanks!" He tottered off.

I poked my head out beyond the door. "Chet? Hey, did room ten leave? They were here when we got here."

He turned back to me, took a couple of seconds to analyze where the LTD had been, shrugged, and knocked on the door of room nine.

We each sat on our beds in the dark room. Time dragged on as we stared at the ceiling, snacked on chips, and discussed ideas to keep Paul busy the next day. If there wasn't snow, I suggested he go to the site where they discovered a huge fossil cache, south of the motel. He feigned interest, removing his knife from his backpack. With dramatic strokes, he began to sharpen it with his new sharpening stone.

A shiver crept through my body.

The generator came back on, and a rush of stagnant air came from the shuddering heating unit. I crawled under the covers with my clothes on and one eye open, wondering if we should call it quits and go home in the morning.

32

The day broke with the sound of water dripping from the ceiling on the top of the television like a metronome. Paul was already in the shower, so I got out of bed to scope out the weather. Everything was coated in crisp white, with the exception of the road. It had been recently plowed and sanded, leaving the asphalt crown sharing space on either side with snow, sand, and ice. The sky was an amazing cobalt blue with scratches of vapor trails miles above.

"I'm going to wait an hour or so for the roads to melt off before I leave," I said, changing into my boot-fit Wranglers, hiking boots, and sweatshirt as Paul emerged from the bathroom. "Don't know when I'll be back from Tower Buttes." I paused. "In case I don't find the medal today, I'm going to go pay for our room for another night, and we can split it, okay?"

"Yeah, sure, not a problem," Paul answered with a nasal voice.

I left to pay for another night, noticing the LTD had returned. The truck and horse trailer had left, replaced by a Crown Victoria dusted with highway snow along its side panels.

Sue was at the desk to greet me. "Morning," she said with a smoker's rasp. She placed her cigarette in the ashtray on the counter before extending her hand of yellowed fingers. She was tall and slender. Her smile showed her coffee- and nicotine-stained teeth behind pencil-thin lips. Gray roots transitioned to jet black hair. Her faded floral dress had a scalloped neckline. She was cordial, asking me how I'd slept while she collected my money. I inquired about a place to eat in town as I put my hand on the door to leave. The diner—"Mickies" she called it—had excellent breakfasts, she said, adding that her cousin, Michelle, owned it. I nodded a thank you. My stomach growled right on cue.

When I returned to the room, Paul declined my invitation to go for breakfast. He said he'd eat some of the food we brought from home. Satisfied, I set out for hot food at the diner, snow squelching under my boots. Ahead, snow topped cars, mailboxes, and bushes but was dulled by rising temperatures. My sunglasses cut the bright reflection as I trudged down the hill following a shallow set of footprints. As I walked, it became apparent that, for all the blowing, the actual snow on the ground was three or four inches deep. The sweet smell of bakery tickled my nostrils before the sign for *Mickie's* caught my eye. The lit yellow square showed bowling pins and a cheeseburger.

I pulled back the glass door, the ding of a bell announcing my entrance. To either side of me were a row of faux mahogany booths with yellow Formica tabletops. In front of me was an off-white Formica counter and black vinyl pedestal stools. A woman with *Mickie* embroidered above her right breast on her short-sleeved red dress told me to sit where I wanted; she'd be right with me. She was a stout woman with strands of white mixed with brown curls and a pointy chin. Wrinkles radiated from the corners of her eyes. A darkened four-lane bowling alley was off to my right, past the kitchen. The linoleum floor showed years of traffic, making it lifeless. Walls were decorated with wooden wagon wheels, wooden hand tools, and wooden yokes. The heavy smell of fresh bread overwhelmed the diner.

Two middle-aged, clean-shaven gentlemen seated at the counter drinking coffee glanced over their shoulders in unison. One had an orange stocking cap, a triangular nose jutting from his flat cheekbones. The other distinguished himself with beefy sideburns bookending soft features set below perfectly groomed Glen Campbell hair.

"Morning," I offered in a cheerful voice.

They responded with a flat, "Morning."

I sat toward the other end of the counter, browsing the limited offerings of the single-sided menu.

"Y'all get stuck at the motel last night?" The one with the orange cap had a bit of a southern drawl. He took a deep draw from his cigarette, flicking the ashes with his thumb into the ashtray.

I rotated my head to answer. "Yeah, I did. You?"

Orange Hat Man continued to look straight ahead. "Nope."

"Hell, no," his buddy chimed in under his breath.

Mickie brought their food—eggs and hashbrowns. To me she said, "What can I get ya?"

I figured if it was good enough for the locals, it was good enough for me. "Two eggs and hashbrowns, please."

Orange Hat Man had more questions, shoveling in his food as he continued to stare straight ahead. *Are you traveling alone? Where you headed? Are you sure you want to go there?* His voice contained a mixture of curiosity and contempt, stubbing out his cigarette butt in the ashtray.

With a guy who works for me. Tower Buttes. Yes, I have to. It's a personal thing for my Grandpa.

Orange Hat Man wouldn't quit. *Sioux land, part of it forbidden.*

Mickie put my food in front of me and grabbed salt and pepper shakers from under the counter. By this time, I'd had enough, so I started to look straight ahead, too. "I got permission from Eagle Elk, Lakota Sioux medicine man."

The three of us ate without further conversation, the diner filled with the scraping of metal utensils on plastic plates. They used hushed banter as I finished eating. A burst of laughter caught my attention. The townsfolk pushed up and away from the counter, Orange Hat Man nodded in the direction of the door, he threw a ten-dollar bill down, and they left.

Mickie came to get my empty plate. "You all through here, hon?" Her motherly nature touched me.

I wiped my mouth and placed the napkin on the plate. "Yes, ma'am. Thank you." As she cleared the counter, I blurted, "Those guys always ask so many questions?"

"Those guys?" She bobbed her head toward the door, placing my check face down on the counter.

I spun around to thumb toward the door. "Uh-huh."

She snickered. "No idea. Never seen 'em before in my life." She pivoted into the kitchen. I threw down three singles and left shaking my head. If they weren't locals, were they law enforcement guys going after the medal? Were these guys at the meeting in Tittle's office? I bet they were, and they'd waited the storm out until this morning. I better get goin'. Jeez, this trip was making me even more paranoid.

The temperature must have risen to almost forty. That, combined with the uphill walk back to the motel, had lathered me up pretty good. Entering our room, I saw a note on top of the television in Paul's handwriting. He was going exploring. *Exploring?* That gave me a good chuckle burst.

I changed into dry clothes filled up my canteen, and grabbed my flashlight, a box of stick matches, and my binoculars. I hopped into the truck, heading north to the four-way stop. No cops or roadblocks. As I headed west, the dazzling sun illuminated the unique shapes of the geologic formations looming in the distance. In short order, the terrain got interrupted by massive Tower Buttes. Weathered and sculpted by wind and water, they rose off the prairie hundreds of feet high like multiple chalky fists thrust skyward in solidarity. The revered feature was a magnificent cluster of shear-walled, mostly flat-topped rock yielding to the occasional spire, and they were surrounded along their base by a two-story band of scree. Anticipation raced inside of me on a track of determination as I got closer. I'd made it that far, and I wouldn't be denied the medal. I needed to stay connected to Grandpa and—should life-or-death circumstances demand it—have the medal as leverage.

I pulled over to the side of the road across from Old Woman spire. Without Joan's description, I would never have recognized the well camouflaged trailhead opening fifty yards to my left. Crossing over the salt-crusted highway with binoculars hung around my neck, I joined a game trail off to the east, trampled by lots of antelope or deer tracks in the melting snow. Following it, I entered a somber grove of ponderosa pines, tall and stoic. The soothing smell of pine filled my nose. The shaded forest floor was covered in a layer of snow, save for the occasional splotches of rust-colored needles where shafts of sunlight penetrated the canopy.

From above, a raven—could have been two—signaled the alarm. Wind sighed through the treetops, the trail weaving back and forth through the blocky orange-brown barked trees. To either side of me, there was a well-defined, recent right boot imprint but a less noticeable left boot print. I picked up two sets of boot prints along the trail—one in and one out. There'd be two sets if it was the guys from the diner, so I told myself my suspicions were unwarranted. Might have been a tribal member leaving an offering at the springs. I knelt to check the animal prints, but they were all going in. The different prints had me perplexed for a beat before I refocused on my goal. The walk was fairly level until I left the pines to climb the switchback path of irregularly surfaced scree. My breathing began to labor as I struggled to keep my balance on the slippery rock. Halfway up, I fell, raking my left shin. Once at the top, I had to turn sideways to slide through a narrowing like a hallway between steep-walled towers. Halting midway, I cocked my head skyward in wonder at the ribbon of deep blue splitting the smooth vertical walls—walls that offered no purchase for vegetation to grow. A bead of sweat—two, three—snaked down my back.

Once through, I stood with my hands on my hips on a balcony of rock to survey the expansive beauty before me, an incomparable sanctuary in dimension and energy. Ringing me were buttes with little slope, differing in shape and size, all taller than they were wide. The impressive structures were dotted with foliage, as if by magic sprung from denuded surfaces, hanging on for dear life.

Colby must have loved being here. I could hear his voice admonishing me, "Take it all in, Jimmy." My walk was pleasant yet caused me a fair amount of nervousness. Was I being watched? In the far distance, I recognized the butte Joan had called the castle by its square shape and cornered spires. I picked up the sweet smell of Dakota sage. My memory flashed back to a smudging ceremony at Standing Bear's years ago.

"Hello!" I shouted. A soft echo returned. Clumps of snow made the meadow look like it was full of marshmallows. Dotted across the meadow floor below, wisps of steam rose from thermal springs skyward before disappearing. Touched by wonder, I understood why the revered area was called "Springs of the Great Spirit."

The game trail descended through the scree before it began to snake through a sun-drenched meadow. Warm rays were uncovering the long grasses and snow-hatted sagebrush of varying heights, none taller than my waist. Intermixed with the sagebrush were a handful of gnarly trunked junipers, making it difficult for me to see ahead. Irregular patches of short vegetation and mud, presumably because of associated geothermal activity, surrounded springs I passed. From nearby, a high-pitched whistle startled me. I spun round to see a pudgy marmot twitch and dart into a crevasse. On occasion, as I followed the lopsided boot tracks, I would notice a freshly broken branch along the trail. Anxiety tingled through my body. I was aware of my own heartbeat and the sound of my breathing, a steady rhythm.

I slogged along to a rise in the trail, where multiple boot imprints faced different directions before they reversed course. A faint tinge of rotten eggs caught my nose, but it floated on by. To my left, multiple tentacles of steam twisted upward from a large pool. My heart leapt at the prospect that I had found the medal's resting spot, but I found no spiritual items around the spring. Beyond it was a unique structure, nestled between boulders the size of a Chevy van. Conical in shape like a small teepee, it consisted of an inverted V opening, and I estimated one hundred two- or three-inch-diameter poles of bark-covered aspen—or it might have been ash; it was hard to tell—at least ten to fifteen feet tall. Leather lashing remained between the tops of the interlocked, forked poles. The structure had started to lean forward onto itself, but I guessed the original diameter at the base was probably fifteen feet or so. I stared at it while trying to imagine it as a home for a Sioux medicine man in the role of a spiritual leader or a sweat lodge from many years ago.

Determined to minimize the blizzard's fury, the sun was high in the sky as I got to a fork in the trail. Scanning with my binoculars, I found no sign of steam or burbling springs where the meadow broadened. Continuing my visual sweep of the area, I caught a glimpse of a mottled, gray-brown sage grouse feeding on the sage leaves before it exploded out of sight. Trusting my gut, I lowered the binoculars and headed right at an increased pace around a wall of tall rock. I was greeted by the pungent smell of rotten eggs. If Joan's description was right, the spring I was looking for should have been about fifty yards ahead, beyond the worn hump of gray rock she'd said was shaped like a turtle. There were springs with puddles the size of Hula-Hoops off to either side as I carefully zigzagged my way toward the gray butte.

My breathing quickened when I spotted the turtle rock thirty yards ahead. Squinting, I thought I could make out a good-sized white dog or wolf sitting on its haunches atop the turtle. Vapors of melting snow rose around it, giving it a mystical appearance. Raising my hand to shield my eyes, I tried to convince myself it was a white wolf. I raised my binoculars, recalling what Standing Bear had said when we'd seen the wolf after leaving the sweat lodge. This animal's outline was blurred, but it was a white wolf, and it was looking right at me, unfazed by my approach. Out of caution, I slowed my pace, peering at the solitary creature. It looked down and behind himself, then back at me—three times. The trail took me through a small, dense grove of junipers, where I lost sight of the turtle rock and, momentarily, my sense of direction. Once through, I reoriented, but the white wolf had disappeared.

I found the spot that had captured the wolf's focus. The warmth of the sulfur spring and the sun had melted the snow from the various spiritual offerings—a small clay pot, bald eagle feathers, elk teeth, a turquoise inlay cross—exactly as Joan had described them. Curiosity got the best of me. What did these items represent? What was their story? Who had put them there? Out of respect, standing with my back arched to face the sun with arms outstretched, I offered a prayer to *Wakan-Tanka*.

I lowered my gaze to the edge of a shallow depression filled with water. Had I gotten here before my competition? A prickle of anxiety rushed through my body. Rings, gently pushed out from the gurgle at its center, obscured objects lying below the surface. A glint of silver-black tarnished metal caught my eye first, the circular shape second. My heart jumped, and my bent legs quivered. My hand stabbed the warm water. The original Thomas Jefferson Peace Medal was mine.

I clutched it tightly to my chest, goosebumps rising on my arms. With closed eyes, I remembered Chief Kakawita's skeletal hand holding it and Grandpa's solemn respect when we'd found it. I squeezed it tighter for the connection I wished to feel . . . Grandpa with me.

Eyes opened; I was super excited to get back to the motel to call Sarah. Elation, anxiety, and satisfaction contended within me. After seven years, multiple states, and thousands of miles traveled, the small medal with the big history was home. Or was it? I took a quick look around and listened. Had law enforcement followed me?

There was no one. My face softened into a smile; my furrowed brow relaxed. Raising it to the heavens, I whispered, "Grandpa."

Holding the medal tightly, I retraced my steps through the meadow, squeezed through the narrow passageway, navigated the scree, and dove into the lingering smell of pine. When I was halfway through the stand, the nagging feeling of being followed returned. I stopped and quickly whirled with fists raised, ready to confront whoever or whatever was following me.

My eyes investigated right to left and left to right as I listened for any sound. The chatter of a pine squirrel scolded me. Movement to my left got my attention. Walking down the scree was the white wolf. Halfway down, its posture slumped, ears flattened. Our eyes met, and it pawed the broken stone three times before sitting back on its haunches. I waited as its eyes fixed on me. Rising up, it let out a penetrating howl, the echo remaining in the air for several seconds. With the wolf's salute finished, it vanished back into the narrow passage.

My heart was swollen with satisfaction, thumping loudly with pride as I continued my walk out on a cushion of air. When I emerged from the tall pines, I was wet and muddied up to my knees. "Yes!" I screamed with pride from a mission accomplished.

A dark cloud of nervousness passed through me as I thought about the Range Detective's meeting in Tittle's office. I'd won the race, and they weren't going to like it.

33

By the time I arrived back at the motel, bright sunshine and rising temperatures had caused the snow in the parking lot to form a small lake. I splashed through it, parking in front of our room. The LTD was there, but not the Crown Victoria, giving me a deeper feeling of uneasiness. Before getting out of the truck, I ran my fingers over the medal in my pocket for reassurance. Exiting to dance between the puddles, I avoided the silvery drops from the shallow pitched roof's drip line. The halo of sunlight around the curtain in our room kept it from being pitch black. Sliding my hand along the wall, I flicked the light switch. Nothing happened. I toggled it up and down, but there was still no light. *Generator out again?*

Skirting under the soffit with care not to stumble on the cracked sidewalk, I found the office door locked. I used my hand to cut the glare as I peered through the glass at the empty reception area. My stomach churned at the prospect of not being able to call Sarah. Maybe there would be another way to get permission to use their phone. I trudged around back. The double hung windows of the owners' living quarters were too high for me to see in. I stood on my tiptoes but was still unable to get tall enough to see above the windowsill. I continued past the idle generator. Turning the corner, I found a back door at the top of snow-coated wooden steps. I grabbed the bare wood of the rickety railing, hoisting myself to the stoop.

Through the door, I heard the murmur of voices, then a whack followed by a woman's scream. "God, no!" *Sue?*

My heart thumped with fear. How should I proceed with this domestic dispute? Was it any of my business? Turning my head to get my ear closer to the door, I heard incoherent, garbled voices. Another whack. A man's laughter. Thud on the floor. "No!" A whimper. Sobbing, muffled voices, a grunt. This wasn't adding up. At the risk of butting into someone else's business, I reached down to check the knob. It was unlocked.

Unconvinced I was doing the right thing, my legs suddenly weakened. I swung the door inward with measured caution. Filtered light through the dining room windows cast a dull pall over the room. I crossed the threshold from reality to a scene out of a horror movie. Sue—gagged and tied to a ladder-back chair—shook her head furiously side to side. Her gag was soaked in blood. There was a one-inch gash below her left eye, her right eye nearly swollen shut. At her feet lay a black handset from the desk phone, its coiled cord wrapped around her ankles. Beyond her was a splatter of blood like sprayed ketchup. Paul had his back to me, kneeling over Chet, who lay writhing on the floor. Paul raised his head to Sue. In a second, he picked up on her facial expression and spun around.

"What the . . . " My voice trailed off when Paul pointed his blood-covered KA-BAR knife at me. He rose to his feet, hair disheveled and hands bloodied. I looked into the eyes of a ravenous predator, regretting I'd twisted the doorknob.

Paul walked me back, closing the back door before pushing me in the chest. "Sit down." He pointed with his knife to another dining room chair. "Over there." I eyed the door to the motel lobby as my escape route, but Paul saw me. "Forget about it."

From behind him, Sue voiced a throaty growl. She squeezed her eyes together so tightly, tears dribbled down the side of her nose. Chet's face, pummeled and unrecognizable, lay in a pool of his blood. One of his ears lay next to him. The sight of him missing an ear caused a spontaneous shiver. Through swollen slits, his eyes found me, the accompanying raspy groan unnerving. The cuts on his hands and arms told me Chet had put up a hell of a fight.

"They wouldn't open their safe at first," Paul said in an apologetic tone, eyeing the beaten motel owners. He extended his arms with open palms like he needed to justify to me why he'd beaten them. "I wanted their cash for extra spending money. Then I'd get my medal back from you and head out." Paul waved a stack of cash in my face. "One down, two to go." His eyes were void of mercy, morality completely absent.

"What the hell is wrong with you?" I shook my head in disbelief.

He stepped in my direction and backhanded me in the mouth and onto the carpet. The sharp copper taste of blood filled my mouth. I dove after his legs, but his reflexes were too quick, and he slashed me, cutting my sleeve open and raking my left forearm. "*Ah*, shit, Paul," I huffed, stumbling my retreat back onto the chair. Fortunately, it was nothing more than a small cut.

"Next time you try something stupid like that, it'll be your last. All right, hand it over." He stepped closer, extending his open palm. "Give me the medal," he ordered. "I know you found it." He put the knife tip under my chin, its point feeling like it was about to break the skin.

I could smell his animal scent. "Just wait a second. Can't we talk about this?" I croaked through gritted teeth, applying pressure to my throbbing forearm.

He used the tip of his knife with added pressure to raise my chin, so I'd have to look directly into his soulless eyes. "Give me the medal." He spoke in a slow cadence, lowering the knife toward my pants pocket. "It's the least you can do after you and your grandfather murdered my dad." The sudden quiet was pierced by the dull clanking of knife tip on medal. "C'mon, hand it over."

"We murdered your dad? Are you high? I mean, get real." I tried to talk forcefully but managed only a trembling whisper. "You have lost your mind, man. What the hell are you talking about?"

He laughed a diabolical laugh, his face racked red with anger. "You're such a fuckin' idiot," he derided. "I was no Ag Econ major. I never worked on a farm. I've been playin' you since I came to town." He tapped the medal again, this time sliding the knife closer to my genitals. "Don't make me."

I took the medal out of my pocket and with great reluctance placed it in the palm of Paul's hand.

A smile of victory filled his face as he ogled it. "Good boy." He put the medal in his shirt pocket.

"Man, we trusted you." I recalled the camaraderie we'd had working the bar, handling money, talking artifacts, and being around Sarah. Things were jumbled in my head. Was this really happening? "How did you know so much about me?"

"Wasn't hard to ask a lot of questions. I did my homework, researched and studied about you and your grandpa for months." He jabbed the knife in my direction and broke into a hearty laugh.

My face flushed with frustration. "You got the wrong guys, Paul."

Paul took a deep breath. He one-handed a cigarette out of his pack, tossed the pack, and lit the cigarette with a lighter. He exhaled smoke in my face as he talked. "Okay, I'm not going to kill you until I tell you why. My dad was Department of Indian Properties Agent Paul Gritzmacher—you remember him?"

My jaw dropped. My brain tried to put the puzzle pieces together. I began to relive the knotted tightness in my shoulders as Grandpa and I were being chased by D.I.P. Agent Gritzmacher and his partner, Agent Calhoun. It was a chase that culminated—I could still hear it—with a thunderous roar of the shale bluff collapsing and their car disappearing with them in it into Lake Oahe below. "Hold on, Paul," I pleaded. "You don't want to do this. I can explain. What happened wasn't our fault."

He twirled the KA-BAR like a baton in front of me, snarling with a mocked stabbing in my chest. I knew from his red face he was about to explode. "Bullshit!"

"Why are you calling bullshit? You weren't there. I was!" I spat, barely able to hold my fear in check.

His lower lip quivered. "Once I found out my dad was out here, I had a reason to live. After years of wondering . . . ." His voice trailed off. "You took from me my one chance at a normal life." He bent at the waist to get in my face and spoke in a calm voice. "So, I decided you'll die slowly. I'm going to use this knife to bleed you out."

His change in tone and body language scared me. He was becoming more psychotic and unpredictable.

Through her gag, Sue let out a muffled squeal.

"Shut up! No one can hear your scream," Paul blasted.

I started to feel a slight twinge of guilt within my panic. "Look, man. I'm sorry about your dad. But I swear to God, he was trying to run us off the road because Grandpa wouldn't give him the medal. We were driving to save our lives." I pointed my index finger at him and scowled. "Your dad lost control of his car trying to kill *us*!"

"You killed him!" he yelled at the top of his lungs, his eyes bulging from their sockets.

"No, no, not true!" I shouted back. "Will you listen for a minute? Please!" I begged. After two beats, I softened my tone. "I mean, I get why you're angry with me, but your old man's driving was the reason the car went off the road and ended up in the water."

"Eye for an eye, Jimmy." He feigned a step toward Sue before turning back to sucker punch me in the gut.

Air rushed out of my lungs. "*Blah.*" Doubled over, I tried to ease the pain by rocking back and forth. I shook my head to regain my bearings.

"Get used to it, Jimmy. The fun is about to begin." He strutted over to Chet and extinguished his cigarette on the back of Chet's hand. "You listening to all this, Chet, my man?"

Chet let out a soft whimper. His wife let out a soft wail, her shoulders shaking uncontrollably.

Paul lit another, leaving his cigarette to dangle from a pinched mouth. He began stomping around the room, talking with a maniacal cadence. "Where was I . . . Oh, yeah . . . After I watch you bleed out, I'm going to take your truck no doubt, find Sarah and cut out her baby . . . to watch her pout." He ended with a sadistic laugh.

My temples pulsed louder as anger rose up my spine.

"I have a feeling it's your buddy Jay's anyway," he added with a broad smile.

He was taking pleasure in torturing me. The torment made my muscles taut, my jaw lock, and my posture straighten. Would I ever see Sarah again? I sat erect and closed my eyes, trying to calm the cobra hissing inside me. A vision of Sarah appeared—she was close to me, sunlight dancing off her jet-black hair, a warm smile, a tiny mole above her upper lip, the irresistible sparkle in her brown eyes. Her eyes were kind, offering peace and providing comfort. The energy of her inner strength crossed through me like a seismic wave. She was holding our baby. I would not let our child grow up without a father present like I had. I would give myself completely to Sarah. A smile came to my face as I opened my eyes. I was prepared to die.

"What the hell are you smiling about?" He took a drag and blew it out of the side of his mouth toward the ceiling.

My vision became crystal clear, and colors in the room became vibrant. For reasons I couldn't explain, an untamed force swelled within me I did not know I had. A surge of adrenaline. The cobra lunged. In one motion, I kicked Paul in the groin, and from bent knees launched an uppercut followed by a left cross, sending his cigarette flying across the room. He staggered back, tripping over Chet and landing at Sue's feet. There was an awkward silence as he pulled himself up, knife in hand, using Sue as a crutch.

He let out a delirious snarl. "Let's have a go, tough guy. It's time you got what you deserve." His tone was inhuman. He pivoted in a crouch, then sprang toward me with his knife extended, slashing the air. "Cut. Stab. Slash. Cut. Stab . . . " Paul chanted.

I grabbed a dining room chair, poking it at Paul like a lion tamer.

Sue let out a suppressed howl, diverting my attention for a split second. A swift glance caught the top of a head flashing past the window. By the time my brain registered it, Range Detective Ross burst through the door, drawing his .357 to assume a shooter's position. He pointed it at Paul, swept the barrel at me, and back to Paul.

"Drop the knife! Drop the knife!" he yelled at the top of his lungs, his face full of intent, eyes casing the room at rapid speed. Veins, purple and swollen, popped out of his temples. Praise God. I set the chair down. Ross's presence allowed my shoulders to release their tension.

Paul stood like a stone statue with his mouth open, squinting at Ross. With a slow gesture, he extended his arm in Ross's direction, holding the knife between his thumb and forefinger to surrender it.

"Drop the knife, Paul, and we can all go home," Ross admonished.

Paul laughed. "Cut the crap." He wagged his index finger at Ross. "You had me fooled." He twirled the knife, landing it back in the sheath he wore attached to his belt. "Put the gun down, 'cause I already got the medal," he said, withdrawing it from his shirt pocket. His face was full of triumph, eyes hoping for the Range Detective's approval.

My brain scrambled to figure out what was going on. A loyal customer, honored soldier, a guy I was proud to call a friend...had sold me out? I was empty, briefly, until a prickling anger consumed me. My enraged heart beat like a bass drum at the prospect that Ross and Paul had been scheming together. "Ross, no," I said with utter disappointment.

Ross's face was stone serious. His unapologetic eyes bore through me before he returned to his partner. "It's over, Paul. Give me the medal."

"Nah, I'll give you the medal on our ride out. Let's get the hell out of here," Paul said, taking a step toward the door.

Ross stepped in front of him, the gun barrel halting his progress. "Only one of us is leaving here with the medal." Ross's face was pulled tight. "And it's not you, Pauly-boy."

Sue's forehead wrinkled with fear. Whatever Chet tried to say was inaudible.

There was a beat of quiet. Paul's body tightened as reality hit. "You double-crossin' son-of a-bitch. We planned this whole thing out. You and me had a deal. Fifty-fifty."

"Yeah, I decided those numbers weren't going to work for me," Ross countered, his gun still leveled at Paul. "I need all of the forty grand. Once they're all dead and your fingerprints are on this pistol, you'll wish you were dead anyway. I'm doing you a huge favor."

With impressive dexterity, Paul pulled the knife from its sheath and lunged at Ross.

Ross unloaded his .357 with a deafening roar.

POP. POP. POP.

A shower of blood and tissue exploded from Paul's midsection, splattering the wall with a mosaic of death. His face wore a mask of blended pain and terror as three ports seeped blood. Paul dropped his knife before reaching toward the wounds, staggered a step, and collapsed to the floor. I retreated, open mouthed, extending my arm to brace myself against the wall. My stomach roiled.

Unfazed, his face a veneer of serenity, Ross walked over to Paul with an air of impunity. He rolled him onto his back as blood leaked out his mouth. He reached down and took the bloodied medal out of Paul's limp hand.

Paul's lips bubbled with blood and mucous, a light quiver of his body evident. "Go to hell." His voice was so quiet I had to read his lips.

"Shouldn't bring a knife to a gun fight, asshole," Ross said, before putting a bullet in his forehead.

This gruesome nightmare I was trapped inside was too much. Would I be next? The determined rise of cold nausea meant one thing. Ears filled with a high-pitched whine, I spun away and puked my breakfast. The smell made me wretch again, louder. I wiped my mouth, turning back to see Sue's ashen face.

"What now, Ross?" My voice broke like a preteen's. My body wouldn't stop shaking. I knew what had to happen next. I forced myself not to throw up again.

"I'm real sorry your baby will grow up without their daddy," he said, looking up at the ceiling. He held his gun steady, its barrel pointed at my chest. "Well, well. My ride out of here is right on time. The pilot thinks he's picking up the two F.B.I. agents you had breakfast with this morning and me. Instead, it'll be me, alone. I sent those two clowns on a wild goose chase."

Sue and I tilted our heads up, too. The unmistakable beat of helicopter rotors sliced through the air. Time was running out. Panic sharpened my senses. In rapid succession, I ran through each possible escape route and dismissed them. *Think.* There had to be a way out. The windows began to exhibit a slight vibration before the rotor wash breezed through the open door. Ross backed up to close the door, but Orange Hat Man appeared in the doorway with his Model 13 .357 pointed at the Range Detective.

"F.B.I.! Drop the gun! Drop the gun!" Orange Hat Man demanded. Glen Campbell Hair burst through the door from the motel lobby, arms extended with elbows locked, his Model 13 .357 steady. Ross tried to spin his gun toward Orange Hat Man, but it was no use. Before Ross could pull the trigger, both agents opened fire.

POP. POP. POP. POP.

Range Detective Ross buckled in place. He hit the floor face down towards me, the medal tumbling from the grip of his left hand. The bitter odor of gunpowder from the pistols floated through the room, joining the smell of vomit and death.

The carnage made me pass out.

34

"What the hell?" I came to, rubbing the lump on the side of my head. Movements around me were blurry. My brain couldn't register the activity around me.

"Easy there, fella," Glen Campbell Hair said. He helped me sit up. "You must be Jimmy."

My eyes darted around the room in an effort to put the pieces together. Things started to make sense again. A couple of emergency medical people were tending to Chet. Sue knelt next to him, quietly sobbing over his body. "Oh, Chet, it's going to be okay," she said over and over.

Orange Hat Man was covering Paul with the cream-colored tablecloth from the dining room table. His legs sticking out beyond the makeshift cover jolted me. My eyes circled up at the agent. "Yeah . . . I must have passed out," I said, dazed. "Who are you?"

"I'm Agent Starr, and over there is Agent Montana. Looks like we got back in the nick of time." He helped me to my feet. "You want me to get an EMT to check you over?" He waved to the beefy medical volunteer. "Medic ... over here."

I was unable to calm my shaky legs and trembling hands. The medal. Where had it gone? My head rotated with eyes scouring the floor. While I continued to search, an EMT wrapped gauze on my arm, checked my pupil reaction, and asked how my head was.

"I'm fine. A little banged up is all."

"Jimmy, you okay? What are you looking for?" Agent Starr studied my eyes before scanning the blood-stained floor.

"I, ah, dropped ... " I turned to look behind me, eyebrows pinched together. "I had my good luck charm with me, and, in the chaos ... I don't know."

"What's it look like?" Agent Starr questioned.

"It's about the size of a silver dollar." A clammy sweat coated my palms. Not wanting to look obvious, I used internal self-talk, wanting to will its appearance ... *It's here ... It's got to be here ...* while my eyes crossed every square inch of the floor.

Chet had been placed on a stretcher. His color didn't look good. Behind me, Sue said she wanted to ride with Chet to the hospital. A medic had to help her walk out the door. She didn't look back.

I took several deep breaths in an unsuccessful attempt to mitigate the taste of purged stomach contents. I scanned the room, hoping the hangover feeling would go away. "Can someone tell me what the hell just happened?"

Starr patted my shoulder. "All in due time. Right now, you sit there and get your bearings. We've got work to do."

I closed my eyes and breathed slowly through my nose, trying to quell the pounding in my head. Starr and Montana were moving about the room, pointing and jotting down notes, just out of earshot. From what I could hear, they were discussing plausible scenarios of what had taken place. Then their eyes settled on me. I spoke in their direction. "What hurts me most is I trusted Paul, and he betrayed me. He worked hard, came across as genuine with his interests in the Indian artifacts he'd find, you know? I thought Ross was my friend." The sick feeling returned. "With all due respect, I want to pack up my stuff and go home." I'd never been so physically and emotionally drained in my life. I resisted the urge to continue to search the floor. For the first time, the medal wasn't my first priority. "I need to make a phone call."

"Try our breakfast joint down the hill." Starr nodded in Mickie's direction. "Stop back before you leave. We'll need to get a statement from you."

I pulled myself together and sleepwalked down the hill toward Mickie's. Behind me, a couple of different high-pitched sirens became less pronounced by the second. I'd never seen two guys get shot to death but was pretty sure the image of their dead faces would remain with me forever.

Mickie stood outside her establishment, a concerned look on her face. "What happened? Are Chet and Sue all right?" she asked.

"Hard to say," I mumbled. "Can I use your phone?"

She started to ask another question but stopped herself. "Use my office phone." She took off up the hill toward the motel.

I dialed Standing Bear's number. Sarah answered.

"Sarah, it's Jimmy."

"Are you all right?" Her voice was full of apprehension.

"I found the medal . . . you're not going to believe what happened next." I assured her I was shaken but okay and there'd be more to tell when I picked her up.

"Thank God," she responded. "Jimmy . . . " She didn't finish.

"What is it?"

With a mournful voice, she told me Barking Coyote had died during the night. "I cried for Howard and Doris. Jay showed up before sunup and led the ritual of placing the white wolf fur hide over Barking Coyote to capture and accompany his spirit to the afterlife. I guess Eagle Elk will conduct the traditional Lakota funeral in a couple of days. Please hurry, Jimmy."

"Did you say white wolf?"

I returned to the motel to let Starr and Montana know I was leaving. Standing on the wooden stoop behind the yellow crime scene tape stretched across the doorway, my brain flashed back to the macabre explosion of guts and flesh. Officer Blanda had arrived with his partner. They were busy photographing, measuring, and taking notes of the dining room. Two black Cadillac hearses parked, and four men in dark suits exited. They marched up the hill with their gurneys. Officer Blanda stepped to the doorway. "Right this way, gentlemen." The scene hit me with a surreal feeling. I involuntarily gagged at the sight and sound of them zipping up both black bags.

"Jimmy!" I ducked under the tape. Agent Starr nodded at a red object on the table. "I think I found your good luck charm. It's caked with blood."

"So, um, you don't need it for evidence or anything, right?"

Agent Montana smirked. "Your token? Nah, we've got all the evidence we need."

Did they know? Was it ignorance or grace on their part? No matter, I picked up the medal and started to raise my arms. My triumphant celebration was met with a zing of pain in my ribs. "Oh, thanks," I said with a quiet voice, pocketing the medal. "I'm heading out. My wife's waiting." *Did I say "wife"?*

"Hold on. We need your statement." Montana was insistent.

I stumbled through the sequence of events. They were attentive, interrupting only when telling me to slow down. I felt like I was describing a movie I had seen—one I wouldn't recommend. "I mean, I just don't get it."

"Let's step outside and get you some fresh air."

On the stoop, the agents exchanged cautious glances before Agent Montana spoke up. "I'll tell ya what I know and what I'm guessing at. It's going to take a while to sort this whole thing out." The agents' unsettled posture and active eyes made me edgy, too. "This case has been unfolding for several months. It's still early, but what we think happened is this . . . " Montana stepped closer to me, using his hands to demonstrate a timeline. "Agent Starr and I got word in our Minneapolis regional field office they were closing in to arrest Paul Van Brocklin in Georgia before he fell off the radar. D.I.P. in Pierre sends out an alert on the teletype about this character asking a lot of questions." He paused to light a cigarette. "We identified him as the same guy from Georgia. Once Officer Tittle got the disturbance call from the campground by Painted Rock, smelled a rat in Van Brocklin, and ran it up the flagpole to Pierre, Bradshaw got assigned to track his movements in and around Painted Rock." He went on to say Paul had been a person of interest in the rape of a nine-year-old in Georgia, questioned about a disappearance of a bank president's wife in Alabama, and served brief prison time for dealing quaaludes.

"Paul told me he wanted to kill me because he was certain Grandpa and I killed his dad," I exclaimed, bracing myself against the handrail for support. I rubbed my rib cage, trying to loosen the stiffness already settling in. "Paul proved to be a complete lunatic. Same with Ross Bradshaw."

Agent Starr jumped in. "As luck would have it for us, we get called in because Range Detective Bradshaw had sent a surveillance photo of Van Brocklin back to Pierre and Minneapolis. We pegged him right away." He shrugged. "That's how we got involved in what ended up being a multi-department investigation. Naturally, Bradshaw was going to be the lead in the collar of this kid." He staggered his feet and put his hands in his pockets. "At some point, Bradshaw discovers Van Brocklin is D.I.P. Agent Gritzmacher's kid. Apparently, since the old man never married his mother, he kept his mother's maiden name." I wanted to ask questions, but the details they had put together on this case left me dumbfounded. "At our last briefing, Bradshaw said Van Brocklin claimed he was on a mission to find his father. When he found out his dad wasn't located with the D.I.P. car, he settled on heading west with you." Starr concluded.

They both set eyes on me. I had nothing to add.

Montana resumed. "Bradshaw told us Paul was trying to get away, so he had a semi blocking the road, which worked out well because of the weather. Bradshaw predicted in our meeting you guys would be here . . . and Paul would have to cut the power and phone lines as part of his escape." Montana opened his palms and shrugged. "It was as if Bradshaw became a puppet master to get the collar and credit for Van Brocklin."

The times Paul and Ross had interacted over the last several months replayed in my head. I swallowed hard before thinking out loud. "And Ross had become one of my regulars about the time Paul started . . . "

Holy shit. At last, I understood why Ross had been hanging around the bar so often. A gray-matter light bulb illuminated and caused me to step back, stunned. It dawned on me that the F.B.I. guys didn't know this was all a setup to get the medal. Chet and Sue had, unfortunately, been caught in the crossfire of Ross and Paul's plan.

"We can't figure out why a decorated war hero and Range Detective would work so hard to collar this dirtbag, and then end up turning the gun on us. There will be a thorough investigation, but maybe we'll never know his motives . . . " Montana shrugged, his voice trailing off.

"Maybe we won't," I added. The F.B.I. guys snapped me a man-nod and said goodbye.

35

Heading to Standing Bear's house, my rearview mirror captured the western sky, which blushed with mauve atop faded orange. Bumpers of snow edged the shoulders of the clear and dry asphalt. The voice in my head continued to ask questions. How had Paul and Ross gotten connected? How could I put into words my feelings of finding the medal—or shortly after, the hornet's nest I'd walked in to? How could I ever trust again? I was certain my physical and mental health would take time to recover. At least I was thankful to be alive. That was a start.

Before my battered body got out of the truck, Sarah appeared on the top step of the porch. She navigated the trampled path in the snow with Standing Bear at her elbow. Sarah and I shared a passionate kiss. Her soft lips and warm body helped me forget my pain. I breathed in all of her. Turning to Standing Bear, I expressed my condolences, which made me feel even more deflated. A tear tracked down his cheek as he thanked me. Standing Bear said Barking Coyote wished to be buried in traditional Sioux clothing with his jeweler's loupes. Eagle Elk would oversee an earth burial, believed to be the way to free his soul, the grieving chief said. Standing Bear's sorrowful expression caused my throat to tighten.

As I put the truck in reverse but kept my foot on the brake, Sarah took my hand with thankful eyes. Tears had formed on her lower eyelid. "I got scared when I didn't hear from you, Jimmy. Scared like never before."

"I was scared, too." I put the truck back into park, and we hugged like it was the first time. With her arms wrapped around me, I started to feel the tension in my body release.

Standing Bear slapped the truck's hood once, like he would slap the hindquarters of a horse, and waved goodbye. We reciprocated a wave, backed out of the driveway, and went down the hill.

The ride back to Painted Rock was filled with Sarah's questions. Some had answers, and some did not. I told her about my experience with the white wolf. We agreed Barking Coyote had been with me. I liked that Sarah was careful not to probe too deeply into the details. When she seemed satisfied, at least for the moment, I pulled out the medal and handed it to her, devoid of the joy I'd experienced when Grandpa and I had first found it.

I could tell she'd noticed the blood and appreciated that she didn't ask about it. She pulled open the empty ashtray, carefully placing it inside. "You think it was worth it?"

I hesitated. I didn't know if it was. This was the second time the quest for the medal had come close to getting me killed. "Too soon to tell," I concluded. "My mind is having a hard time comprehending the last couple of days."

"Would you do it all over again?"

Again, I paused, this time driving a few miles before answering. I was struggling to find answers for her . . . and me. "Good question," I said, eyes forward. "Yeah, prob—oh, I don't know." I grimaced, adjusting my posture and trying to get comfortable. Arching my back to the left and resting my left forearm onto the door's armrest helped take pressure off my aching ribs and throbbing arm. "That's a little better."

"Are you in pain?" She tilted her head, eyes of concern directed at me. Her hand softly touched my thigh.

"I'm sure my ribs are cracked or bruised. It hurts when I inhale, and I might have a chipped molar from when he backhanded me." My tongue caught a rough edge. "The self-defense course Pastor taught us didn't save my life but may have helped me stall for time." There was brief silence except for the hum of rubber on asphalt. "What gnaws at my guts is . . . I was duped so entirely. I bought Paul and Ross's lies. Every damn one of them." I shook my head. "How was I so stupid?"

"No reason to beat yourself up, Jimmy. Paul was a dangerous conman. I feel as deceived as you do," Sarah said with genuine sympathy. She reached to take my right hand. "Ross wasn't who he pretended to be either."

We bumped off the bridge and weaved our way through Painted Rock to our home. While Sarah began to unpack, I cleaned the blood off the medal in the kitchen sink. Once dried, I stared at it, unable to escape the sight and smell of death. My head fought for understanding over all I had been through, but my soul danced with gratitude that I had survived. I wrestled with the pain or pleasure conflict of the medal while taking step after painful step to the living room.

With my brain fog lifting, I found myself staring at a five-by-seven picture atop the bookcase of me and Grandpa taken at my high school graduation. I picked up the picture, and my eyes focused on Grandpa—full of health and happiness, wearing a toothy smile. "The medal can rest easy here next to you, Grandpa." I put the picture back and placed the medal next to it. "Here's to happy memories of you." I paused and took a step back. "Now it's time for me and Sarah to move on with our lives. So, keep an eye on it for me, will ya?" I knew he heard me.

A few days passed as news spread of the shoot-out and deaths at the Crook Motel, forever to be remembered as my personal Hell. Sarah and I began to get our lives back to normal. My aches and pains—both physical and mental—began to melt away. The medal never came up in conversation with our friends, neighbors, or customers. We avoided the media. "Too soon, too painful," I said.

The talk in town was all about Ross and Paul's treachery. I told Sarah my theory was that Paul and Ross had used each other. Paul had agreed to split the money he would get from selling the medal he'd stolen from me. In return, Ross would find a buyer and get them to Mexico, where they'd be free. I surmised Paul had figured early on, or always guessed, his dad had died in the D.I.P. car. Agent Gritzmacher's body was never recovered. We found out from Agent Montana that Chet died on the way to the hospital. Sue's recovery could take months or even years, he said. She remembered nothing of the ordeal, and might never, he said. The term he used was "traumatic amnesia." Turmoil aside, I did manage to run a few errands for supplies we needed in Pierre—one, in particular, I was desperate for.

The steel-gray darkness of an early Saturday morning had segued into a clear, bright morning. It was a morning that reflected my outlook as I prepared the scrambled eggs and bacon for Sarah.

I had our kitchen table set, complete with a bouquet of brightly colored flowers from Darcy's Flower Shop.

"What's going on in here?" Sarah stood in the doorway, her baby bulge conspicuous under her draped nightgown.

For theater, I bowed in her direction and pulled her chair out. Sweeping my hand, I directed Sarah to her chair.

"What's the occasion? It sure smells good." She giggled, and once seated, she said, "You are nice to do this, Jimmy."

"No occasion. I wanted to make you breakfast," I responded over the sizzle of bacon.

Steam rose from the pan of scrambled eggs as I turned off the burner and scooped them into a clear Pyrex bowl. I placed the bacon on a paper towel spread on a plate before grabbing the carton of orange juice from the fridge. We both dug in—forks scraping, bacon crunching, and gulping orange juice in between bites of egg.

"I have to tell you something." My palms got moist, and my hands began to tremble.

"Oh, God," she lamented, holding her fork above her plate. "There had to be a reason for all this."

"No, no. Hear me out," I tenderly pleaded. We both set our forks down. I pushed back from the table, crossing my arms on my chest. "The last few months have been pretty crazy, you know."

"Uh-huh," Sarah agreed, rolling her eyes. "For sure."

"In between all the chaos we've had in our lives . . . I've had a lot of time to think. One of the things I've had to acknowledge is that by avoiding a commitment to you, I've been selfish."

Sarah's forehead furrowed; her smile went flat. She curled her hair behind her ears.

"I remember when Grandpa was in the hospital, he said one of his regrets was he never dedicated his full self to his wife, Grandma Phillips. He said it was the biggest mistake of his life."

Sarah took another drink of orange juice. "You didn't tell me."

"I don't want a halfhearted relationship for us." I stopped to consider what I wanted to say next but couldn't find the right words.

"Me, either." She jerked her head backward. "Why are you telling me this? Jimmy, are you having second thoughts about getting married?" Her tone was piercing. "Is that what this nice breakfast is all about?"

I began to get choked up. "Let me finish." I looked deeply into her big brown eyes. "Like I was trying to say on the way home from Standing Bear's, it's time I step up and accept my responsibilities, you know? It took the sweat lodge with Eagle Elk and my talk with Pastor Dawson to open my heart and mind ... Sarah, I do value you, and I know our relationship is good and pure. It is painfully obvious to me now."

Sarah's eyes welled with tears. She reached across the table to clasp my hand. "*Okay* ... but ... is something the matter?" Her face wore an uncertain visage.

"I love you. I love us," I responded, my smile growing with the moment at hand. I pushed completely away from the table while maintaining our clutch. I told her how the prospect of not seeing her again and a fatherless child had thrown me over the edge at the motel. A comfortable pause settled over us. We locked eyes, Sarah's face full of empathy. I squeezed her hand. "I realized I have deep, deep feelings for you I didn't know I had. I mean, our baby would have lost a father, you know." The corners of my mouth rose. "And you would have lost your future husband."

Sarah looked stunned. I locked on her eyes, waiting for the realization of what I had said to register. Her widened eyes became filled with joy. She chanced a radiant smile.

With graceful flair, I withdrew the ring from my pocket and dropped on one knee.

Her eyes darted in bewilderment. She drew in a big breath and held it, both hands covering her mouth.

I presented the brilliant diamond ring. "Sarah, will you marry me?"

She exhaled, bursting into tears and nodding her head. "Yes! Yes!"

I slid the ring onto her left ring finger with difficulty.

"It'll be fine until we can get it sized," Sarah acknowledged. She laughed. "My fingers are kinda fat." She extended her arm with her fingers pointed up, letting the ring twinkle in the kitchen light.

"I think I've loved you since the first day I saw you carrying my cheeseburger and fries at The Caboose eight years ago," I said with a delighted smile.

Sarah got up, and we embraced. "I felt it, too." She tipped her head back, looking up into my eyes. "I still feel it."

ACKNOWLEDGMENTS

First, I'd like to thank all of you who read the first novel, Bad Medicine. Your words of encouragement kept me going through the tough stretches of writing this sequel.

I'm deeply indebted to Kim Suhr, Director of Red Oak Writing, for her continued support and suggestions. She is really good at teaching this writing craft thing. Kim also possesses the patience and tact to work with a well-intentioned beginner like me. I appreciated her praise for my work.

Special thanks to the brave souls who were my early readers—my brother Steve, Sue, and Ross. The input from Pastor Lance O'Donnell regarding Jimmy's marriage quandary was essential to get that scene right. I hope I can be as helpful with his writing. Doctor Pat Sims added pertinent information I needed for Sarah's pregnancy. My talented cousin Dave's early suggestions to get me back on track and focused on the medal were needed and appreciated. The Master Editor was clutch, again. My advance readers deserve praise, too. I salute Karen, Lisa, Lauren, and Mark. Thanks for your time and generous reviews.

Shannon and her talented team at Ten16 Press worked their magic to get this in your hands. Bravo.

Behind every writer is a group of supportive people. In my case, that's my wife, Christa, along with Ashly, Rex, Lexi (the map maker!), and Brad. They prop me up on a daily basis.

Finally, to Mom and Dad: With faith and courage, you made the South Dakota prairie our family home for a bit. Thank you.

ABOUT THE AUTHOR

Pete Sheild is a graduate of the University of Wisconsin and Marquette University School of Dentistry. He is a member of the Wisconsin Writers Association, The Historical Novel Society, and Red Oak Writing. *Remnants* is the third book he has published, and it is a sequel to *Bad Medicine*. His first book, *Sermons From Thy Father*, chronicles his dad's journey into ministry and contains sermons from his first church in Redfield, South Dakota. His debut flash fiction piece, *Playing with Sticks*, was published by *Gastropoda Literary Magazine*. He and his wife, Christa, live in Oconomowoc, Wisconsin. He is retired.